The Ten Commandments

The Ten Commandments

Edited by
TOM WAKEFIELD

SERPENT'S
TAIL

Library of Congress Catalog Card Number: 91−67836

British Library Cataloguing in Publication Data
The ten commandments.
  I. Wakefield, Tom
  823 [F]
  ISBN 1−85242−232−7

First published in 1992 by
Serpent's Tail, 4 Blackstock Mews, London N4
and 401 West Broadway #2, New York, NY 10012

Typeset in 10½/13 pt Palatino by Setrite Typesetters Ltd,
Hong Kong
Printed in Finland by Werner Söderström Oy

CONTENTS

For Malcolm Johnson

Acknowledgements
My thanks to all the contributors for meeting their
deadlines and providing a wonderful correspondence.
Gratitude to Robert Collie, Patrick Gale, Rose Collis
and Deirdre Clark for editorial assistance.

The text of the Ten Commandments I have used is
taken from the Authorised Version.

T.W.

I suppose that various interpretations will go on forever with regard to biblical lives, biblical stories and biblical laws. Both Cecil B De Mille and the present Pope have asked us to prescribe to their imaginations. Can Charlton Heston's Moses be accepted more easily than the present Pope's statements concerning abortion laws and the Nazi Holocaust? Either way, a believer has to be more free-range in his/her thoughts than the wildest chicken to find palatable seeds in these interpretations. And what of the Commandments? Do they all make good sense? Do they enhance human values and proffer sound, social tenets? I think, for the most part, they do.

In the selection of authors, I felt the need for diversity both in cultural background and religious belief. Hence, there are writers here from no less than six different countries. Catholics, Jews, Anglicans, Methodists, atheists and agnostics are all represented.

Here are ten stories written around ten laws and brought into the setting of modern lives or modern memories. They owe little to Cecil B De Mille or the present Pope but I hope that they might make you laugh, cry or think. Fundamentalist thinkers have hijacked these rules for their politics and their forms of social control. These stories suggest that they do not have a copyright.

Tom Wakefield

◆

The Missionary's Pay Day

ADRIAN WESTON

◆

*'I am the Lord thy God, which have
brought thee out of the land of Egypt,
out of the house of bondage. Thou shalt
have no other gods before me.'*

◆

Lee came back to town in a cloud of dust. It had been the same ten years before and again ten years before that. That was the only way anyone ever arrived in Wyuna.

The car dipped and bumped over massive tumours in the road, bottoming badly as it hit Main Street. Pieces had been falling off the vehicle from the moment the last of the bitumen had given over to the first of the corrugations and the pall of red dust had become all pervasive. She'd be surprised if there was much of the car left by the time she returned it to the pool, for all that it was new and emblazoned with Australian Design Awards.

For the last mile or so, she had been slowing down, trying to catch her own landmarks: a rusted windmill driving a rackety pump, drawing water from the bore — water that tasted as though it could strip the enamel from the inside of a bucket and introduce a dozen cancers to your bowel. Behind a derelict mine head, she could just see the roof of the Lake View Hotel. 'No lake, no view,' she said to herself, remembering. It was surprising that it still had a roof.

Lee had lived at the Lake View for a few months on her first stay in Wyuna in 1960. The heat and stink had driven her off the reserve when she had wanted to write up her notes. To her surprise she felt afraid there at nights and watched in the days. It didn't seem a happy place. Living in the desert was always strange, but even in the wildest places she had seldom felt that way; it was more the way she felt in cities. In the end she had been glad to go back to her caravan on the reserve.

A few months later, the Lake View was annexed by the agricultural research station to house the single guys working there. They held a party and Lee went to it. She got friendly with one of the scientists (that lasted for a while) so she went there quite often and slept over sometimes. Even so, even with company, it remained an unhappy place.

Now, Lee wondered whether anyone was living there. The research station had closed since she had last been up north and in the past the place had only been kept a bare step this side of dereliction. Small sections had been brought back from the brink several times, and even twenty years ago the top floor had been a death trap. If the place had at last become a hulk, some cowboy would probably have made off with the fittings and fixtures to flog in the city. None of them had even thought of that in 1960. 'More fool us,' thought Lee, recalling a crazily baroque brass bedstead that had stood alone in one of the first floor rooms.

On Main Street everything looked the same. It appeared such an unchanging town: there had been little noticeable difference in the two ten-year gaps between her previous visits. The street was wide enough to turn a bullock train or a team of horses and dead empty. It was only notionally a street, being a full mile long and having but five buildings on it. You could say they were well spaced out: Wyuna was open plan. There were voids, massive gaping voids, and beyond those the emptiness of the desert.

Wyuna hadn't always been empty. There had been a huge transient population during its gold rush, living in tents and humpies around the core of important buildings. A man named Gunn struck gold and the area was deluged with prospectors. Then some more was found plus enough other minerals to open a few mines and sustain the appearance of prosperity for a couple of decades. There had been three hotels in town at its height: the Lake View, the Station Hotel and the Grand Hotel. The Station Hotel burned down back in the 20s and was never rebuilt. The trains had not reached Wyuna anyway, so there wasn't much point. Some of the old bushies still liked to talk about the fire, though, as if it was still news.

'Blokes were getting drunk on the fumes. The fireman couldn't hardly stand he was so bloody pissed. The joint went up in minutes,' they would say. 'Crying shame that so much good piss went to waste.'

Lee loved that story and must have heard it fifty times.

There were no remarkable incidents in the Lake View's history. It faded out over the years until the early 1950s when its last owner died. No one wanted to buy it as Wyuna was practically a ghost town by then. The last of the Lake View's regulars (all six of them) drifted quietly over to the Grand on Main Street and stayed there. With only the one hotel in town things were more companionable, even though the Grand's long front bar would be less than half full if every man, woman and child in Wyuna and for miles around should turn up at once. That was excluding the Abs from the reserve, which Des the barman did as a matter of course. He'd sell them piss in any quantity though — port at twenty-five cents a four-litre flagon — but only from the corrugated iron lean-to round the back. Des had no need to state this restriction, it was just the way things worked in Wyuna. The same way that none of the white population would ever want to go and drink in the shed with the Abs. And as Des employed a young aborigine to work there, he didn't even have to sully his hands doing business with them.

There were only fifty whites in town and over five hundred aborigines on the reserve. But that didn't figure. The missionaries were the only ones who had cause to be involved with the Abs and, as Des would point out, the missionaries didn't drink. Des probably raked in far more over the trestle in the shed, even at twenty-five cents a time, than he did over the slab of the front bar. Such was the status quo.

Lee had to tolerate Des. At first it had been important for her to cope with the missionary too, but it remained so with Des: it would not be possible for her to live and work in the area if she didn't get on with the only barman in the only hotel. Her position was tenuous enough as a single white woman, nothing to do with the mission, working on something weird *and* living with the Abs. She made no sense in Wyuna's scheme of things. This time, she was going to have to fit in a little more readily as she was planning to take a room at the hotel, at least for a while. No caravans. No camp beds in derelict buildings. Those were her personal conditions: concessions to being twenty years older and to her private ghouls.

A small pack of dogs was circling the car as she slowed again to a near crawl. They danced up to and away from the vehicle, barking at the back wheels. They were feral, at least half of them noticeably dingo. The working dogs from the stations were kept well away and people didn't like them, but equally did nothing about them. The odd station hand would take a pot shot with his gun from under the hotel verandah or out of a truck window, but on the whole they bred and barked. Lee was afraid of them, though not as much as she had been. She had to work hard to remind herself that there was no rabies in Australia.

The dogs' barking was louder now than the engine or the cassette Lee was playing. In some towns it was cats that had gone feral. There were occasional stories in the papers of feline monsters as big as an alsatian, picking off the livestock at their leisure. Lee couldn't help thinking even that would be preferable to the dogs.

The dogs only came so close to the hotel before turning and running away, settling in the dust in the few scraps of shade around. Lee saw that she had been watched as she pulled up in front of the building and the dust flurried. There was someone standing under the verandah, looking towards her, taking in the unfamiliar white car with government number plates and a dent in its fender where she had struck a roo at dusk. It was an old boy watching her. A grey beard with a stick and not someone whom Lee recognised. It was going to be hard being a stranger all over again.

Lee's allegiance was not with the town, and never had been. It was with the reserve and her Abs. She called them her Abs in the way that anthropologists appropriated the racist terminology of the ignorant and turned it into a joke to show their own cultural superiority. Lee supposed that it was as offensive to say 'my Abs' when talking casually with her colleagues although they had different terms for their professional discourse.

Lee's skin made a peeling noise as she separated herself from the car seat and got out. A huge circle of sweat on the back of her shirt made it cling to her and the seat of her shorts was just as wet. The car was supposed to be air conditioned but that had given up completely the day before. That's how a stay in Wyuna was meant to go.

She said 'G'day' to the old man, nodding but not looking his way. It wasn't on to be friendly, not like that. You just slouched by without too much recognition, even if it was your brother or father you were passing. You *could* talk when you got to the bar, or if you were watching another man with a horse or a machine or a dog or some significant beast. Then you could turn and say, 'What do you reckon about that?' and the bloke would snort or say, 'Piss all.' But you still wouldn't let your eyes meet.

Inside the bar, the air was a bit cooler, but clammy. They had one of those evaporative cooling plants mounted above the door, running with the sound of a severely broken fridge which pumped air into the room that only felt light and fresh if you stood directly in front of it. It added humidity to the room, but not much else. When Lee walked in there was one man sitting on a stool at the bar, with his back to the door, watching television. Now that was a development. When Lee had last been there it wasn't possible to pick up the radio without expensive equipment, let alone television. Des stood behind the bar, also watching, holding a glass and a cloth, but he did turn towards Lee and nodded. She had forgotten just how much slow nodding passed.

'G'day.'

'G'day.'

Lee sat down at the bar.

'I'll have a schooner,' she said. A mineral water would have suited her better than the beer, but she had to begin playing by the town's rules. If she didn't drink, they couldn't talk.

'What's the chance of some food? I know it's late for the kitchen, but anything'll do.'

Des looked at her for a long careful minute.

'I reckon Dot could find you some sandwiches.'

Des went off to test his theory, leaving Lee to contemplate the stranger's back or the television.

'I didn't know you could pick it up out here,' she tried.

'Des got a VCR,' the back replied. And that was that.

The sandwiches Des eventually brought back for her were tinned ham and processed Kraft Individual Cheddar Slices between staleish white pre-sliced bread. The bread must have come a long way.

'Have you got a room free upstairs?' Lee asked. It was unlikely that he wouldn't have.

'Yeah.' There was a very long pause before Des went on, 'How long d'ya want it for?'

'Few weeks. How much?'

'$35 a week, dinner and breakfast. Piss'll cost you extra.'

'Piss extra. OK.'

The deal was struck. Before leaving the city, Lee had had to remind herself of the vocabulary and the etiquette. She had dined with some colleagues just back from doing fieldwork up the Birdsville, which was possibly even worse than Wyuna. They had sat out in their garden as the night grew darker, eating and drinking at a table under a huge fig tree, running through the idiosyncrasies of life out bush. Rod had suffered particularly, having to give up his vegetarianism in this land where meat was all. He'd had to sit in countless station kitchens while 'the beast' was butchered and cooked for him. Coming back to the city he had made an immediate appointment with the doctor, convinced that he had developed an ulcer at best. Lee had laughed and laughed at their stories, but she had had to steel herself at the same time.

There were other reasons for her to be prepared. There would be private undertones and personal fears. Despite the surface of stasis, Lee knew that there was going to be much change, hard change for her to come to terms with, particularly out at the reserve. At least the mission was gone. Lee had told herself that she could not come back to Wyuna while the mission was still there, not after her last stay. But it was the changes she would find inside people, her friends, that she feared, even though she had long predicted what would happen. The missionaries' legacy and society's legacy.

Lee had tried to keep in contact with Wyuna during her absences through the network of aboriginalists. She knew some people who worked with another community about 100 miles west of Wyuna. They were a slightly different language group but they had strong kinship links with the Wyuna mob. Bob and Alice had been in the field there recently and they had warned Lee.

'At least the mission has gone,' Alice said on the phone. 'There is that.'

She would have to go and take a look around the mission, stand in those buildings, if they were still there, and see how she felt.

Her final conflict with the missionary had come at a time when Lee had believed that a miracle was taking place. It came in a year when the desert flowered.

A spring rain appeared from nowhere. It fell on the cracked and barren soil, laying the dust. At first Lee thought that it would last only for minutes. That was what her experience of rain in the desert had been, but it fell long and hard into the night. The children on the reserve ran about in it and shouted with joy. A small fat child called William, who often sat silently on Lee's knee, stood ankle deep in a mud puddle with his tongue out, tasting the drops. Later, Lee lay still on her bed in the little caravan as the rain continued to batter the metal roof, the noise too loud for her to read or write or think. Faintly though, in the darkness, she could hear voices, music and barking dogs coming from another part of the reserve.

Some of the men had started drinking and getting rough, she thought. There would be injuries before the night was out. There always were, regular as clockwork on the days when the missionary gave out a small allowance to buy 'necessities'. On those days all the men got in the back of a couple of trucks and headed to town, to buy their piss at the shed. Later in the night the trucks would weave their way along the track with a drunken mob and a good supply of piss. It could turn very nasty. The pattern was set that way. The missionary doled out the money with an ever increasing quantity of morality, but Des just dropped his prices a little. He reckoned that if the Abs didn't buy it, no one would. He was probably right. It was foul stuff. The day the rains come was the missionary's pay day, but the last there would ever be.

The rain must have stopped some time in the early hours of the morning and the water soaked into the soil, pooled under stones and coursed along forgotten creek beds. Waterholes came back to life. The rain had moved across the north of the State in a great unbroken sheet, covering hundreds of miles. Buckets-full fell. An hour or two more and there would have been disastrous flooding. To the west of Wyuna there *was* some flooding, a few roads washed away and some livestock drowned, but it was only localised. The rains had stopped in time. In the morning the miracle began.

By the time the sun was well up, thousands and thousands of acres of the dead land had begun to bloom. As the morning progressed, every tiny patch of ground bore some fruit. It defied belief. Lee opened the door of the caravan and stood where she was. She had never hoped to see this. As she breathed the air she could feel and taste the change. The constant powder of red dust that gave its arid bite to every breath you took had gone. This air was clean and new.

Lee got her boots on and walked out onto the pliant ground. It was sticky with mud. Lee had been in the desert for such an age that she had almost forgotten what it felt like to walk on soft soil. She only had eyes for the ground at her feet.

Of all the people on the reserve, Topsy was the only one Lee wanted to talk with. She was possibly the only one who would ever have seen the desert in flower before as she was easily the oldest person on the reserve. Topsy had learned a little English of late, but preferred to speak Warlpuri which she did in short staccato bursts. It had taken Lee a long time to be able to understand her, but now she was one of Lee's best sources: Lee was working with kinship systems and Topsy carried genealogies in her head that went back to a generation that had never seen whites. Lee estimated that she must be at least ninety. She had been brought out of the desert very late, so she was one of the strongest links with the past. She had known more than any of the others to begin with, and she had forgotten less. Topsy was also bright, funny and wicked. Lee loved her unreservedly.

Lee wandered around for over an hour looking for her, all the time her joy grew at what was happening to the desert.

'Seen Topsy?' she asked over and over.

'Nah,' was the reply but always with a suggestion: 'Try at Jindies,' or Billy's or Joey's, or 'over there'.

'Hey lady!' a young handsome boy, widely known to be trouble, called back after her. 'The missionary's out to git you.'

Lee turned and grinned, 'I'm not afraid of the missionary.'

The boy laughed and tilted his pelvis, rocked back on his cuban heels. He was called 'Sleepy' on account of his permanently half-closed eyes and his belief that there wasn't a woman in the State who didn't want to sleep with him, given the chance.

'See you around, lady.'

'See you, Sleepy.'

Eventually she found Topsy sitting on the ground by a new water hole, digging with a stick, looking for food. Topsy greeted her. She had her knees up practically to her ears. Her legs were skinny as twigs although the rest of her was large. A lot of the elderly aboriginal women had these amazing legs, thin enough to close your hand around. It didn't look as though they could possibly stand without toppling over, but they did. They could squat for hours, too. Lee envied them this ability, growing stiff quickly herself, having long lost most of her limber.

'You've made that missionary mighty cross.'

'Have I, Topsy?'

Topsy just laughed. She didn't care about the

missionary or any of that. She went back to poking about the hole with her stick, then grubbed in with her hand. It was a root that she pulled out and popped into the plastic bag tied to the belt at her waist. Topsy always carried a gathering bag with her. All the women did, even the young girls. Once they would have been woven bags, now they were the plastic ones from the store. But the gathering continued. It was the men who did the hunting, which took them further afield than the women. But the biggest difference was that at the end of the day the women always brought in enough food for a meal, whereas the men often had nothing to show for their time. 'If we only ate men's food, we'd starve,' Lee had heard Topsy say to Christmas and they had both sat back and cackled. Both Christmas and Topsy had long since lost their husbands and neither of them thought much of the men. Christmas had a son in his late twenties, but she was even scornful of him. It was his generation that had suffered most by way of the reserve. He didn't really understand the land and he drank and fought, but he was fairly harmless in comparison to some of his contemporaries.

Topsy and Lee sat quietly for a while, smiling at the sun, which had broken through to illuminate the scene. As well as plants, the rains had brought insects to life and even frogs would come: there were tadpoles swimming in the waterhole. All the seeds and eggs had been set into the hardened ground, waiting for the rains. Lee had read that some of the plant seeds and the spawn of one species of toad could remain for decades, maybe even sixty or seventy years, always ready.

Topsy became pensive for a time and then she began to talk to Lee. She told Lee that this had only happened twice before in her life. Once, when she was a young woman and all the salt pans turned to lakes again with fish swimming in them and birds coming to them from the sea, and once before that when she was a child. She couldn't remember that herself, but she had been told. The story was much as a story from the dreamtime. Lee sat silently by her while she talked and thought, 'This really *is* a miracle.'

Lee always learned things from Topsy, but for once there were things growing around them, literally before their eyes, for which Topsy had no names. This plant and that plant, Topsy had never seen before. She would only smile to them and hold out her hand flat, touching a petal or a leaf the way that a child approaches something wholly unfamiliar but lovely. Some of the plants looked quite prehistoric with ugly fleshy leaves and extravagant, loose-petalled flowers. The variety of shape and colour was enormous. Most of the plants had such short life cycles that they had to compete violently to attract the insects to pollinate them so they could leave behind fertile seeds for the next distant rains. It was impossible to accommodate the speed with which this happened, and that only the day before this had been bare earth.

Over the waterhole some dragon-flies skimmed.

Lee and Topsy fell back to silence until Christmas joined them. She squatted down too. She was wearing a bright yellow dress with an apron tied over it. The apron had a Christian homily sewn across it. The missions had guilds in the depressed outer suburbs of the cities where housewives and unwilling daughters sewed and embroidered for the benefit of 'our poor black brothers and sisters'. Christmas saw Lee looking at the garment. 'Mission gave this me. God made it himself, must have,' she grimaced. Christmas always spoke to Lee in English, even though Lee was talking

Warlpuri to Topsy. 'What you done to the missionary, hey? He's spitting for your blood, Dr Lee.'

'I just did what I thought right, Christmas.' She had to admit that she knew he wouldn't like it.

'Isn't that what he always says to do, anyway? "Do what you think is right, Child. Don't be swayed by the ministries of others," he says. Though I reckon he ain't talking 'bout himself when he says that,' she laughed again. 'Reckon it's you, Dr Lee, he means most often when he says that.' She paused. 'Silly fucker,' and she and Topsy roared. 'Silly fucker' was a phrase that always made Topsy laugh.

Another woman turned up and Topsy and Christmas went off with her. Lee went back to her caravan. All she wanted now was to see what would happen next, whether this really could continue.

That night Lee wrote letters. She was filled with a compulsion to record the detail. She had taken photographs, of course, but she didn't have any faith in what they would show. She had seen photographs of deserts in flower, but they had merely looked like flowers and sky, beautiful – yes – but not like this. Lee wrote to her sister, 'It's biblical, it's like a miracle. I walk through the desert in a trance and find myself thinking that this must have been how Eden felt or what it was like to arrive in the promised land. It is because everything, except for the ground itself, is new. It has just been made. I have never seen anything like this before and I very much doubt that I will again. Not if I live to be a hundred-and-one.'

When Lee went to bed and slept, she dreamed of herself passing forever through this landscape of flowers and grasses growing out of bright red soil, but her dream had nothing in it that she had not seen in the day. When she woke she felt like she had been walking for the whole night, but had remained fresh. It had rained again and the horizon seemed to have moved closer. There were huge red desert peas that had not been there the day before, and there was a suckered ground plant that had produced sharp yellow, flaccid petalled flowers in the night. She could hear some frogs calling to each other.

The reserve was spread out and tatty. Humpies made of cloth, bark, plastic and corrugated iron, various sheds and huts, as well as some caravans and trucks with no engines or wheels, were all lived in. There were a vast number of broken vehicles, three or four functional ones, and as many dogs as there were in Wyuna, except that on the reserve the dogs all 'belonged' to someone. At the furthest point from Lee's caravan and at the point closest to Wyuna, were a school house, the mission house, the mission hall and a shed where the people from Wyuna Store opened once a week. Like Des, the reserve represented their biggest, if least affluent, market, but they couldn't afford to ignore it.

The rains had gone a long way to hiding the squalor of the reserve. The new greenery softened the worst of the edges and obscured much of the rubbish lying around, most of which was resolutely unbiodegradable. Suddenly the place looked almost picturesque. It was quite a transformation. The missionary would no doubt be taking credit for it having happened, Lee thought as she took a folding canvas chair from the caravan and walked with it away from the reserve. This feeling of burgeoning spring had taken from her the impetus to work for the second day. As it had done before, the sun broke through and Lee wanted to continue to contemplate. She did carry a notebook full of genealogies, but only as a token. She had to carry some sort of talisman of her studies.

She put the chair up facing away from the reserve and Wyuna and sat down, feeling like a pioneering woman. The unfamiliar sounds of the desert growing all but obscured the fainter noises of people on the reserve. For that brief time she was totally alone in the world and at peace.

That is why the shock was all the worse when she was grabbed from behind and flung bodily towards the ground. She only just managed to get her balance, get on her feet and turn.

'Heathen! Evil woman! Satan's child! You've done the devil's work for him and you are proud of it. You stand there puffed full of your scorn and your wicked ways. You know what you have done!'

The missionary's rhetoric had impressed Lee the first time she had heard him hold forth, even though she had loathed what he was saying. He didn't normally lay hands on except as a sign of healing, nor espouse violence directly, but this man of God was leaning dangerously towards her.

'Get away from my land,' he said, 'and stay away from my people.'

He was only a little shorter than Lee, but he inflated himself and she wondered if he would hit her and if he did, how she would retaliate.

'I will see you gone,' he finished.

'Doug, please. You know I was doing what was right and fair. It was quite legal. You were defrauding the community. You'll be lucky if the social services don't bring charges against your organisation, particularly if other missions have been found to be doing the same things.' She was holding her hands, palm out towards him as she spoke, like a text book illustration on conciliatory body language. She tried a different tack. 'Times have changed, Doug. You can't go on in the same way anymore. Whatever your beliefs, they have human rights, civil liberties.' Now she felt as if she was preaching too. Why didn't she go the whole way and quote Rousseau or Marx, tell him that they, too, were individuals? She didn't because of his glazed eyes.

'*You* are the sort of woman who brings VD to the natives.' He delivered this line with a gesture like a thunderbolt and went, leaving an air of threat behind him and the words 'I'll see you gone' shouted once more.

It was an extraordinarily unreal feeling, standing there in the sun, in the never-ending field of waving flowers with a deckchair fallen at her feet. Perhaps she was a little bit afraid of the missionary after all.

People always talked about the missionary in the singular, even though there were several missionaries and members of their community. They made it sound as though the missionaries had one collective mind, acting and talking as a single entity and in a way they did. Doug Brunt was their leader, guiding light and driving force. He was a big man in a little man's body and while he was not attractive, he was charismatic. He knew no uncertainty and was strong and determined in every way: admirable qualifications for a missionary. He was certainly not one whose soul had known dark nights.

It was inevitable that one day Doug and Lee would come to blows as they were completely at odds. Doug's whole purpose, given by God, was to bring the aboriginal community into the way of the Lord, into righteousness. To do that they must give up their heathen practices and wear modest clothing, among other things. Most important, however, to Doug, was for them to cast off the mantle of their polytheism: he had made some study of their culture and beliefs, so that he could better 'know the evil of it'.

In the beginning Lee had made some attempt to be at peace with Doug. She had had problems with missionaries before in Papua New Guinea, where she had done the fieldwork for her doctoral dissertation. Her own brother was a missionary there and her father, who had been a lay preacher at a dissenting church for years, would have been an evangelist if he hadn't become a civil servant. Lee had run through almost every possible conflict at her own family table. She knew well what crossing a missionary could mean. She decided to be cautious. Like it or not, approve or not, Doug and his crew were part of this community and a good anthropologist shouldn't make too many waves and particularly not when an absolute newcomer to that community.

On her first long stay in Wyuna, back in 1960, Lee managed OK. She went to one or two of Doug's meetings, to get the measure of him and because he had asked her.

'Come to one of our Sunday prayer meetings, Dr Lucas,' he had said to her in the Wyuna Store. 'We welcome anyone who is prepared to come and listen,' he added in a chilly and unwelcoming tone.

Lee smiled her thanks to Doug and said that she 'just might do that', adding Doug to the list of hardships that had to be endured in Wyuna. She ran through the difficulties she would probably encounter in dealing with him, not least of which was the fact that each of them was trespassing on the other's territory. For the moment, she tried to give him the benefit of the doubt. Her life would be much easier if he turned out to be the sort of non-interventionist missionary concerned with the aborigines' social and physical plights but remaining discreet on the spiritual front.

Of course, Doug wasn't that sort of missionary. Lee took up his invitation the following Sunday. She made her way across the reserve, joining a group of mainly women. They were all 'dressed' for church, some of them even wore hats. Very few of the garments either fitted or suited their wearers and the effect was highly bizarre. To Lee it was depressingly similar to her brother's congregation in New Guinea: formerly laughing eyes cast demurely to the ground, warm bare skin clad in nylon, sweating. It gave her a very bad feeling.

The mission had a long tin shed of a chapel beside the mission house. It was painted white throughout, with a wooden crucifix on its gable and another inside, high on the end wall above a bare table. There was a single chair placed beside the table. This was also almost identical to her brother's mission.

'We are all going to pray for you tonight, Lee,' her brother had said to her, a tear of sincerity in the corner of his eye. 'Come and join us.' Lee had shaken her head and left.

'I hope you'll be saved, Lee.'

'I hope you will too,' she had shouted back, allowing venom to colour her voice. 'Why,' she had thought, 'did he have to come here to do his work?' Her brother was one, she suspected, whose motives were spite disguised as goodness. 'I *am* prejudiced,' she told herself repeatedly and without conviction.

Doug Brunt entered the mission hall with quiet dignity and one of the mission women at his side carrying a tumbler, a jug of water and a Bible. The mission woman sat on the chair after placing these three objects ceremonially in a row across the table. Doug took his position with his hands behind his back and spoke, eyeing the congregation levelly. He spoke with intensity and some sort of passion. Lee soon saw what he was.

Doug was a man of the commandments. They mattered deeply and literally to him. He warmed a while to the general theme of evil, but it was going in one direction only. There was a detour via drink, bad language and general lewdness. But Doug grew an inch or two and glowed (Lee suspected that he clenched his buttocks together, although she couldn't see) when he came home, so to speak.

'I am the Lord your God,' he spoke in a low voice. 'I brought you out of Egypt where you were *slaves*,' the volume rose. 'Worship no other God but *me*.' That last pronoun, that *'me'*, Doug really meant personally. It was *the* commandment, the one that defined everything and, as Doug expanded, Lee had a flash of foresight of more trouble.

'You have been brought out of the desert, where you were slaves to ignorance and immorality, into God's love. You *must*,' and Doug's eyes slid around the room, 'give yourselves wholly to that love and leave behind the demons of your past. False idols of the dreamtime must be cast aside.' In Doug's imperfect understanding of the dreamtime (the aborigine's creation myths, peopled by wonderful dreamtime beings, the animals of Australia, large and beautiful) he was presenting his aboriginal children with a clear equation: 'You have this...or...that' and if 'this' is everything that is right then 'that' must be everything that is wrong, idolatrous and sinful. This man in his white, pressed shirt (although even the righteous sported sweat stains) with two small gold crosses pinning down the wings of his collar, saw as his God-given duty the destruction of the culture of Wyuna's aboriginal population. He and Lee could not but be enemies — they had no choice. Listening to Doug preach, Lee felt as though she was being pelted with those old stone tablets.

For that year Lee trod lightly on the reserve's earth. She did return to the mission hall one more time to join the gathered group praying for their brothers and sisters who still walked in darkness and lived as heathens as if they had never been brought out of the desert. She also went to the thanksgiving tea on Easter Sunday. The spread of food guaranteed a good turn out of righteous and unrighteous alike (Doug and his helpers beamed with benevolence for the day). But apart from that Lee and Doug kept well away from each other, although Lee learned that Doug tried to dissuade people from talking with her.

Of course, in 1960, Lee had no choice but to be careful. The state and the missions were mutually supportive. The Federal Government's aim was for the assimilation of the aboriginal population: the mission's part was to take huge numbers of aboriginal children from their mothers at birth and to place them with middle-class urban white families so that they might become 'members of society' in a God-fearing white country. One way or another Australia was still pursuing its infamous 'White Australia Policy' and how, then, should it accommodate its indigenous black population in a humane way?

Lee was in a doubly difficult situation. Her research was government funded and she was coming to work with kinship systems in a community with a whole generation missing. On that first visit there were virtually no small children on the reserve. It was as if the whole community had become infertile on a given day. No doubt that would have solved the authorities' dilemmas very neatly: in some areas less than a century before they had tried to deal with the aboriginal question by distributing blankets infected with white man's ailments, wiping out whole groups, their languages and customs. In Tasmania, ever pragmatic, they had simply rounded up the whole lot and shot them. These measures obviously wouldn't do in a modern, civilised country, but they were still trying. At that time, there was still not much Lee could do besides staying quiet and getting on with her work before it was too late.

A decade later some tides were beginning to turn, and Doug was forty and balding. Lee took this to be a significant incidental detail. She could see that Doug was feeling the ground to be less steady for him. He still knew that he was wholly right, but the problem was that fewer other people could see this: he was suffering from an attack of the prevailing social mores and that made him testy. He and Lee argued almost at once, and then again. She hadn't been back long when she shouted at him from above. Leaning out of her truck window she called him a barbarian and Topsy, who was sitting at her side, roared her approval at Lee's tone. 'What a fucker,' Topsy said in English and Lee let in the clutch with a bang, leaving Doug literally eating their dust. The decade that had passed was a big one, out there. There were even children back on the reserve.

It was the missionary's pay day that did it. That ritual had been going on when Lee had last been there, but she had not pursued it then. But a few weeks before the rains came and the desert flowered, Lee had been at Sunshine's camp with fat William on her knee looking like a happy brown buddha. Sunshine, William's mother, was married to Billy, a Wyuna man, but didn't come from Wyuna herself. She often saw fit to pass comment on events that everyone else took for granted.

'Won't see much of Billy tomorrow,' she said to Lee, resignedly.

'Why?'

'Missionary's pay day.'

'Sunshine, do you know what the missionary's pay day is? I mean, do you know where the money comes from?'

'God and the Government.' Sunshine gave a rare sneer, one that was reserved for authority and, sometimes, Billy. 'Government gives it to the missionary to give us. Guess God gives it to the Government.'

'How do you know it comes from the Government?'

'It's the DSS. Missionary came round with forms with our names on. We had to sign them so that the missionary can get us money.'

'Did you read what the forms said?' Sunshine read well, if you gave her the time.

'Nah. Missionary said we didn't need to. He told us what was on it.'

Lee had to stamp on the anger she felt. There was no point in letting it well up now. She knew full well what Doug had been up to. She had heard of it happening before – the Hermansberg Mission had been notorious but she hadn't made a connection. The Hermansberg Mission had claimed benefits on behalf of the aborigines living around the mission who, largely illiterate, had signed or marked whatever was given to them. That was what white men did, wasn't it? Peddle meaningless pieces of paper. The mission then had a considerable amount of extra money at its disposal.

'So,' thought Lee, 'that is the path Doug Brunt follows.'

Lee had to act. She could not let him continue. As well as affronting every principle Lee valued, it was fraud. This man thought he could trample his way over the indigenous culture without blinking and then proceed to dictate financially, control every last detail of their lives. She could hear his 'me', his 'I', the words of his commandment echoed in her ears.

It took a trip across the desert to Port Augusta and a couple of appointments to sort it out. Lee was astonished but elated when she climbed back into her four wheel drive with a bundle of forms to be signed and returned as quickly as possible. Her trip to the DSS office was merely confirming their suspicions: she didn't have any persuading or arguing to do. Private enquiries about the functioning of the mission were already being made and Doug's monopoly was broken. Simple.

If only it really was that easy.

Ten years later, at the bar of the Grand Hotel, with a schooner of beer in her hand she wondered more about Doug. What had *he* felt when he was removed from the reserve? When land rights were granted by the highest in the land and the reserves became self-governing aboriginal communities? She must find Topsy and ask how he was removed. Was it with a polite little note: 'Your services are no longer required'? Or was it rougher justice that was meted out to him? 'Out on your ear, eh, mate?' Perhaps it was a case of the missionary's own words being acted on — false idols being cast down. She hoped so.

'Give us another, Des.' She held out her glass with a flush of confidence.

'Sure, mate. Hey,' he leaned over the counter, 'haven't seen you round for a while.'

Lee smiled. 'Yeah. I've been out of town for a bit.'

'You're the one that was slung out on your ear by the missionary, that one that thought he was God almighty.' Des snorted a short laugh in her direction and went back to polishing glasses.

Lee had stood in the middle of that vista of waving grasses and flowers with the upturned deckchair at her feet. She had stood still and imagined that she was swaying so gently with the slow wind from the north. A hot dry wind it was. Doug Brunt counted for nothing, she had thought, and she was part of the landscape. That was what she had felt then as his threats vanished into the sky. Eventually she had walked off and spent a normal day, a happy day sitting talking to some of the younger women, playing with their children and gathering seeds and stems, petals and leaves.

In the dark she made her way back across the reserve to her caravan, untroubled.

They were waiting for her there. She walked softly, slow steps and absorbed in thought. A truck's engine started and its lights came on. No figure appeared cloaked by the headlights, arms spread. She didn't hear his voice intone 'I will see you gone' low and intense. But then she hardly needed to. What Lee remembered as the last sound before something hard and heavy hit her over the back of the head, was the crescendo of a thousand desperately mating frogs.

Lee's luck was that she didn't die, that she wasn't driven miles and dumped in the desert. Instead she was dumped in the back of her own truck, her caravan hitched up to it and towed to the far side of Wyuna. It was left beneath the Lake View Hotel, on the road south. Lee and her concussion came round to see the shadow of its roof line moving slowly across the old mine head. The murder that had been done was of her work. No trace of her papers remained in the caravan.

It would take anyone a decade to recover from that.

Lee left the Grand Hotel after she had finished her sandwiches and beer. 'Water off a duck's back,' she told herself and got into her car. 'Pissy little thing,' she called it. The department was stupid to have replaced its four wheel drive trucks with soft-bellied family sedans. She backed on to the track with wheelspin and not a glance over her shoulder and headed for the reserve. She drove outback style, one hand at the top of the steering wheel, her right arm lolling out of the window and her foot flat to the floor. The rush of sand and stones against the vehicle's underside was therapeutic. 'It won't last a month,' she had said with scorn at the budget meetings. 'Have you ever *been* out bush?' she asked the guy from the bursar's department, already knowing his answer.

A stone the size of a boulder hit the floorpan.

She would find Topsy, she must, and talk with her. Find out what had passed and fill in all the gaps. Topsy would be there, she was sure.

The reserve was nearly ten miles from the Hotel and about a mile from its edge an even bigger crowd of dogs gathered, circling and leaping. She headed for where Topsy's humpy had been. She had to crawl along, the pot holes and corrugations almost impossible to negotiate other than in a truck. She went so cautiously that the dogs lost all interest: there was no competition. Topsy's humpy was in a depression behind a ridge of rock like a dinosaur's back and well screened with salt bush. There was a track just wide enough for a vehicle. A squat, savage looking dog started to go mad as her car approached, but it was chained up. Then a short old woman, Topsy, surely, emerged from the humpy, looking angry, fit to kill. She was picking stones and beer cans up from the ground and hurling them at the car with surprising accuracy.

'Hey! It's me. Dr Lee. Topsy! Stop!' She nearly swerved into the rock by the end of the track, ducking under the barrage. Topsy dropped her arms to her side as Lee stopped the vehicle.

'Dr Lee. I never thought it was you in that government car. Thought it must have been the social workers.'

It was then that Lee realised this was not Topsy. Topsy would have spoken to her in Warlpuri. No. It was Sunshine, looking ninety now at least. She couldn't be much over forty.

'Sunshine,' she said 'what's happened to Topsy?'

They sat for the whole afternoon and the evening by the fire that Sunshine had going round the back of the humpy. Sunshine had some emu meat which they cooked and ate on its own. Topsy was dead, had been at least six years. Christmas was sick, real sick, away at the hospital. She had started drinking too and then got bad and the doctor had to come for her. The list went on and on.

'Remember Sleepy?' Sunshine said and Lee nodded thinking of the boy in his shining cuban heels. 'He can't. Can't remember nothing, who he is, where he was yesterday. Nothing.' Sunshine looked at the fire.

This was it. This was what Lee had feared and known would be there. Bob and Alice and plenty of others had warned her. 'I've stayed away too long, it's too late now,' she thought. This was what they had been brought from the desert for − she could hear Doug's words again − a God that wasn't worth shit. And when that had gone there was only the drink left.

The fire had burnt down and it was time to get back to Wyuna. She'd see plenty more of Sunshine over the next few months but for the moment there was one more question she had to ask.

'When the missionary left, what happened?'

'Oh. He went quiet,' and Sunshine laughed, 'real quiet.'

Worried about Dolores

MICHAEL CARSON

◆

*'Thou shalt not make unto thee any
graven image, or any likeness of any
thing that is in heaven above, or that is
in the earth beneath, or that is in the
water under the earth. Thou shalt not
bow down thyself to them, nor serve
them: for I the Lord thy God am a
jealous God, visiting the iniquity of the
fathers upon the children unto the third
and fourth generation of them that hate
me; and shewing mercy unto thousands
of them that love me, and keep my
commandments.'*

◆

*D*olores stepped into the porch of St Patrick's cathedral, searching in her bag for her mantilla. Finding it, she took it out and shook it. Then, deftly, with great care, she bobbed her head under the little canopy of the cloth and let it settle itself down on her short black hair. She tied the two ends she had been holding loosely under her chin, dipped her hand into the holy water stoop and crossed herself. She stood for a moment, feeling the holy water trickling down her forehead. She closed her eyes and breathed deeply.

The cold water was a wonderful shock to her after the muggy heat of the July New York street. It calmed her immediately. That in itself seemed a miracle, and she walked into the cathedral nave with confidence, feeling that here she would be able to make everything work out. Here the miracle she required, the big one, would happen.

There were not many people in the cathedral. Four or five old ladies dotted about the hundreds of pews, a tramp mumbling to himself under the eighth station of the cross, a few tourists rubbernecking, a woman sitting smiling behind a table covered in Cafod brochures.

Dolores walked half way up the nave, then genu-flected in front of the tabernacle, before taking a short cut along a row of pews to the statue of St Thérèse, to whom, she had decided, she would pour out her troubles.

Many had been to the saint before her that day. Many came every day to the statue of the young nun of Lisieux who had promised after her death to drop miracles on the earth like roses. The statue stood behind two dozen burning candles: a smiling girl in a Carmelite habit, holding a crucifix to her breast, while with the other hand she dropped the promised roses down her body, past her rosary and on to the earth beneath her feet.

Dolores put fifty cents in the collection box, took a candle from the tray and lit it, holding the wick next to one already-burning plea. Then she fixed the candle into the bottom-most space on the candle-holder, hoping that her humility would endear her to St Thérèse, make her pay more attention to her than to the more confident candles burning a jot nearer heaven. She knelt down on the prie-dieu, rested her elbows on the shelf, her fingers crossed like woven rattan before her chin. Dolores looked up, through the soft candle-light, to the kindly wimpled face of the saint.

'It's me, dear St Thérèse. It's Dolores. I am sorry to bother you. I can see that you are busy. But every time I come you are busy, so I suppose one time is no worse than another. I am not even sure that you are the saint I should be approaching. It is habit, I guess. When I was younger, when I was innocent, it seemed fitting to come to you for help because you were young and innocent when you died. You, like me, had never strayed far from your village. Dying at twenty-four with all those innocent sisters around you, I always thought you would understand the problems of a young village girl like me. Ah, but St Thérèse, I did not know then what was going to become of me. I could not see the miles I should have to travel, the houses of strangers, the insinuating touches of men who held my passport and the future of my family in their evil hands. St Thérèse, I could tell you stories! The good die young, they say. I think I have many years ahead of me. I sometimes look in my *Dictionary of the Saints*, trying to find one who had sinned as I have sinned, who would not be shocked and horrified by what I have to say. There were, of course, many and I do pray to them in the quiet of my room. But here in the cathedral I must take what is on offer. Many go to St Joseph over there. But he is a man, although a most exceptional man. He took Mary back and believed that she was a virgin. No man that I have ever known would believe that. He would think that what the angel had told him about Mary and the Holy Ghost was a lie. He would get up and take off his belt to beat her, or maybe use it to sharpen his knife upon. No, pretend I didn't say that! What do you know about such things? But another side of me thinks that you do understand. You promised to drop roses on the earth. Everyone comes to you. They must teach you a lot. It is such an unfair exchange, though. You drop roses while we throw up filthy stench into your saintly face.

'I hate to think that all the requests of poor sinners here below may be stopping you from enjoying heaven. But perhaps it is possible for you to continue in rapture in God's sight while still paying attention to our needs. Even here on earth some people can do many things at the same time. Mrs Duke's children can listen to their Walkmen, talk to one another and still kill the soldiers on the television with their computer guns. I don't know how they can do all these things at one and the same time. If I am ironing in the next room and hear the bang of their toy guns and the cries of the dying cartoon soldiers, I find that I am losing concentration and will forget to iron a cuff. Mrs Duke doesn't seem to worry about distractions either. She can talk to a friend on the telephone and switch channels on her television set and massage cream into her face and make sure her cup of coffee warming in the microwave doesn't boil over. All these things she can do. That is why I suppose they are all so rich in New York. They can do things in half the time. A simple Filipina like me can do only one thing.

'I'm sorry, St Thérèse, I am such a gossip. I only meant to say that if people down below can do many things at the same time then you in heaven may be able to listen to our prayers and requests and problems while at the same time enjoying everything heaven has to offer. Yes, I am sure you can do that. I mean, heaven would not be heaven if you were denied it every time you had to listen to a request. Anyway, thank you for your attention. I am an unworthy sinner. I know that I do not merit any of the roses you have promised to send down to the world.

'Yes. I, Dolores, am a wicked girl. I keep thinking that maybe I am wicked because I am poor. But that is no excuse, is it? I sometimes look into my mirror and wonder why men see me as a girl who is prepared to be wicked. I never wear dresses cut more than half a little finger below the neck. I refused several of the dresses that Mrs Duke offered me for that reason. Mrs Duke wears very revealing dresses, but she is a good woman and no men ever take advantage of her. But it seems that ever since I left my village men have seen me as the kind of girl who is available.

'I thought when I came to the Duke household that things would be different. Mr Duke is a doctor, as I am sure you know. He has beautiful white hair and was interested in everything I told him about my life. When I said how I had been treated when I was sent to Arabia I thought he was going to cry. He kept saying, "O my gosh, O my gosh!" And I did not tell him everything. I only told him how one of the sons had forced me to be impure. But there was much more to say. I could have told him about the agent's man in Manila. The agent laughed when I said that I was an honest girl and a teacher of English in my village. He knew I was poor. He knew that my whole family needed me to get a job abroad in order to support them. He knew he had the power. I wanted to say no. I have always wanted to say no, but if I had said no I would have lost the jobs, and my family would have lost the food from their mouths. So I said yes.

'If Sebastian knew he would be angry. I know he would not marry me. He might take a knife to me and end my life. But what can I do? I have to stay away from my country. I have to send money home. And I am just one of millions.

'St Thérèse, you must have heard this story so many times before. Perhaps it makes you yawn. No, I'm sorry, I did not mean that. I know that you are interested in all our problems. The sisters always used to tell me that a prayer did not need to be full of words. Perhaps I should just say: "*Another Filipina.*" That would say everything. And here I am babbling like I babble when I meet another Filipina maid on my night off. Of course we don't talk like I'm talking now — well not all the time. We also talk about Green Cards and going home and what is happening there and how we can send our money or the things that relatives are always writing and asking us to send them. That is one of the biggest problems, St Thérèse. People think that because I am in rich New York I have got plenty of money to send them all the things they do not have. I try to. I send pens and books and little gadgets, but grandmother wrote me asking for a dehumidifier. I did not even know what a dehumidifier was, but grandma knew because there is a consumer programme on Manila television called *Whatever Next?* and they showed grandma a machine that takes the water out of the air and grandma has been obsessed with the idea of it ever since. She keeps telling mama that she would sell her soul to the devil for a dehumidifier because a dehumidifier would take water out of the air and make her breathing easier. Also — or so mama says — the water that is taken from the air goes into a little plastic receptacle and tastes like the water from springs in the mountains of Palawan. I do not judge grandma harshly, dear St Thérèse. She has worked so hard all her life and has had little chance to buy comforts. Now that she has a relative in America it is natural that she should do her best to receive favours. For grandma I am, perhaps as you are to me, an invisible benefactor. But already I send them every dollar that remains from my wages. How can I send money for a dehumidifier? They think I am like the rich New Yorkers. Perhaps Dolores knows how you feel, St Thérèse. I too feel besieged sometimes.

'You must be so busy and yet here I am going on and on. I saw a picture in a Filipino newspaper last week of President Aquino praying to you in a Manila church. Poor President Aquino! I can only imagine what a long list she presented to you for your attention. What a headache! She must not only pray for the repose of the soul of her dead husband but for all of the millions of Filipinos she is in charge of. Listen to her, dear saint. Listen to her first. I am only one.

'But I do have a problem — I mean apart from the *real* problem. All our prayers are answered. Did not Jesus say that? So what did you do when Ferdinand and Imelda Marcos prayed to you? They had everything on earth that anybody could possibly want, a million times more. But what they did not have was the love of the people. I just do not understand, St Thérèse, how a leader would not care about what the people thought of them. Would our love not bring them more satisfaction than all the jewels and shoes and real estate in the world? Imagine what we would have done for them when they died, had they really loved us and worked only for us! We would have set up shrines to them, had masses said, named streets after them, cherished their memory as blessed. But I have seen what they did with the money they stole. Ferdinand and Imelda loved it more than all of the millions of poor Filipinos. How can this be? Explain it to me. I want to understand. I say a prayer for Imelda. She cannot go home. I ask you to teach her the right way.

'I think I am babbling so much because I am really afraid to tell you what I need. Let me tell you what has happened. Last week Mrs Duke went out with the children. They were going to spend the day with friends in Connecticut. Dr Duke came in and started talking to me about my life in the Philippines. I told him how poor we are, how everyone is dependent on me. I told him about grandma and her aches and pains. I also described Smokey Mountain, where Sebastian searches with a stick through all the rubbish of Manila and takes as prizes the things that I throw down the Duke's refuse chute twice a day — tears in my eyes at the thought that the objects here are without value, while on Smokey Mountain the uncovering of a can would make Sebastian's heart beat faster. Dr Duke said that my story made him ashamed to have all that he had, but I told him that everything in the world is as God intended and that anyway he had been very kind to me. Then, St Thérèse, he walked over to me where I was sitting ironing, and stroked my hair. I was not anxious. Actually I looked at his gold Rolex and did a sum about what it would buy for me back in Manila. It made me giddy. It would, of course, buy everything I dream of. I do not think it means much to him. He throws it on the bedside table each night as I throw cans down the refuse chute. Perhaps with less care than that. Anyway I was not scared when he stroked me because it felt like a father comforting me. But then he pinched my cheek, leaned down and kissed me. "Please, Dr Duke," I said. "I am a good girl."

'"You forget," he replied. "I've heard your story."

'Now, St Thérèse, this is the part that I know you are going to hate to hear, you whose holy purity was a byword throughout France. But if I do not tell you I cannot tell anyone. I have been used before. In Arabia the father and his brothers, even the eldest son, thought that because they were rich all they had to do was click their fingers and I would do it with them. I resisted then but they knew their way through my defences, through every defence of workers from poor countries. "We will report you to the Ministry of Alien Labour for insubordination and theft." They had the power. I had visited Filipina maids in stinking prisons, their only crime refusing to give the men what they wanted. But these men were like children in their sex. They were so excited and afraid that it was over before it had begun. A few stabs, a moan and stickiness. I would watch them, St Thérèse, watch them completely detached, and think, "So this is what manhood is! So this is why they strut up and down in their white angel-suits! They hide their women away for this! For this they worry about the honour of their women as we worry about food for our children! They have an ugly tap which needs to be near something warm before it can jerk out its sticky poison." They allowed me the luxury of feeling complete contempt for their need, for their whole sex. They were like nasty children who needed to piss badly. Usually afterwards I only had to wash my outside.

'But with Dr Duke it was different. Much worse. You see, I respected him. I would never have bared my soul to him if I had not thought I could trust him. He was almost like a priest to me.

'Anyway, St Thérèse, Dr Duke went over to the video machine and put a tape in. Then he came back to where I was sitting watching him. He undid his flies and took out his thing. He turned to the television and zapped it on. First, for a moment, we were watching *Golden Girls*. I like the grandmother and, despite the sight of him there with his thing out, I was trying to think about what grandmother was saying. But then the picture changed and I saw a fat white man on the screen, his thing big and near the camera, with girls who could have been Thais or Filipinas writhing all over him, kissing the big thing and making him moan. Dr Duke was watching the video, playing with his thing, which was very long, but soft. He would look over at me from time to time, hissing. "I'm going to get me some, I'm going to get me some. My tight little slut sitting like a good girl with her ironing! I'm going to get me some!" He fast forwarded the video and I almost wanted to laugh because the old man looked so funny when he started to lie on top of one of the women. His fat bottom just went up and down like a clockwork toy. Then he returned the video to normal where the man was standing and a young girl was kneeling in front of him and he was doing it into her mouth, holding on to her ears. He watched that for a minute or two and then he came over to me. His thing was still not hard. They need to be, St Thérèse. It's a biological thing. Unless they are they can't do it. I thought you ought to know. He stood me up across the ironing board from him and lay his thing down on it. "Bow down and kiss it, then take it in your mouth until it's hard! Go on, Miss Green Card, Miss Third World Guilt, Miss Abused Teacher, Miss Virgin and Martyr Among the Pots and Pans, get down on to it and show me what you're good for!" He grabbed me by the shoulder with one hand, then put his other round the back of my head, forcing me towards him. I bowed down. My nose was full of snot from weeping and I wondered if I could wipe it on the shirt I was ironing. I saw the thing against the gingham ironing-board cover. I did not think. I had the iron in my right hand and suddenly he was screaming. He let me go and tried to pull the iron off his thing. But I was pushing down in the way I sometimes have to on badly-creased cotton. I am sure you know all about ironing cotton from your work in the convent. It can be very stubborn. Anyway, I think I may have been screaming too. He started lashing out at my face like a drowning cat. I drew back and he was screaming on the floor. On the video screen the girl was fighting to get away from the man's huge thing but he was holding her tightly by the ears, growling, "All of it, bitch!" I looked at the girl, then I looked down at Dr Duke writhing on the floor, screaming.

'I turned off the iron, went into the bathroom and washed my face. I then returned to the room where Dr Duke was. I telephoned for an ambulance. Dr Duke's Rolex was on the table. I looked at it. I suppose that I was trying to distract myself from the sight of Dr Duke on the floor. I did not want to look at him as I thought it might make me feel pity. The watch was such a small thing. I remember that I saw each link of the bracelet and imagined the things just one link would buy for us back home. I saw the tiny gold needle of the second hand and heard it tinkle on to the tiny scales of a Manila jeweller. Dr Duke continued to scream but I thought I could hear the Rolex ticking.

'I am still shocked at myself. I, who hate to see anything in pain, who would pray for the goats of Arabia with their throats cut thrashing about on the ground, did not feel an ounce of pity for Dr Duke screaming on the floor. I could not be moved by what I had done with my hot iron, just as he could not be moved by what could be done with his ticking Rolex. I know it is wrong and unchristian and diminishes me but this is an eye-for-an-eye world, an Old Testament world. Only from the poor are the turning of cheeks, the spreading of legs, the smiling beatitudes of passivity, expected.

'Anyway, St Thérèse, you can imagine the rest, I think. They took him to St Vincent's hospital and I telephoned Mrs Duke to tell her there had been an accident. I said he had been ironing a pair of trousers and had somehow burnt himself. Mrs Duke said, "He's been *WHAT*? He's never ironed anything *IN HIS LIFE*!" But it is strange how things work out, St Thérèse. Almost miraculous in a way, because when Dr Duke came round that is exactly what he told his wife! What else could he tell her?

'But even though our lies coincided Mrs Duke did not believe it. I think, perhaps, she discovered the video in the machine and suspected the truth. On her return from her visit to St Vincent's she took me aside and told me to pack my things. She would give me a month's salary. I just nodded. I had been looking after the children, watching the boys zapping the television channels, daydreaming. I often do this, St Thérèse. All the time in the Dukes' house as I dust or tidy away the children's toys and clothes, I will look at an object and see its cost transferred to my family. I sometimes like to imagine that I have a machine in my hands, like they have to close the drapes or change the channel on the television. But instead of changing channels my machine transfers the value of objects across continents. Why does somebody not invent such a machine? I could zap Dr Duke's Rolex and lift our family up. Anyway, I just nodded.

'St Thérèse, I know there is no magic machine. But I have you, St Thérèse. You must be my magic machine.'

Dolores began to weep at this point, for the moment had come when she had to tell the saint the thing she had come into the cathedral to confide, to ask for a miracle.

'So, St Thérèse, what I need more than anything is a new job. Please help me to find a new job. You have helped me before. Please do it again. Intercede with Jesus and His Holy Mother for me! Ask them also to stay the hand of the US Immigration men. They do not understand the problems of the poor. They will put me on a plane back to Manila. If they do that my life is finished, the lives of all who depend on me are finished.'

Dolores looked hard into the unblinking eyes of St Thérèse. She had heard stories of the eyes of statues leaking tears when the poor poured out their troubles. In Sablayan on the island of Mindoro a statue of St Martin de Porres had wept tears. A reporter had recorded the tears with his video camera. Dolores had seen the tears oozing from the saint's eyes, dribbling down his body to form a puddle on the marble floor of the church. Thousands of pleading people had come to the church. Many had been the miracles. She watched now, hoping that her plight would move the statue of

St Thérèse to tears. She gazed at the blue eyes unblinkingly until tears came to her own eyes. No, St Thérèse was not deigning to weep. But that did not mean that she had not heard. Had she heard? She tried to unask the question, feeling that it would insult the saint if such a doubting question were allowed to reach her. Then she remembered that she had asked St Thérèse to intercede for her with Christ. Perhaps she should talk to Christ in the tabernacle before she left the cathedral and returned to the apartment to collect her suitcases.

Dolores made her way to the centre aisle and walked towards the high altar, on which stood the tabernacle. Her shoes clicked on the marble and the sound echoed around the cathedral. She began walking on tiptoe. Then she bowed her head, daring neither to look at the tabernacle nor consider the Godhead within it, hidden in the form of bread and wine. Usually Dolores only approached the saints, who then approached God on her behalf, because she did not feel worthy to approach Him directly. But today she was desperate.

The sanctuary lamp glowed. A flame flickered from the wick on the surface of the golden oil. Each flicker, she had been taught, spoke the sentence: *Jesus is here, Jesus is here*. The sisters had told her that. She had told her own children in the village school that. Staring at the lamp, a lamp half the world away from the one in the wooden church in her village, a lamp which flickered in the same way, she felt in the presence of miracles. But, not daring to direct her gaze at the tabernacle itself, Dolores continued to pray.

'Sweet Jesus, I am sure St Thérèse has passed on my plea to you by now. I am so sorry to keep bothering you all. It would be OK if I were good myself, but you know what a wicked sinner I am. But you were friends with Mary Magdalen. I am a poor girl, Jesus. One of millions in my country. Our poverty forces us into sin. We give up our homes, our honour and our purity so that our children may eat. In Japan, Arabia, England and America, we marry, maid, teach and are prostituted. This is the fate of the poor and powerless. *Dear Lord, Father of the Poor, forgive me and help me to find a new job.'*

Dolores repeated the last sentence of her prayer again and again, kneeling at the altar rails. She did not immediately take notice of the tumult at the back of the cathedral, the voices raised, the winding of cameras, the flash-guns popping. The repeated last sentence brought tears to her eyes once more. She stared through her tears at the curtains of the tabernacle, sending a beam of pleading as strong as anything the Duke children zapped at their computer, through the silk curtain and the metal doors and the chalices, to the Godhead hidden within, nestling in a solid gold chalice under the disguise of unleavened bread and New York State wine.

Then, quite suddenly, she heard the noise. Robbed of concentration, her thoughts pushed back to her suitcases in the Dukes' lobby, Dolores stood up. She genuflected in front of the altar and turned to leave the cathedral. She tiptoed back up the central aisle, seeing through the gloom a scene of mayhem. A woman was coming towards her, on her knees. Behind the woman a jostling group of people, pushing, straining, using their elbows and whispered shrieks, to get a better look. Dolores stopped when she realised that the woman on her knees was Imelda Marcos. Her arms were outstretched and it seemed to Dolores that those arms were coming to enfold her, while they kept at bay the wild people behind. A glittering rosary was hanging

from the white-gloved fingers of her right hand. Imelda
shuffled towards Dolores, her lips moving. Tears had
leaked over the barricades of her mascara and were
coursing black down both cheeks. Dolores stared at
the apparition. She had stopped in the centre of the
aisle, eyes wide, her head full of the glittering celebrity
on her knees before her. Imelda seemed to be looking
at Dolores, begging her forgiveness. For the briefest of
moments Dolores thought that this was how her prayer
was going to be answered. Imelda Marcos had been
made aware by St Thérèse of her crimes against her,
her family and all the millions of struggling Filipinos.
She would stop in front of Dolores and beg her forgiveness, perhaps give her one of the stones from her
brooch, her rosary or her flashing earrings. A perfume
of roses filled the air. Dolores was practically fainting
away from the perfume, from the feeling that here she
was in the middle of another miracle, and this beyond
any chronicled in her *Dictionary of the Saints*. A thought
came, a thought that she knew had been given her by
sweet St Thérèse. After Imelda had wept apologies and
promised her a job and the making of restitution to
the Filipino people she, Dolores, would lift Imelda to
her feet and together they would go back to the altar
rails to weep tears of joy, to pray in tongues of burning
gratitude. Imelda would auction off her baubles. She
would take the magic remote machine and zap the
buildings she owned in New York so that their value
was transferred to the poor in the Philippines. The
buildings would be dissolved. Each brick, window
frame, floor tile, light fitting, door, mirror and drape
would fly up high into the air, dance gloriously across
the ether and softly fall on her homeland. Houses for
the poor would be formed by these things. Schools
and clinics and workshops click into place. The New

York skyline would look no different. The missing buildings not be missed. Rather, more sun would beam down into the cold canyons, warming the city's stony heart. From the sites of the buildings springs would flow that would cure the sick. But more than that, just as the scales had fallen from the eyes of Imelda, so all in New York would see that dollars were not worth chasing. Only Beatitudes were worth effort.

And the strange gods Imelda had worshipped at their shrines on Fifth Avenue and in the glittering grotto of the Trump Tower she would sell, divide, melt down and transfer the proceeds back to those who longed. Then, dressed in a simple dress, owning one pair of shoes, Imelda would accompany Ferdinand's body home. The forgiveness of the people would sooth Imelda body and soul, provide a million times the satisfaction of all the bank accounts, bonds and baubles she had, while under the devil's influence, acquired. Perhaps one day in this very cathedral people would kneel down to pray in front of the statues of St Ferdinand and Imelda. They would be The Patron Saints Of Those Who Think They've Seen Everything.

Dolores smiled through tears of joy at Imelda shuffling towards her. Only twelve feet separated them now. Dolores imagined once again what she would do when Imelda arrived at her feet. She would reach down towards Imelda and offer her arms to her, would get down and enfold the penitent, would lift her up, cradling her as she had cradled for so long the babies of strangers; tell her that everything was all right, heaven hers. Together they would return to the tabernacle, to the plaster statue of St Thérèse and, sisters and magdalens both, offer prayers for the repose of the soul of Ferdinand, even for the swift recovery to health of Dr Duke. For would not Imelda's penitence reach

Ferdinand in purgatory, Dr Duke in St Vincent's, and swathe them in its balm?

But then a bodyguard elbowed Dolores out of the way. She was pushed against a pew and saw that Imelda's eyes had not moved. They wept still, but their gaze had not been fixed upon Dolores at all, but the golden tabernacle on the altar.

Dolores sat down heavily in a pew. Imelda shuffled on past her. Cameramen ran down the side aisles of the cathedral, jumped over pews as if they were so many hurdles in a race, shooting picture after picture as they went. She heard the cameras winding on, saw intense white flashes behind her closed eyelids. The flashes turned into suns shining down on Sebastian as he foraged with his stick on Smokey Mountain, a cloth over his nose. He looked up at the suns, then out at her. The cloth fell from his face and she saw that he was screaming. When Dolores, anxious to awake from her nightmare, opened her eyes, she saw Imelda Marcos kneeling in front of the tabernacle on the high altar of St Patrick's cathedral — where hides the God of the Poor — thanking Him for the miracle.

◆

His Name

STEPHEN GRAY

◆

'Thou shalt not take the name of the Lord thy God in vain; for the Lord will not hold him guiltless that taketh his name in vain.'

◆

I thought I would have no difficulty with the preamble of this story: I do not normally use His name for evil purposes, would fully expect to be punished for misusing it. Let me run this through in the less clear but more familiar language of my childhood: I should not take the name of the Lord my God in vain.

Which I assume is a *lot* more serious matter than our father's use of blasphemy, cursing and even obscenity: 'Oh bloody f——ing Jee—— Cripes,' — stressed for effect, red in the face, that's how he would thump it out as he failed to get the engine re-started. Our mother gave a tired sigh, equally strong in its power of deprecation, at our dilemma: clinging to his leaking canoe in some wild lagoon with the tide running out at a rate of knots into the Indian Ocean. 'Boys, close your ears and look at the view.' 'Never mind,' my younger brother would say, 'we all got to die someday.' 'He picked it up in the war — how to curse and be a bully, and *use the Lord's name in vain*,' she confided in us. 'Going to get the women and children drowned first...' We were being tugged towards the big sea, father sworn to a standstill. 'I'll try,' I perked up, winding the greasy rope around the head... and it started and my father exclaimed, 'Good boy, *you* are a son of mine.' We puttered ashore, disaster averted.

I was learning that more than the badmouthing of your average unhappy war veteran was needed to provoke divine retribution. His kind of language was just *not used*, especially in front of us. Some far greater misuse of His name was being held back to be tested.

I would not be remembering any of this had not that younger brother of mine — called David — not tried to recreate so exactly how our father treated us in the way *he* treated his own two little boys in turn. Family history repeats; my heart bleeds. I suppose the next will also chain-react to keep this thing going, and little Joey will defect, as I did. I simply gave up, David got to develop all the dubious property — in my case only the beach house is of special interest — and my half in cash is long drunk away.

'Uncle Joe, why don't you have a family like Daddy and Mommy?' (young Davey, son of, son of).

'But *you* are my family, guys — blood is even thicker than kith and kin. That's how it works.'

'Ma said you can't have a family cause you drink too much,' (Davey's brother, the one who will defect).

'Don't be silly, how can boozing be connected to things like that?' (I'll say one thing for these boys, they as yet lack guile).

'Shall we go fishing, if your mother'll trust us?' *They'll* do any fishing; my hands tend to flutter. I shouldn't slang Carol, my sister-in-law; she is the one who found me my night-nurse in the city seven years ago, when she went up to give birth to the second of these. It's hard to explain why the night-nurse stayed on: accommodation in Hillbrow is *so tight*; bit like Box 'n' Cox, he's out when I'm in, which is only officially so: unofficially, I miss Reggie and his great soft hands and his woolly hair and his great big floppy gentleness. I should be so lucky. Where may we be together, apart from in the closed circle of that other family one has?

Couldn't bring him here to throw him to these white Christian sharks.

Talking of sharks, my God, they are right — little Davey: 'Rugger toof! Jees, just check the dorsals!' '*Ragged* tooth, you total dweet!' Sure enough, up the Mbashee estuary comes this almighty scavenger of the deep, cruising for a jawful of washed up cow in the mangroves, I suppose. The boys throw it with stones (South African English). But I say, 'Rather don't,' (also), respect and respect, and they desist; they pull in their lines and we watch rather awed as the ragged-tooth beats against the glittering tide, then goes upstream.

But that's not enough for my brother Dave: 'Do you think I'm going to let my kids play there with a thing like *that* in the lagoon?'

'Leave it, Dave,' but I have only to say leave anything to its own devices for him to have his speedboat down the slips and now I'm meant to stand in the bows with a harpoon; this is really no way to handle alcoholic withdrawal.

The frenzy wears off a bit when he's out of sight of his wife and those poor kids. He jams the rudder round and switches off. 'Which way did you say it went?'

'Haven't a clue, how could I? And now that you've alerted the whole estuary. Dave, you like to make such an awful he-man racket, just like your bloody father. Why don't you go with the flow a bit, like they used to say?'

'Sorry, but I don't like Carol and the boys to be threatened. Anything harming them sets me off.'

'But they're not remotely being harmed.'

'You wouldn't understand. How could you?'

'Back to the same old thing: I may not have a family

of my own, but I remember how it feels to be part of one: you, Momma, Dad in that leaky canoe, and Dad fucking over-protecting *his* family and we were drifting out to sea right there.'

'And all it took was you to sort it out.'

'Yes. So you do remember that.'

'You never did stop telling us all it needed was a simple act of faith.'

'Ugh, I'm sorry.'

'You were like that then.'

'Oh God, how embarrassing.'

A generation on and could this be leading back to a forgiving brotherly clasp? — the kind of gesture I could make only after much liquor and he perhaps could never make at all.

'So you do remember.'

'You were quite my hero then, in some ways.'

'*That* didn't last so long.' I was slurring my words in sheer terror that I would slur them if I spoke (if you know what I mean).

'No, I'm convinced the root evil is our father didn't want us at all!'

Oh please. The lagoon lapped against Dave's varnished boat; at least he didn't get the engines farting and firing.

'He never wanted us. He'd much rather have stayed a white warrior after doing Rommel in the desert, just stayed on doing the Congo and Kenya and all that. Die in his boots, a Salusa Scout. He didn't want that wife and settle down bit. After killing blacks so hard he wasn't ever right to settle down, except to raise us boys to help him kill more blacks.'

As usual, having unblocked my tongue, I had sluiced off in the wrong direction.

'I don't think we're going to find this thing now,'

said Dave. Nevertheless he started up.

On these speedboats there is a safety device in case the driver gets bounced overboard; a rubber plug on a line tied to his ankle. I pulled this and the twin-screws cut. 'Talk to me, Dave, just tell me things: it's a beautiful evening, we haven't been... stuck out on a lagoon together for most of our lives...'

'It's getting chilly, let's go back in.'

'To more of Carol's carrot-juice, no thanks. This is the perfect sundowner, bobbing with my young bro in this hilly green; I mean, you do have access to paradise, you know. I'd say you live like *very* few people can afford to in the rest of the whole world.'

'Dad saw to it.'

'Dad did not see to a coastal estate with company helicopters, or anything else of the kind. Dad just left you an inaccessible ruin in the interminable bush and a few blocks of city shacks.'

Dave put finger to lip, pointed. 'My God...'

'Yes...'

'Hit the fucker, what are you trembling at?'

There was the muddy silver monster, mouth open over several chins for a strike.

'Trouble with you, Dave — you really do have no faith: never had, never will. I challenge you to jump into the muddy brine, right now.'

'Ah come on Joe,' (four stressed monosyllables).

'Dad the daredevil would have; survivor of a thousand deaths.'

I could see how afraid — and scornful — Dave was; too full of his own importance to risk his precious body as bait. I felt like shoving him overboard, let him feel his own fear.

Instead, in a sort of bored disgust, I flopped over backwards myself, holding my nose until I'd come to the surface, and then reaching out for the shore at, for me, an amazing pace, not really aware of the shark-infested water, the speedboat making its infernal racket behind me. Just swimming as best I could where the sun went between the burning green Transkei hills, mudsnappers flicking about in the roots; and finding some firm shore where I could slosh out and at least squeeze the water from my shirt-tails: Carol coming up, 'You've really upset Dave; the one thing he did *not* want was to get his own brother eaten or drowned. Surely you understand that, dammit.'

'I'm not eaten, I'm not drowned, Carol. I even still have a sense of humour.'

'Look at the example you set for the boys; why do you do it, just to rile him; you have no excuse.'

'He has no guts.'

'Guts! Well, if that's guts, Joe, I'd like to know what you think of as brains!'

All right, carrot-juice.

Within the week we had to photo Dave and the ragged-tooth at the winch; not that a thing that long could be weighed until it had been cut up. Dave's trophy for the season.

Carol was not yet like our mother, but she was showing signs of becoming. The only time Dave took any interest in his own domestic life was during the Sunday barbecue: sprinkling the sausages on the grill as if that would damp them and Carol took the pitchfork from him and stabbed free spurts of fat; he gave a goofy grin. Then Carol stood behind him where he sat with his shandy, her elbow on his shoulder, and I could see the way their bodies responded to one another. He very much loved and admired her, depended on her for everything: sausages pricked, standards maintained and raised, neat collar and tie, even the plants to bloom, the fish to swim. Between the two of them, the young ruffians choosing which way to follow — their father's or mine. Women never were in the running. Our mother died of her servitude; Dave doesn't remember that; she just got tired of the weight of her terrible husband and rolled over and departed.

When you're living inside such a story it is hard to pinpoint the blasphemy: trying to speak the unspoken, maybe; utter the forbidden name of God in a compromised position, to say the least, in a part of my life which is off the record and shall stay that way. Obscenities so shocking you would neither believe nor, I doubt, I could verbalise. But that is not the point now. What I wish to explain here is how that terrible defiance lurks in my affluent and extremely successful family, and how my brother's activities seem so much more offensive to me than I know mine do to him.

For a miracle, he did visit me in the flat — once. The phone went at about five; you've got to believe this, he said his private jet was having a service before he flew to, I don't know, Taiwan at midnight. I said oh good, why didn't he come right away, we were having an early dinner anyway as Reggie had to go out to work (to slave his black ass off) — as usual.

'Who's Reggie?' says my brother.

Hadn't I told him? Hadn't his own wife explained all those years ago?

Why, Regina the Queen of Upper Cross Hill, from whose hands I'd been receiving wafers and blood, the private nurse who'd stayed on and with whom I shared even my title deeds. Did he not know how *difficult* this had been in bad old apartheid days; and now even worse among predominantly blacks, so he was *not to be surprised* when he got to the foyer and pressed 1005 the place was described as occupied by Mr *and Mrs* Swabalala, for decency's sake.

'What time does this other person go?' he replied.

'Soon as we've eaten,' I said; 'he's on at seven till dawn. Night watch — has to hold their hands as they go. He does that best; they expect it of him, too.'

Reggie took the phone. 'You Joey's long-lost brother... having your jet cleaned out, I hear. Joey's told me a lot about you and always shows me the Christmas cards... No, he's dying to see you... He's just taking all the bottles down to the skips in the basement to make some room in here: yes, we have our own one for clear glass and one for green glass and there's a smoky brown. Recycling for crippled care. Just about everything we do is for charity: oldies on walkers and hydrocephalics, autistics...' Dave must have said they sounded interesting. 'Oh, we have the AIDS helpline as well and I do counselling for them; no, not AA, AIDS which is this new disease we get, right, that's the one; I do counselling for people like that and all, or just lonely people who want advice...' Reggie hung up. 'Your brother says he'd certainly like to meet me, I sound so socially useful! Pity I have to earn a living as well.'

I brought in the tray with two bowls of soup and croutons and a fresh salad. We sat opposite one another in the last winter sun for the day.

'If he puts me under any blackmail, you know what'll happen — relapse isn't the word.'

'Don't you dare.'

I toasted Reggie in sparkling grapejuice. 'Why do you waste your time with such a has-been, Mr Reggie and the Pledge — when you could be — Thailand tomorrow, New York the next? In one of my brother's soap operas. You could find so many richer men than me to live off.'

But Reggie just doesn't hear temptation, isn't interested in anything much outside our funny life together. Takes the tray to the sink, washes out. Laces up his sexy Stryker boots and bounces off to the wards to help them through. Thank God I found him before anyone else. Start up the Mantovani: my life is in his hands; if he were to drop me, see how I'd fall; he is indeed extremely good at his job. He is the only person I have ever deeply — well, loved.

They miss one another by minutes; my brother has seen to that. I let him in and warm the third bowl of soup and throw about the remains of the salad.

No, not to worry, he won't stay long.

Not stay long... he must have pressing business indeed if after all these years.

He does have; he shows me: he pulls out what to me is a tobacco-pouch with cute little drawstrings and he looks for a well-lit, dust-free surface. He will not drink of our glasses, lick of our spoons, and now the flat is too clogged with dust for him to pour his diamonds out. Three times I swipe the shelf in the bathroom down of toothpaste and mouthwash; this surface is indeed extremely well illuminated to distinguish one prescription from another. I have to agree they are absolutely exquisite; not touch them, I have *greasy fingers*... hereditary, subliminal grease, I suppose. Held up in tweezers, can they possibly be worth so much, how much did you say, oh the *lot as a whole*... cut diamonds; these things ought never to be allowed out in daylight.

All right, now he would have a little soup.

'How's Carol?' I said. He said Carol was fine and,

although she didn't want to lose them, the boys were both coming to Johannesburg: little Davey to Law School and the other to 'drop out and learn the business from the ground up' — a hard procedure considering the nature of the business: parachute-making, and then the whole nylon and silk industry. (There had been a scandal over boys in the border-war baling out only to find their big Dave-spun webs unravelling in mid-air. Dave was still sensitive about it, although he had weathered several assaults on his integrity since. I just followed all that in *Business Day*.)

'Carol'll be lonely.'

'Sure will, now the main purpose in her life is gone.'

'Does Carol know you say things like that behind her back?'

'No, of course not.'

'Do you sleep around now that she has no function and you're away so much? I suppose with your photo of her and the lads on the bedside table, it's sort of OK.'

'There isn't time for that. I don't think you realise how deeply I'm in.'

'Whatever that means. Dave, I don't want to know, but don't you just — have a heart-flutter occasionally about — someone that comes along — other people are so beautiful — and touches your fancy? Not even a special person, a thing maybe? Just something unpredictable? To throw your eye off the fax-machine a bit? I mean, other people would enjoy sleeping with *you*, you know.'

Dave had his eye on the photo of Reggie as Carmen Miranda and yes, that was his brother with the pineapple bra holding up his brother's lover's peacock-feather train (the night he won 'Miss Stag's a Drag' at the Dungeon, and I was his runner-up). This must have had some effect on Dave; he'd been poking his tongue in and out of his cheek until even I was getting embarrassed.

'You once said,' he muttered, 'you must not take our father —'

'I must or you must —'

'Well, I — but generally —'

'Not *our* father, you dolt: it means take whichever one you/I/he holds sacred and *misuse* it. The commandment comes in the first person, but it means do not go against the beliefs *you* proclaim, thou hypocrite, otherwise *you* are a wilful sham and deserve to be punished for it. You may lie, but it means you mustn't live that lie knowingly as well. Is *that* why you came to see me — for some stupid post-religious, post-apartheid, post-everything else — moral advice, O brother mine?'

'I didn't love our father.'

'I beg your pardon.'

'I hated him.'

'Oh and I'd say you've only now realised your whole manic energy is based on hate for your father and not love; oh come on, Dave. He was a disgusting man; are you surprised you loathed him?'

'He shouldn't have given us life!'

'Um, maybe he shouldn't have given *me* life, my darling. But you're so exactly what he wanted you to become.'

'How does it happen that two so different — you know — from the same?'

'Christ, Dave, only now are the big questions of your early teens catching up on you in advanced middle age? Oh p-lease. You'd better go, you'll miss your plane.'

Well, in his case the plane would wait. We sat and watched *Hill Street Blues* until he phoned down to his car (yes... golly-gosh). Hate got him a lot further in the world than love ever would me! Oh gee, oh gosh, the heavy-handed irony of soapy fate. If I had known I really would have given him more care.

It's not that I check on him or, heaven forfend, wish to cramp any of his style, but when Reggie does come to bed at five or six or seven a.m. I have in a way been waiting up for him and the long night may now end for us both. 'Brr, you should have seen my brother; he had this packet full of rare stones....'

'I did, I saw him get in the lift as I got out. I said, "You must be Joey's brother"; looks exactly like you, bit fitter; one mieliepip and another.'

'Peas in the pod is the European expression.'

'Your paunch is a bit, bags under eyes; I say he has a hairier chest, but otherwise —'

'You couldn't tell us apart... All quiet tonight?'

'As the grave.'

'Thank God for that.' Then I suddenly sat up: 'You saw him? You saw him, the evil bastard: that man is evil, evil, evil...'

'Looked OK to me.'

'What did he say to you?'

'He didn't say anything because he didn't know who I was, obviously.'

'You wouldn't let a chance like that go by.'

'Quite correct. I said: "You must be Joey's baby brother, and I'm Reggie his lover," and we shook hands; well, fingertips — brushed like that.'

'Did you tell him how well you're doing in accounting, now that you're getting personal tuition?'

'Joey, he wanted to go up in the lift I'd just stepped out of. Finger-light, just a brush.'

'Evil bastard. You don't have to know much of his personal flight schedule to realise what he does for a living. How come he can go where *no one* else goes?'

'Parachutes in, I suppose.'

'Pays to travel with a little pouch of crêpe de chine,' (the billow of the sac is referred to)... The touch of fingers; they come, they go...

When the *Sunday Times* business section phoned me six months later, that was the first I heard of my brother's demise... gone down over some diminishing rain forest or melting ice-cap or over the boiling ocean, without trace. All I could say was: 'I don't believe it; he'll be back.'

Did I know how many companies he'd left? I had no idea. With how much capital? None whatsoever.

Did I know he'd left what was his to leave, lock and stock entirely to me? I said I'd better talk to his wife Carol, surely he'd have left some of the barrels to her. And to the boys.

This was what they called a conference line; they added Carol in. 'Joey, it's quite true what they say. We have stuff to make do with — you get the business, you know.'

'Oh Carol, I am so deeply sorry, after all you've done for him, and how you two were together.'

'I know. See you at the funeral then. I'll be all right.'

'What funeral, if there isn't a body?'

'You have to have one, nevertheless.' Carol gave a horrible sob. The *Sunday Times* intervened and I told them to put her back on. They lost both of us. Quote: 'Brother in Dark over Empire, Widow Mourns.'

During the next hectic weeks I discovered only some of the extent of my late brother's operations: dark, hateful, secret industries which even he could not have fully controlled. Layer and layer would peel off, clue after clue: munitions again, nerve-gas — a new spoiler without a name. People in the know were just *too scared* of what he could already do to stop him doing worse.

An exception should be made in my brother's case: he should repeatedly be brought back from the dead to stand trial for his crimes against humanity. One little life was not enough to pay in punishment. To put none too fine a point on it, South Africa had long given up on decent practices in an open market; was used to flush detestables; survived dirtily; would have fallen long ago if there were limits to misuse of the Lord's name. I don't even know how to express my disgust for my family and for my country that let them so flourish.

I phoned Carol often; always she'd say she just didn't know. Instead of now feeling lonely, she felt more and more excluded.

Thank God — once again — I had Reggie: that's all. If I was pressed for any one of a thousand crucial decisions, I'd stammer, I'd stutter and mutter, I would wait until I had consulted *my* business partner!

At least we would get our heart's desire out of a small eddy in this tidal flow of cash: the fully equipped R & J Centre where generations of patients could have their inevitable way to the tomb eased, at least that; at least not an end in the gutter where others more fortunate could tread them down without mercy; punish them for misusing His/their name (Ex. 20, 7). Anyway: the R 'n' J Crisis Clinic, as all sickeningly young males-only know, stands ready to receive them for contusions and crashing on the corner of Lower Cross and 3rd, 24 hours every day (no charge). R 'n' J C C is far more sophisticated than your old VD clinics (nothing that long-lasting penicillin couldn't cure); this one has every piece of equipment from laser ECGs through to smokeless incinerators... Sometimes when you see the array it is hard to believe it is intended to do the human body good. 'Burn, baby, burn,' says Reggie, my co-founder and lifelong fellow shareholder, and I remind him: 'No, Reggie, the point is atone, baby, atone.'

With the clinic open very conspicuously and everyone knowing how wealthy we were, people flocked to consult us. Reggie was kind and thoughtful, as always. But I had shot from being a back-room accountant who worked from the bedroom of his flat into being this sort of storefront adviser. My old clients with corner cafés below now wanted to convert to delis, and if I thought they were hard-working enough I would assist; if not, advise them to sell out to blacks! Most I recommended sell; some I cashed up for them. *Nothing for free*. I had not had a relapse into the bottle, either; life was far too exciting as my late brother's humanitarian wing.

The reckoning had to come. Making money was too much fun to last. We kept the flat; Reggie kept his range of employment. But now he had an extended African family he had not heard of before, stretching from the Cape to the Zambesi – they all had demands: rent and fees to pay, children to place, funerals and weddings – about none of which Reggie had even been kept informed before. If he was away discovering his heritage, I took his shift as a telephone counsellor, and that's how I discovered the little light of my life.

'You are new to the city, have lost your father tragically recently –'

'Um, and my older brother's such a horrible, you know – butch, er, trying to disinherit me –'

'And you're coming out in the usual painful way; you do not wish your mother to know of your feelings. Just to complete the picture, do you by any remote chance have a gay uncle, too, kept in the family closet?'

'Er, oh my God...'

'Look, just come up to 1005 High Cross and I'll tell you probably more than you want to hear. Don't feel bad about it; it had to happen sooner or later. God does not sleep. It's a common enough story.'

When Reggie got back from evident blood-letting in some tribal reserve: 'My God, if it isn't Joey's late brother's little second-born coming out to greet his uncle and his friend after all this time: now isn't that the cutest, darndest thing. Why, I remember you da day you were born —'

'He just talks like *Gone with the Wind*; he learnt his English from the video.'

'Sabona, Reggie,' said little Joe, and their fingers touched and Reggie, temporarily stuck for words, patted the pillow alongside him on the couch, for the eighteen-year-old piece of family to lay down his weary limbs.

And it had to happen, despite the age-gap. They sort of fell for one another (but couldn't confess it, could they now?); became inseparable, experienced many exciting things together about which I was not meant to know, not even to be interested in. Reggie dropped all his worst jobs and got himself driven around to distant parts these days. I had other people's accounts and the TV. I should have felt we had acquired a child; I felt I had lost everything.

This was the first time in my adulthood I was lonely. I had incessant phone-calls from secretaries of bosses or visits from one or another director (always late), and really would rather have liked some friendship and moral support. Routinely I said no, I would not budge... but I wanted to, I wanted a complete change.

So it was time to call Carol and bring this thing to an end: I told her (we discussed many things freely) I wanted a fortnight with both her sons and excluding her at Mbashee (where last we fished together), with all the usual catering and facilities, but no intruders, and I would settle the line of succession once and for all. I assured her she need have no fear. She wanted to remarry, so a settlement would ease things for her, too. But little Davey was then skiing in Switzerland with the daughter of Hoechst and she had high hopes; I said I didn't care if he was windsurfing in Haiti with the son of Siemens — he was to be at Mbashee on the 20th. The 20th it would be. I wanted all the keys, no secrets. But Dave kept nothing there; oh yes he did.

Reggie and I were flown down in a no-fuss way, and what a thrill for him; we were made welcome as though the place were already ours. Mbashee had not changed, but Transkei was of course under military rule by then... which meant a police guard in the bushes. The Pan African Congress had made its boast that any whites holidaying on the Wild Coast would be slaughtered on or before Easter weekend; this seemed a perfectly reasonable way to gain access to power. That lone family palace over the tidal lagoon looked wonderfully remote. I thought of my cussed father and tolerant mother and freckled Dave as we tossed about in the homemade boat (no money in those days), and now — time's manoeuvres — there came the two hearty grandsons, waving up to the roof-balcony, heartbreakingly beautiful in the fuzzy sunset. So at ease with one another, with us. So easy-going: 'Uncle Joey, *Uncle Reg.*'

Their father had indeed meant to spend more time there: we dug out amounts of documentation and quite enough firepower to defend half the coastline. That's how he worked: secret deals; bullets. 'Do you like it, young Davey?'

Davey did not know if he liked it or not (was not used to it yet), but his attitude was that since he obviously represented the straight line of the family, he should get control. I said that my crooked body was not dead yet; I would retain the central string of the businesses until I was completely sure which way the net should go. This put everyone on their best behaviour.

With so many guns and deferential looks around, I wonder they didn't just shoot me. They had reasonable opportunities: while Davey was teaching me to fish off the bows of the speedboat up-lagoon where no one would know. (Maybe I was too good a cook of the shad I caught and, to my great delight, slit open; and I'll tell you, unfrozen fish does not smell fishy. Maybe Davey thought I would give him some last lessons.)

'Uncle Joey... what do you think? We sell, for the strip-mining? It'll keep three hundred people employed for thirty years. The dunes'll grow back.'

'Only in a thousand years. You know I think the answer to strip-mining is no, and no means no.'

'OK, so what do you approve of? Do you approve of anything that shows some endeavour? First time I've heard a business is too moral and all to be a business at all; man gotta live, Uncle Joe.'

'So why not just shoot me as an old windbag?'

'Why are you doing this?'

'Because *your father* wanted me to punish you for his sins, that's why.'

'Aw, Uncle Joe....'

They nearly shot Reggie; not the two nephews, but the Transkeian guards who were on to protect us from the PAC, for goodness sake. One evening we had been playing cards and Reggie gets overbored, decides to liven up the party in Carol's beach-gear with the tape-recorder playing Judy's greatest hits. They nearly shot him for being a *black man* playing a white whore. These bruisers have no sense of humour.

They shot one of their own; boys will be boys; it was an accident when one got the jitters down at the jetty. We had to get his fatigues off on the kitchen table and find the slug. The man seemed indifferent to pain; no, he was extremely brave. He took a double brandy. He, who had every reason to blaspheme as the bait-knife dug under his ribs, did not; he merely went: 'Hoo, mama...' to Reggie with a dishcloth round his nose and in washing-up gloves. Little Joey at his side, holding a saucer to receive the metal piece.

In such a godless world it occurred to me that is all we could do: save the men from themselves. Little Davey was taking the sight of blood badly; I had to hold his head back for air, then push it between his knees. That's how his father started, and his father before him — over-sensitive to physical realities. So shocked when blood flowed, so grateful it wasn't his own — fear, really, kept them having it spilled, any blood except their own.

'My decision, Davey...' I said the next day. 'Let's not prolong this.'

We were all getting into the speedboat. The man with the bullet wound made a stirring motion with his good arm and smiled faintly. He meant the ragged-tooth shark was back in with the tide, in the muddy water just ahead. Davey wanted to throttle, but held back in order to hear what I would say.

'This stays as is, for us to play mad Schweitzer and Nanny the Nurse; we'll probably retire here, and little Joe is welcome whenever he wants; well, you all are, of course, specially your mother.'

'Agreed.'

Reggie and his little one-piece sylph held their noses, whooped with glee and bomb-dropped overboard.

'They're swimming in and amongst a shark, you know,' said Davey. He cut the engines, kept an eye out.

'Sometimes it's hard to find the right cord to pull, at the right moment,' I said.

'Sure thing,' said Davey, infinitely unimpressed.

'You get the rest, with due provision and in trust and so on and so forth, for the rest of your days,' I said.

'As from when?'

'From this moment, a verbal agreement is binding, you know.'

'Sure, sure. And there's only one thing you wish to add.'

'There is, you're right.'

'I will not use your name for evil purposes again; honest to God, I swear.'

'Thou shalt not take my name in vain, ever again, you mean.'

This is the difficult bit — how it ends.

Dreadful child — blue eyes turned skyward, his fingers crossed firmly behind his back. That way he thinks it does not count. His name is not little Davey any longer.

◆

Watch out,
the World's Behind You

JOSEPH MILLS

◆

*'Remember the sabbath day, to keep it
holy. Six days shalt thou labour, and do
all thy work: But the seventh day is the
sabbath of the Lord thy God: in it thou
shalt not do any work, thou, nor thy
son, nor thy daughter, thy manservant,
nor thy maidservant, nor thy cattle, nor
the stranger that is within thy gates; for
in six days the Lord made heaven and
earth, the sea, and all that in them is,
and rested the seventh day; wherefore
the Lord blessed the sabbath day and
hallowed it.'*

◆

'*A*nd on the *third* day,' William said,
'...we got The Dog.'

'The *Dug*,' Robert corrected.

William opened the Harrods Super Deluxe Photo Album at a double page spread headed THE DUG in individual silver letters. Beneath which: photos of Robert and The Dug, William and The Dug, Robert and William and The Dug.

'Oh and there's us seeing ye aff at Central Station.' Robert's ma pointed the picture out to her husband. Mr and Mrs Murray were sitting either side of William on the big settee; in front of them a coffee table supporting a huge pile of photo albums. The table was a pretentious affair which William had dared Robert to buy. Instead of legs to support it, there was a big bronze Hercules shouldering the smoked glass. He seemed at that moment to be sweating. Certainly the bronze was glossier than usual. Robert sat opposite with an upside down view of the proceedings.

'That's a gid yin,' Mr Murray said, looking at the Central Station photo. 'Who took that wan?'

'That's one of mine,' said William. 'I take all the arrivals and departures; Robert takes all the important ones.' He slid the picture out of the tinted protective cellophane. 'Gorgeous, isn't it? You should see it on the projector.' He handed it over to Robert. 'We really *must* get the slides out later.'

Robert examined it. Yes, it really was a great picture: Robert's ma and da with The Dug on Renfield Street, at the corner of the station. William had stood well back up the street so he could get into the picture the big neon IRN BRU sign which William, a twenty-one-year-old Southerner, had decided was the nexus of all Glasgow, Scotland, just as the COKE sign on Times Square was the centre of New York, New York.

As always when he saw those neon night photos of Glasgow — even more so when it was the aerial post-cards kaleidoscoping the city — Robert found it hard to believe that he was looking at the same place he'd grown up in, a place that corresponded much more, he was sure, to the old black and white tenement pictures they didn't seem to take as much any more. But William's picture really did, Robert remembered, look great on the slides, where you could lighten and darken the scene so it was even better than the real thing, like a memory.

'Remember,' William said, taking the photo back, 'that was the night we were going to London.'

'Of course I remember. It was only two months ago. Show them the new fire in the bedroom.'

William snapped the album shut.

'Do you want to see it now?'

Robert's parents dutifully stood up. They always deferred to William's English middle-class politeness; through enchantment, claimed William, through cultural intimidation, said Robert.

'We turned the fire on earlier so it could build up to its best effect,' said William as he led them away, turning back to Robert. 'It's probably warmer in there.'

Robert turned the photo album around and flicked through the pages.

God, all this nostalgia.

But he had been trying to remember something himself.

The kitchen door was open. He couldn't help noticing the overflowing laundry basket waiting to be emptied; the hoover plugged in and ready to rock; half-written letters and unpaid bills on the desk.

Fucking Sunday. The rubbish tip at the end of the week, where all the undesirable chores of life pile up, demanding immediate attention. How could anyone like a Sunday?

Sundays

Robert had always hated the last day of the week. He had got off to a bad start with Sunday right from the beginning. It first became distinct to him as The Day Before School, throughout which the week in prospect lingered at the back of the mind like a death sentence — whether he had homework to do or not. Having to do Sunday chores was bad enough — although compared to the nine to five of weekdays it should have seemed like heaven. Worse was the depressing realisation that the weekend had gone, all too quickly, and there was the huge five-day sentence in store before another. Curiously though, once he actually started serving the sentence it was never as bad as the anxiety that preceded it. But, of course, he forgot this every Sunday, as completely as a reincarnated soul is said to forget all its past lives.

Mass was always the low point of the day. Robert went dutifully, although he didn't know why he had to. Neither did his parents, but when he asked they told him: 'Because you're a Catholic.' His Protestant friends didn't have to go. They probably loved Sundays. They never had to make the big decision: Morning Mass or Evening. Neither alternative was attractive. If you left it till night time you had it hanging over you all day; if you got up early, the day was that much longer, *and* you had to mingle with all the Happy Sundays, the ones who went to mass because they enjoyed it, not, like the majority, because they were terrified of Hell.

Mr Murray always got up for the 10 a.m. show, which made Robert feel guilty, since Sunday was his da's only day of rest, the weekdays being spent taking the place of a piece of machinery in a factory, and Saturday afternoon working part-time in the betting shop. The countdown also began for Robert's da on a Sunday, the countdown to Friday night, when he would be in the pub, young.

Everybody's young on a Friday. Friday is blind youth — all that time in front of you! Saturday, with Sunday on the horizon is middle-age; Sunday, old age and death. Monday to Friday night is the dutiful pre-independence period, when we grudgingly do what others tell us, because we think it will be good for us in the long run.

Robert looked through the double glazing on to a late afternoon Glasgow Sunday. Depressing stillness. Nearly all the shops shut. An early winter sun dying painfully.

He left the lights down low and switched off the photo album lamp. It should have been one of those sultry Barry White/Luther Vandross soulful moments, like the ones they try to evoke in the ads for 20 LOVE SENSATIONS. Instead, being Sunday, the atmosphere cried out for a bland waiting — room soundtrack: sterile saxophones, tuneless muzak getting nowhere by intention. Cheap nostalgia.

Robert had another look at the Central Station picture of ma, da and The Dug. William's furry glove was clearly visible by the edge of the photo. He could never quite take a flawless picture.

Something about the glove.

What *was* he trying to remember?

He dug out some of his old Woolworth's photo albums: Robert Abroad.

By leaving Glasgow Robert had managed to obliterate Sundays altogether, but the process had begun before that. Choosing jobs that involved shift work meant he worked through the weekends, getting paid double into the bargain. And there was the reward of sweet midweek holidays: getting up at eight in the morning just to go out and buy a big 'Sunday' breakfast and watch all the zombies at the bus stops. Somehow all the normal Sunday things became luxurious during the week: the long lazy meal, three hours over papers and magazines, black and white 40s films. So it wasn't, he discovered, that he hated not working. It was that all-encompassing Sunday rut that was so hard to endure, when everyone, no matter what the circumstance, is expected to come to an abrupt halt for twenty-four hours and take part in the great collective rest.

Take the worst aspects of Christmas and New Year − the obligation to walk slower, smile for nothing, reflect − multiply by fifty-two. Answer: Sunday. *The Day The Earth Stands Still*.

And not that he hated the prospect of a working week. At least not since he found a job that suited − the photo-journalism that ultimately destroyed the Sabbath by taking Robert here there and everywhere until there were no more days of the week at all, just assignments and in between assignments.

Here there and everywhere eventually became New York, whose inhabitants, at least those worker ants that Robert mingled with, could ignore pneumonia if it got in the way of progress; so Sunday was a piece of cake – or rather, Sunday was Central Park jogging, performing, hosting, spectating, culturing, *doing*.

He made a lot of money there.

'There's a rerr heat aff that fire, Robert,' his ma said, coming out of the bedroom. But she still made for the big Real Coal affair in the living room, rubbing hands. They had obviously set the bedroom fire too low.

'We've made this smaller bedroom into a gym,' William was saying, leading Mr Murray there. The tour had only just begun. Robert's ma quickly left the fire to follow them.

The money embarrassed Robert, after all the early poverty – which he could now review with the same sense of detachment usually summoned up for his snapshots of Third World Misery.

Tenements

Snap One: the outside toilet, unlockable door hanging open, overflowing with used toilet paper and urine, beetles crawling up the walls. Snap Two: Brother, two sisters and parents sharing a cramped room (males) and kitchen (females). Snap Three: The same rooms two months later with the furniture rearranged to make it look new. Snap Four: The raganbone man handing over a few shillings for beans and cheese biscuits on the day before payday. Snap Five: His da, furtive, embarrassed, handing over the pay packet at work to Robert on Friday afternoon because they couldn't afford to wait till he got home.

Even though he had easily managed to buy his parents' council house for them, clear off all their debts and free them from money worries until the end of their days, Robert still felt guilty. He had more money than them and he always would have. If he gave them every penny he had they wouldn't know what to do with it. He could never make them as consumerist as he had become; as his generation and class was becoming he discovered on his return to Glasgow in the 80s. They were too old to get on that roundabout.

'What time is that now?' Robert could hear his da asking. All the clocks and watches in his parents' house were running either too fast or too slow, to varying degrees, so that you had to check all of them at one go to calculate the exact time. But only Mr and Mrs Murray knew the rates of imprecision, so the secret of time was theirs in their own home. Outside of it their watches were useless.

'It's only just after six,' William said.

He'll be worrying about missing the news, Robert guessed. Mr Murray was an absolute news junkie. He watched all the main programmes on all channels – one o'clock, five-forty, six, seven, nine, ten, *Newsnight*, and all the in-between bulletins, from TV A.M. to *Through The Night* on STV. Like so many working-class pensioners, untrained for a life of leisure, he had a thoroughly informed opinion on all those issues of the day he could do zero about. Except vote every five years, in a country that had been voting in huge Labour majorities throughout the decade and had been 'democratically' governed by the Tories for its troubles. So zero right enough.

Robert's da almost escaped back into the living room.

'Oh, but one last thing,' William stopped him. 'You must see in here.' He took them into the little studio they had set up: a dark room for Robert, and a wall of tape machines, synthesisers and video equipment for William. The plan had been that together they would create avant-garde audio-visual poems. But William hadn't counted on Robert's art burn-out from his years in Greenwich Village. As far as he was concerned,

Lennon was right when he said, 'Avant-garde is French for shit.' So William had to settle for a video collage of Robert's best pictures, synchronised to William's beat. And thus was the creative fusion of their relationship achieved, not to William's complete satisfaction, but well within the time limit set for it.

Robert pitied his poor parents having to sit through that. And his sisters and bemused brothers-in-law seven days earlier. Embarrassed friends the week before that. This Remembrance Sunday was definitely becoming a fixed routine.

When had it begun? It must have been on the Anniversary. Four weeks ago. Six months they celebrated. To the day. According to plan. They were where they said they would be six months before. So it wasn't only a period of time together they were celebrating, but a success. A job well done.

It was definitely something about the early days Robert was trying to remember. Maybe as far back as Day One, the day they officially charted the beginning of their life together from; or further back still, the few weeks before that (which William chose to ignore), that limbo spent cajoling Robert into marriage, into *bed* for god's sake. The weeks that those who weren't there never believed existed.

No one who saw the sandy-haired twenty-one-year-old William with the stencilled-in stomach muscles would ever have imagined that he would have to *pursue* a reluctant Robert, twice his age, greying, balding and thickening all over. None of what friends Robert had left at the time believed it, any more than they believed his claim to have been celibate for the ten years before he met William. Celibate not just in any old decade, but in the fun-loving, hedonistic 80s, when the British were just beginning to learn about conspicuous consumption — or at least were beginning to learn to yearn for it. But it was true. And he wouldn't have believed it of himself in the 70s. When he went quite mad.

Robert's 70s

For a working-class Scot to make big money was reason enough for merrymaking — they celebrate enthusiastically enough on factory wages — to travel, even more uninhibiting. But to let loose a near virginal faggot on The States Of Desire in the decade of The Golden Age — *well*. Robert enjoyed The Dancers and The Dance to the full. To the extent of addiction really. But being addicted to sex, love, drugs, money in those places at that time was like being 'addicted' to tea or beer in Glasgow. You would never have dreamed of looking at it as such, since the medicine was so readily available, and nobody was asking you to watch the dosage.

Ironically, the one narcotic he did attempt to be Scots-thrifty with — love — was the one that proved the hardest to kick. Sex, drugs, booze, money were all consumed in copious amounts with never a thought to the morning after. But he did try to economise on the currency of Romance: the looks, gestures, declarations, tears and admissions, attempting to save something for some far off Right Time.

'Postponing happiness Robert, *really*,' William had said when he told him all this. 'How *very* middle class.'

And of course the plan was doomed to failure. Love was the one thing that couldn't be rationed or controlled, and the overdoses, withdrawal pains and eventual immunity had ultimately led to his austere decade. But it was the thing he gave least thought to that started him off on the road to abstinence.

Sex had at first been easy, uncomplicated, fulfilling. And safe — until the little bug arrived, whenever. Somehow he had been one of the lucky ones, but if he hadn't tired eventually of the consequences of over-indulgence the bug would certainly have found him too. For Robert got everything going. Friends watching him prepare for a night on the town would joke: They're out there waiting for you Robert, all those little germs and bugs with the big red 'R' on their backs. He began to get fed up with the increasing number of weekends which had to be endured in agony before he could get hold of his doctor; days spent passing razor-blades through the bladder, and clawing at red skin (why did he always ignore crabs until it was too late); bedtimes spent drifting in and out of nightmares at the thought of those creatures living off him, even after he'd given in and shaved every hair off his caveman body. And come Monday, the flesh-rending cures were just as bad — 'A mild stinging of a transient nature' indeed. His doctor had begun to tire of Robert's indulgence shortly before Robert did, signalling his lack of sympathy by yanking foreskin back, and demonstrating just how heavy-handed you could be with a cotton swab.

'I knew the Scots had to be famous for something,' he would complain sarcastically.

Robert was giving the Homeland a bad name. He decided to slow down. And when the physical illnesses were compounded by more severe emotional ones, he decided to stop altogether.

'He's dreaming of Alberrr again,' William said. The tour was over and his parents had been brought up to date on WillyRobertland. They brought tea in with them.

'It's no ferr leavin' William to do all this himself,' Mrs Murray said.

'Five minutes,' said Robert, 'and you'll have my undivided attention.' He locked himself in the bathroom.

His head was buzzing with unanswerable questions.

What am I trying to remember?

Why all this reminiscing?

What else is there to do on a Sunday?

Do angels spend eternity gazing down from heaven at their imperfect earthly shadows?

Longingly?

How Robert's 70s ended

1979: he was falling out of love with love. He had endured one too many hello/goodbyes; and all that other nonsense: please stay/better off without me, I/you need more space/time/relativity. He had experienced, directly and indirectly, too many emotional couplings, too many insights into the whys and wherefores of Romantic Love. Like a scientist nearing the end of an experiment, the data was becoming all too familiar, trial results repeating themselves over and over again. Far from rationing love, by the end he was consuming and processing it at an alarming rate. An attraction that could have sustained itself for several years at school in mystery and luxurious frustration was now digested and excreted in a week or a night, so efficient had his emotional metabolism become. No sooner did he begin some attachment than he rushed to see the end of it, rose in one hand, telescope in the other.

This state of affairs had come about through necessity. He had decided he needed to stop loving because he was too sensitive to romantic failure. The non-starters or enforced partings were bad enough. Even worse were those grey areas when agonizing choices had to be made: whether to maintain a difficult but intense relationship or not.

Torture.

It was then he wondered why everyone made all the fuss about sex and none about love. Why did authorities meticulously define sex crimes but ignore love in their law books. The consequences of sex — VD, pregnancy, AIDS — are so foreseeable and preventable that it's impossible for a consenting, careful partner to be unexpectedly affected by them. But how many emotional virgins are trapped by experienced cynics into passionate affairs, only to be dumped by the expert when he tires of what was, for him, a diversion, for the virgin, everything.

'Alberr' — Albert — had duped and dumped Robert. Had he been warned, he would have thought twice. Had someone said: You will fall in love with Albert, but he will never be able to fall in love with you, then he would have taken precautions. But he was not a consenting adult, and he bitterly told those who would listen that they should take the pretty police out of the toilets and put them in cafés and wine bars where love crimes were being committed every day.

Albert, contrary to William's belief, was not the major entanglement, simply the first of many disasters — those attractive intellectuals and artists who fascinated him with a language which seemed way above his head (until the same quoted authors turned up again and again, the same quotations); the models and B-movie actors who turned out to have brains in inverse proportion to beauty.

He learned. It became easier. And be began breaking hearts himself, knowingly and without consent. And he got sick of himself, after all those moralising Catholic teens. Anyone, it was now obvious, could be a puritan in a block of ice. And then he began forgiving himself, and all the others, and ended up feeling calm, all-knowing. And middle-aged. 'Another Brick in the Wall' was the appropriately bland tune that was number one the day he dramatically decided to have a rest from it all: New Year's Eve 1979. At a mad orgy of Village People lookalikes in New York. Which left him with yet more germs and bugs with the red 'R' on their backs; but this time the creatures were much more tenacious. Which, in retrospect, was a blessing in disguise: he would surely have fallen back into old habits but for the enforced three month layoff. After which he realised that he did not miss the sex as much as he would have thought, told himself to grow up and get on with Other Things.

Robert's 80s

Success in his career intensified his resolve. The assignments were already mounting up since he switched from journalism to showbiz. All the contacts he'd made led to contracts for pre-production work on major movies. Making a small fortune became the biggest kick of all. And then he found himself in with one of the echoes of the Warhol crowd, where celibacy was chic in the early 80s, and you had all the drugs to help.

And just as the notion of dipping his toes back in the water emerged there were the first rumblings of the AIDS volcano and he decided to wait just that little bit longer till they got it sorted out. Then it got worse and he was convinced he had it. He had a test. It was negative, which was a surprise, a relief, a message. The doctors had their four-year plan for a vaccine or cure; he had a similar length plan for lifelong financial security. His plan worked, theirs didn't. They were still saying 'four years' almost a decade later. And throughout that decade the chance of moving from positive to full-blown moved from one in ten to nine in ten, and he decided he didn't trust his willpower, having never practised 'safe sex' in his life. Anyway, the rest would do him good.

No. It wasn't anything to do with that period either he was trying to remember. It was definitely to do with William and him and Day One.

Robert joined William in the living room. He was not, as Robert had feared, showing off their joint address book: look how many people we know! They had decided very early on that Good Friends were a must-have component of the population of their world.

Parents were in the kitchen. TV was on.

William handed Robert a cup of cold tea. 'What's with all the off-stage philosophising?'

'I don't know. I feel as though I've got a tape loop of The Robert Murray Story reeling through my head today. It's all your fault,' − he indicated the photo albums piled high − 'And all this grand tour nonsense.'

'Well we worked hard for it. Why not show it off?'

Robert sipped the cold tea and made a face. He sat down, back, and closed his eyes. William sat beside him, took his hand and rubbed it vigorously.

'Now, now. We don't want to lose you again. I know the Scots are supposed to be dour and impenetrable but this is ridiculous.'

Robert opened his eyes and sat up. 'Sorry. Sundays just make me feel so lazy.' He opened one of the earliest photo albums. 'I bet you didn't realise what you were taking on back then. I bet you thought: nothing else doing tonight, so I'll take on this old thing, even though he's twice my age, balding —'

'Attractively.'

'Greying —'

'With distinction.'

'And putting on weight all over.'

'*Very* attractively.'

'You make middle age sound... attractive.'

'You make it sound like Lourdes.' William measured the considerable expanse of Robert's shoulders. 'I thought you were James Bond.'

'Only because you were in a Scottish gay bar.'

'No. It was the hairiness that did it. First I noticed the arms, then the bits peeking out over the top of the T-shirt. I thought: I bet he's got that fab Sean Connery chest. I could see you had the build. It doesn't matter how heavy you get with bones like yours.' He offered Robert a plate of cakes.

'I'm not into that type at all,' Robert said, taking the plate.

'*Now* you're not. What about before.'

'I suppose it's more attractive when you're younger. Come to think of it,' he smiled and licked all the cream out of a huge cake, 'I used to *love* Jean-Paul Belmondo when I was your age — those big French Kissing lips.' Robert had a repertoire of teases he could practise on William: the mention of anyone called Albert, of course; Albert cakes, Albert Square (through which *any* reference to *Eastenders* became suspect); *Alberto Balsam*, Prince Albert and any connectives; anything French.

'So you found Jean-Paul in New York and I found Sean Connery in Glasgow.'

'— as James Bond,' said Robert, opening a photo album. 'Life imitates Art.'

'Imitates life,' said William, pointing out a picture he had taken of Robert dressed up as Sean As Bond.

Robert studied the picture, feeling better about himself. Quite sexy: shirt and trousers tight in all the right places, good strong shoulders and neck, big dark-eyed glare. He could have come all over a picture like that twenty years ago, when he really was into the Jean-Pauls, Redfords, Newmans, and, well, almost anything older than he was. When the last thing he wanted was a fragile, middle-class English boy. The accent alone would have put him off at that time, when it was still associated with authority figures or Scots trying to act posh. But he lost those prejudices abroad, when he discovered you could be rich, educated *and* unpretentious. And the Socialist English were becoming defensive about the Scots' perceptions of everybody south of Manchester being Thatcherite yuppies. You could be sure their distate for such people was one of the first things they let you know about themselves. It was certainly one of the first things Robert found out about William that first night.

How Robert's 80s ended

It was going to be just another night in the Waterloo. Robert had continued to frequent gay bars throughout his celibacy, with friends, a sister or two, his mother. The brother had long before joined the Yups down under with his Economics degree. (When asked if she had any children other than Robert his ma would invariably reply: 'Two girls and an insurance salesman.') It was all just a good drink and a scream in the 80s for Robert. If ever he felt the old urges return he could easily remind himself of the many benefits of celibacy, the principal of which was how much easier it was to relax in gay bars with no concerns about success or failure, no anxieties about looks or performance.

Ironically, predictably, this relaxed aura was transmissable and made Robert seem much more approachable than most of the other customers, whose assumed air of nonchalance was exposed as fake by their ever-attentive eyes and ears, their acknowledgement of every entrance and exit. So the greatest drawback of celibacy turned out to be the necessity of dodging the evening's drinking partner at closing time. He often felt like a pop star trying to escape after the concert at which he's just spent two hours giving the illusion of eternal availability. An illusion he would repeat with a different audience every night. If Robert didn't make good his escape, there was indignation bordering on violence. Especially with older, plainer types who were more pushy since they lacked the self-assurance of the attractive youths who thought all they had to do was wait patiently and they would be asked. So even if Robert hadn't already decided to join the party again he would have chosen to speak to William, the only youngster there that night.

'Do you remember the first night we met?' Robert asked William as his parents returned to the room.

'Oh God, do I!' William rolled his eyes theatrically, turning to Mrs Murray. Mr Murray had sat in front of the television.

'He starts rambling on about the Berlin Wall coming down, and how much everything was changing and he was stagnating, and if he didn't touch another human being soon he'd explode.'

'I was really drunk.'

'And after all that it was four weeks before I even saw him in his underwear.' William looked a bit embarrassed by what he had said, remembering the company. But Robert's da seemed engrossed in the religious TV programme, and his ma knew more than

William did about that period, by virtue of the drink and gossip sessions Robert and she had indulged in since he came back from abroad.

'I was beginning to think you were going back with Gordon,' she said.

'No. There was no chance of that.' Robert turned to William. 'Gordon was just another person, he wasn't as special as I made out at the time... *he said defensively,*' he said defensively.

Gordon

'I met Gordon in Boston in '78. You've seen his picture.' He nodded towards the cupboard where the old Woolies albums were kept. 'I bumped into him — literally — a couple of months before we met. He was the first old affair I'd seen in years — one advantage of making all your mistakes in one continent then leaving it for another.'

It had been running into Gordon and his new lover that convinced Robert that his period of celibacy must end. He had turned the corner into Sauchiehall Street one night and come face to face with that stunning face, the wild blue eyes, gelled back black hair; Gordon's face, framed by night colours, seemed to have picked up only a few laughter lines on the journey from twenty-three to thirty-five. The night colours tinted the white T-shirt Gordon had on. And they were both wearing shorts at eleven p.m. And it was summer and hot and the whole scene brought back desire from the dead just like that.

They were on a European holiday, just off to Bennets. Their obvious happiness with each other intimidated him, filled him with jealousy. He declined the invitation to go to the dancing, but couldn't help kissing Gordon lightly on the cheek as they parted.

The collision seemed to have jogged Robert's senses back into action, because he found he was hypersensitive to Gordon's musky smell in the warm evening air, his firm tingly skin, aftershave taste.

Twenty minutes later he found himself moving along the Glasgow streets at jogging speed. He stopped, noticed he was almost at Partick, miles from where he was headed. This unthinking, heart racing, blind running had only ever happened twice before: the first time when he got the contract for his first job abroad, the second when he just missed being run over by a truck.

First night

'You looked so confident that first night,' William said. 'As though you owned the place.'

'He's spent enough money in it!' Robert's da said. 'He'd be as well fucking owning it!'

Robert ignored him. 'I was terrified. That's why I drank so much. As soon as I decided I was back on the market again all the old places became frightening. Even the good old Waterloo. It was like walking into your classroom on exam day — you know how you start noticing things you never did before —'

'— lopsided pictures,' said William helpfully. He was always amused when Robert began getting dramatic.

'And don't forget I was forty-three, not thirty-three. I was afraid I'd wasted the best years of my life.'

'That was a great film,' Robert's da said. They were singing hymns on the TV.

'Liza Minnelli!' said William. 'That's how we got talking.'

'She wasn't in it,' said Mr Murray.

'Judy Garland, yer thinking of,' said Mrs Murray.

'No her either,' Mr Murray said. 'It wizny that kinda film.'

'No. Robert had just put a Liza Minnelli record on the juke box. "Losing My Mind". And I said, Oh that was great on *Top of the Pops*. And he said —'

'The best thing since "Starman",'

'Another great film,' said Mr Murray. 'Jeff Bridges —'

'— Who's a doll,' said William. 'Anyway, that's how we got talking, about this record. I said I had been really disappointed when it went down the chart from six to seven since I had been listening to the top forty specially because I thought it was going up to number one.'

'And I had been listening to the same show, with the same thought, and we both realised we'd been experiencing the exact same emotion the year before at exactly the same time. Me in Glasgow, he in London.'

'What did we do after the Waterloo?' said William.

'Burger Bar,' said Robert's da. 'Heard it.'

'Just you keep watching the priest on the telly telling ye what to do,' said Robert. There was the usual pious figure of the cloth, dispensing moronically simplistic parables in a condescending voice.

'God, who the hell do they think they're talking to?' Robert said.

'*Me*,' said William.

'You're not telling me you get anything from that.'

'Who would you rather be listening to — the Marxist Minister for the God-awful truth, no matter how depressing?' Robert's da was nodding in agreement. 'I mean they're not doing any harm. At worse they're just telling nice fairy stories to cheer people up.'

'Proves my point,' said Robert. 'You tell children fairy stories; why do they have to make it so obvious they're talking down to you? You don't talk to an adult like that − or an equal.' Robert was sounding more bothered than he actually was. He had only brought the subject up because it was the one thing that William and his da could gang up on him about, giving at least the illusion of some sort of bond.

'We're not back to the old tyrannical middle classes abusing their power over the lower orders are we − like in the Burger Bar.'

The Burger Bar Story

'He looks at the menu,' Robert said. Mr Murray turned off the TV.

'He looks at the menu, and there's about a dozen dishes with little pictures next to them. And one without a picture. So he has to ask about the *one dish* that isn't pictured. I mean it was something like deep fried pineapple burger and he had no intention of ordering it. He just had to show that he was the paying customer and was going to make sure he got everything he was due. That's so middle class. Why do you always have to remind yourself of whatever power you have?'

'Firstly,' said William, 'It's not middle class, it's me − my sister's just like you − she would eat a pickled rat if it was put down in front of her rather than "make a fuss". Secondly − what about the working class? What about the chip shop?'

'That was just one particular guy − to use your own argument.'

The Chip Shop Story

'We'd been standing in this chip shop ten minutes before the assistant showed his face. I could see him in the back telling his pals, "Am no servin' him." Then when somebody else came in he served him before us!'

'It was that stupid fairyish pink scarf roon yer neck.'

'That widnae go doon too well in Argyle Street, William,' said Mrs Murray.

'That's right: it was gay prejudice, nothing to do with class.'

'Rubbish. As soon as I open my mouth in this place I get the big chip on the shoulder treatment.'

'Or chip shop in this case,' said Robert. 'It's your Englishness that annoys us anyway, not your class. You're paranoid.'

'So are you.'

'I'm surprised you ever agreed to meet each other again after all that,' said Robert's da, irritated. He hated listening to stupid arguments, unless he'd started them himself.

'I didn't think we'd ever meet again,' said William. 'If we couldn't even manage to buy something to eat together without an argument...'

'But strangely enough we met again the very next night. In the very same place.'

'Well I had just moved to Glasgow, obviously I was going out every night to get familiarised. What was your excuse?'

'The heating broke down.'

'Like tonight?' said Mrs Murray, rubbing her hands.

'Oh I'm sorry,' said William, jumping over to the central heating gauge. 'I keep forgetting the coal fire isn't enough for a room this size.' He glanced over at Robert. 'And the weather here is so changeable.'

'A wee dram's the quickest way I know of heating the blood,' Mrs Murray said. 'Right Robert?'

'A wee hauf,' Robert agreed, was the very thing.

They opened a bottle of whisky. And spent twenty minutes arguing about what music to put on. Mrs Murray (The Carpenters) won, but she couldn't get over the novelty of the CD remote control and kept changing tracks.

'God this is what Robert and me did the second time I met him — argued all night about what records to put on the juke box. Then I asked him to go home with me and he refused. I thought I wasn't his type.'

'You were, sort of, by then.'

'You thought he looked like that boy, the blond one in *Brideshead Revisited*.'

One of the problems with Robert's alcoholic confidences with his mother was that she often regurgitated his confessions with scant regard for accuracy. Especially on her third whisky.

'No. I never liked him — the look of him, anyway. Too smug and spoiled.'

'That poor boy,' said Mrs Murray, shaking her head. 'Oh the drink's a terrible thing.' She downed her third whisky and headed for the bottle.

'That was the only thing that was interesting about him,' said Robert, 'the drink, the melancholy, rebellion.' He turned to William, smiling. 'Until I saw that programme I didn't realise that middle-class people drank.'

'Oh, come on.'

'Well, I didn't know they *enjoyed* it.' He was laughing but William was getting annoyed. He knew Robert didn't give a toss about creed, class or country but he couldn't stop arguing back if there was someone else there.

'He wasn't middle, he was upper class. And anyway he can hardly be said to have enjoyed it —'

'Don't take that aff!' Mrs Murray shouted. Mr Murray had gained control of the CD player and was trying to eject Carpenters and inject *Cabaret*. Mrs Murray went over to stop him.

'So,' William said. 'You were hoping I'd be a tear-away lapsed Catholic alcoholic —'

'— with a *huge* dowry.'

'But it surely wasn't the fact I wasn't that put you off sex.'

As he said this, William had a terrible sense of *déjà vu*. He knew what Robert's reply would be and what he would say after that. This had all been sorted out the day they agreed to go with each other, but more and more they were going over old ground, as when they had re-examined the perfectly functional old fire in the bedroom with ever greater scrutiny, willing some hitherto unnoticeable imperfection on it.

'I was terrified of AIDS — especially with a Londoner, and a youngster. I mean, *I* could never have been careful at your age.'

'But we "youngsters" are more scared of people your age. And what's London compared to Edinburgh?'

'That's mostly straights. Anyway, Edinburgh's not Glasgow. You're as bad as the Yanks. They think Scotland is part of England.'

'It's a miracle right enough we did eventually get together.'

Day One

William was convinced that the only thing holding Robert back from taking the plunge into the whirlpool of sex and love was the simple fact that he had left it so long. But it took him four weeks to persuade Robert. Four weeks of endless drunken conversations in the pub or at Robert's home. Conversations with no con-clusions. Robert would always put the case for the defence first (which was basically his life story up to that point). But before William could state his own case, before Robert even finished his own story, the alcohol gradually made useful conversation impossible: in the pub the music demanded ever more attention, at home, drinking spirits, they simply fell asleep. Court was adjourned.

Of course, William eventually worked out another line of attack. He realised that Robert was intentionally dodging the issue. On those nights at Robert's house when they drank themselves into a stupor he would awake, thirsty, at dawn, to find himself shoeless and blanketed, lying on the couch; Robert's bedroom door was firmly closed. He never tested it, but he would not have been surprised to find it had been locked as well. Robert never lost control no matter how much he drank. He knew exactly what he was doing.

After four weeks of this, William stopped Robert's monologue one night and condensed the rest of it into a few sentences, ending with 'and now it's 1990 and you have a very simple choice to make.' They were at home. It was only nine o'clock. Robert had no choice but to listen.

'Don't tell me you can't have sex with me because of AIDS. You know I've been on the scene less than a year, that I've never done anything stupid. What do you want – a certificate to prove it? Even if we both had tests we could go right out the next day and get fucked stupid. You know we can do it safely. Or we can do anything; and trust each other. I'm willing to believe your story. You have to trust me.' William refilled Robert's whisky glass. 'Coping so far?'

'Go on.'

'But I think that sex is the least of it. I think you've just got so used to being in control, of living this bland, safe lifestyle that you're afraid to rock the boat again. You're afraid you won't be able to cope with the emotional traumas that were difficult even fifteen years ago, when you were more confident that something else would make itself available. Am I on the right lines?'

'More or less. But you don't realise how *tired* you can get. It's different when you're younger, jumping into affairs with your eyes shut. But I know what's going to happen. It takes a lot of energy.'

'You see that's your problem. You think you know everything.' William was annoyed. 'How can you possible know me? How can you be so sure things will continue to happen the way they always have?'

'OK. You've stated the problem. What's the solution?'

'As I said before. You have a simple choice to make. You can *never* have a sexual emotional relationship with someone else again. Or you can. That's what it boils down to in the end. Your circumstances aren't going to change in any way to make it easier – quite the reverse, as you know yourself. Either you take a chance or you don't. If you don't take a chance now you're saying you're never going to take a chance ever. For the rest of your life.'

The fact that Robert's fear had nothing to do with AIDS was proved that night when they finally did have sex, and 'safety' was the last thing on either of their minds. They both awoke the next morning, lips bruised and numb, dicks blistered and swollen ('Wish they would stay that way').

'I think that was a perfect lesson in how NOT to do it safely,' Robert said. William smiled: he knew now that Robert trusted him. They stayed in bed till it got dark. Which, in fact, was only two hours after they awoke. But a romantic two hours.

And productive. They made up there and then their

plan for the next six months. They would get married. They *were* married. They would make this marriage work by leaving nothing to chance. Pooling their respective experiences they decided on all the factors that were essential for the perfect relationship and worked out a battle plan. Communication was, as all good agony aunts tell us, essential. Day One was, conveniently enough, since they were in bed and had exhausted the only other two things you could do there, Talk Day. Each had to tell the other of all previous affairs: good, bad, mediocre and why, why, why.

'What do you want more than anything in a lover?' William asked first.

'I better not say. It's too sugary.'

'Tell All. Remember?'

'I hope you're not diabetic.'

'Come on. I'm getting interested.'

'Shh,' Robert said, and drew back a curtain above the bed headboard which revealed windows throbbing beneath a rain waterfall. 'Someone to listen to the rain with.'

'You're right. It is too sugary.'

'I want a divorce.'

Day Two

On the Second Day, William bought Robert a little toy James Bond ring. Robert got him a Wizard of Oz watch. 'It was the nearest — portable — thing to Liza Minnelli I could get. You either wear this on your wrist for the rest of your life or the video of *Cabaret* round your neck.' William read out the inscription on the back: For giving me the heart, the brain, *de noive*.'

Day Three

On the Third Day they were moving William's stuff

into Robert's house when a pack of mangy mongrels crossed their path, examining William's possessions with dirty paws and scarred noses.

'Dugs!' screamed William in his best Billy Connolly accent. 'And look — there *is* always a three-legged one.' Sigh. 'A genuine three-legged Glasgow dug.'

On the Third Day Robert brought home Rusty, The Dug. And William saw that it was good. And the creators of this little world were beginning to feel pretty damn pleased with themselves.

And then it was fixing up the house, installing the gym, helping each other get fit, the abortive attempt at co-creativity (whose relative failure was really a success, of course, since it showed them the parameters of their life together), the dual record, book, video collection, the search for friends who could fill the spaces their divergent interests created — musicians for William, journalists for Robert. And so on. For six months. And on the Seventh they rested.

The Seventh

On the Seventh they looked at photo albums. And drank whisky. Which was running out, according to Mr Murray. Robert served up the last drops to his parents before they left. The TV was on again. Iraq's invasion of Kuwait. 'The beginning of the Holy War,' Mr Murray was explaining, that he had been predicting all along would be The Next Thing.

'Thank God you're not taking pictures in places like that any more,' Mrs Murray said. Robert wondered if he was thankful. If he'd rather be taking pictures than looking at them.

After the parents had gone, Robert shoved on an old Velvet Underground LP. On the record player.

'What's wrong with the CD?' William asked.

'I want to hear the LP, with all the clicks and pops. Twenty-three years I've had this, and I can remember where every scratch came from. You'll never be able to do that with a CD. They're *too* perfect.'

William brought in coffee from the kitchen. 'You won't be saying that about me in twenty-three years. I bet people would buy CD versions of other people if they could, to keep them perfect.' He began to sing:

'Another fine edition of you oh yeah, and boys will be boys will be —'

'Roxy Music. *For Your Pleasure.* 1973.' Young people were always impressed when you could identify pop stuff, Robert found.

'I must have heard it in the nursery,' William said.

It did not escape Robert's attention that William had just made his first ageist joke at his expense. He hoped they weren't going to get into one of those stupid Sunday night arguments again. The last few weeks it had been the same: too much drink, days of tension and irritability building up, demanding an outlet. Who started it this time? Me, Robert decided. Stupid dragging out The Velvets like that. He kept forgetting these days how much the age thing affected William in a way it no longer did him, despite the occasional (occasionally truthful) protestation to the contrary. He'd gone out with all age groups and had come to realise how little it really mattered if the older guy had more experience/knowledge/lovers than you; or the young guy less lines/body fat/grey hairs.

That remark about a 'new model'. Maybe William really did think he was getting bored with him. The daft thing was, this was supposed to be the best time, the secure time.

Robert had announced, excited, on Day One that they should send out invitations there and then for their first anniversary party to prove how confident they were that they would last together. Then he got carried away and the party was to be only six months away and by then William would have a job, the house would be sorted, everything would be just right. And it was. But before everything was just right, Robert would have been more sensitive to William's anxieties. He wouldn't have started blabbing on about Twenty-Three Years Ago without reassuring him that Now was better than ever.

There was a long, loud crackle from the speakers.

'*Watch out the world's behind you*,' sang William, along with the record: 'Sunday Morning'. Surely a contradiction in terms, he thought. He too was examining the discontent in the air.

Complacent; resting; retired. He never thought he would ever associate those words with Robert. But he couldn't help thinking that something *was* behind them. And it was Robert's obsessive fault: ten years indulgence, ten years of deprivation. Six months 'getting things right'. For what? So they could spend the rest of the time getting it wrong? But it was his fault too. He had worked at least as hard as Robert and rested as hard now too.

Strange, William thought: Robert had always refused to take those big, sickening wedding photos with all the diverse generations, grudges and jealousies, frozen together in false unanimity. And now here they all were trapped in the same glossy charade: the lovers, their parents, relatives, animals, friends, possessions, labelled and stuck in a scrapbook, preserved in transparent foil.

Work.

Rest.

There would have to be a bit of creative fusion again. This time he would insist.

In the bathroom getting ready for bed it occurred to Robert at last what it was he'd been trying to remember all day. He had awoken that morning anxious and paranoid, thinking that things were slipping away from William and him. Then, like the marriage guidance counsellors tell you to do, he began to try to remember the thing that had been good about their relationship in the early, successful days, the thing that had convinced Robert to go with William, despite so many misgivings. He got into bed still trying to remember this thing, feeling almost as anxious as he had that first night together.

Then William did the thing he had done that first night that convinced him.

He held his hand.

It wasn't one of those perfunctory, Oh-it'll-be-all right-you'll-see squeezes you give to a dying relative; William had turned round in bed, in that moment just before sleep, with no conscious effort, and entwined all five fingers round Robert's. It was a prehistoric, animal gesture, which requested and granted re-assurance in one movement. It startled Robert now the way it had done that first night. It said: *Come on*. I belong here and you know it. It was a gesture that existed before language, one that revealed its inadequacies. A picture worth a thousand words. Or a month of Sundays.

Robert looked down at the hand. William was still wearing the Wizard of Oz watch.

It was Monday.

◆

The Stag

TOM WAKEFIELD

◆

*'Honour thy father and thy mother: that
thy days may be long upon the land
which the Lord thy God giveth thee.'*

◆

When I was thirty-five or there-abouts, I visited a man of fifty-four. He was the bachelor uncle of a friend. He had left inner London to live in semi-retirement in the Sussex countryside. The house was a two-bedroomed, pebble-dash cottage. A white wooden fence enclosed the small but adequate garden and the interior of the place exuded a simplicity, a considered untidiness, and quiet style which I found most appealing.

The man (whose name I have now forgotten) seemed to reflect the qualities of his household both in appearance and demeanour. We ate scones with home-made raspberry jam at four in the afternoon and in the early evening we sat in the garden together and drank chilled white wine. We didn't talk a lot, there were birds offering sufficient and pleasing intrusion over the Burgundian Court music which drifted from the house. It still feels good to say those names aloud – the names of the composers – Grenon, Fontaine and Binchois.

This was one of those rare moments when I felt entirely at peace with my past, my present and even my future.

'When I am over fifty, I shall be like him,' I thought. 'I'll be as complete as he is. My life will probably not be shared with another single man and it will be sweet and pleasant to be alone.'

I even remember looking forward to this inevitable ageing, relishing my vision of it with my imaginings.

Now that time has arrived and I am not in the rural idyll that seemed to beckon. The Sussex countryside is still beautiful but it fails to tempt me away from the inner city. I reckon that I'd look bloody silly wearing shorts and a straw hat and if I started making my own jam, my neighbours or friends would think that I was going mad. I have Grenon, Binchois and Fontaine on a tape but rarely play it.

Although I live in a capital city, I do not venture a great deal from the area where I live. Highbury Vale has become my village. I am curiously unaware of the football crowds. The stadium hosts forty thousand or more sports invaders. I ought to see or hear these people but I don't seem to. Two or three times a week I make a sortie out from all that has become familiar to me. Just once a week, I visit another single man. I have done this for the past five years and during this period I have come to know — and then say goodbye to — six of them.

Today, I'm going to visit the seventh one. It might sound as though I have been involved in a number of tidy but casual romances. This has not been the case. All the single men have died, and comfort, not romance or transient passion, was the purpose of my visits. But... But this present single — this one — this one is so different.

I seem to have discarded all the rules of counselling. I hesitate... I hesitate because there is a romance, of a kind, between us. I enjoy the anticipation of seeing him, as well as being in his presence. I am enchanted by him. I visit the hospital with no sense of duty, it is a joyous event for me, it is something to look forward to.

I give less attention to personal appearance nowadays. For the most part, I have to accept that I look distinctly shabby. I now find myself checking over details before I leave the house. Have I locked and bolted the door to the garden? Is the side gate to the house locked? Check: central heating timer, water in cat's saucer, front door keys in pocket. Do I have three 10p's with me?

I pause for a moment to look at the coins. Often I hear on the radio and the television — read it in some newspapers — that the country is doing well. That more people own more things than they ever did. Perhaps this may be true, yet I could never have imagined, until this last decade, that I would set aside coins for beggars before leaving the house. This is England. Hope and glory do not extend to everyone.

I know that I will see beggars on the way to the hospital, it will be miraculous if I am not accosted by two or more when I leave the Tube stations or when I enter them. A strategy of not seeing the poor or trundling past them as if they were not there has a bad effect upon me. These Victorian Values we have been exhorted to return to don't suit me too much. For the most part, they seem to be based in pretence rather than honour.

'Good morning. I hope you don't mind me talking to you like this but you have been granted a very special opportunity today. It's a chance to join us this evening; I can promise you, if you come along, your whole life will be changed.' A young man in a smart, well-cut, grey suit with a face so even-featured that it leaves the visage unimpressionable, bars my progress towards the Underground ticket office.

He thrusts his arm forward and offers me a tract of some kind. He smiles. His teeth are small, cream and even, and I notice that his hair is cut short. There is a parting down the left side, which resembles a scar that has been left behind by a meat cleaver. I take the piece of paper from him and step to his left side. He moves too, so that once again he confronts me.

'Are we doing the Palais Glide or The Gay Gordons?' I ask him. He does not comprehend this reference to dance steps; they are not part of his history.

'I can see that you are a family man. I expect that you have grandchildren. Come and join us... for their sake. Hell is nearer for all of you than you might think.' As he delivers his dire message, he beams yet another advertising executive smile at me. I wonder if he has false teeth, they are so cream and so even. He continues to talk, to obstruct. 'Do come and join us. *He* said, "I will make you fishers of men if you follow me." Will you follow Him? Will you join us? Do you know that Hell is close?'

I want to say:

'Your Hell is blocking my path,' but I don't. I say, 'Excuse me. Please let me pass. I am not a father, I am not a grandfather. I am a single man and I am in a hurry.'

'Would you like to make a contribution?'

This time I am too quick for him. I dart past him, get my ticket and do not look back. I hear his voice as I reach the top of the escalator:

'Good morning. I hope you don't mind... how close to Hell...' His voice recedes as I descend.

On the train, I remember that I still have his message clenched in my hand. It informs me, in the most celebratory terms, that one of the largest and most beautiful cinemas in Europe is now to become a sort of supermarket for Christian Fundamentalism. The literature is more political than spiritual, the words bounce about my head and it feels as though I am being emotionally and intellectually stoned to death. I put an end to this assault by screwing the paper into a tight ball and placing it in my pocket.

I emerge into the daylight and give my first 10 pence — not to a man but to a woman who is standing at the Underground station's exit. Her age is indeterminate. Lank, matted hair falls across much of her face. The hunched shoulders, the layers of ill-fitting, wretched clothing, the sores about the mouth, the seeing but dead eyes, give her the aura of someone suffering from permanent concussion. The odour about her is foul. There are thousands like this in London now. It has become a harsh city. Community care? What community? Must put this out of my mind. Set myself a task. Something mundane. The walk to the hospital takes fifteen minutes. I'll count the number of dogs.

There has to be an excess of dogs in London. I have counted fourteen in this short distance. Most of them were not of a small variety; the majority were large, and one was huge. There were three yellow-eyed Alsatians, one not on a lead. The dog and its owner claimed all the territory of the pavement, forcing human pedestrians into the gutter as they passed. A Dobermann and its human counterpart ploughed past travellers like me as if we were on holiday from a concentration camp. A Dalmatian excreted huge steaming turds on the footpath whilst its minder pretended that nothing was happening, and a Staffordshire bull terrier snarled disapproval at everyone that came within a yard of its owner.

If all the dogs in London rebelled and went completely wild, they could destroy the city. Are these animals protector-companions? Or do they reflect an aspect of their owners? This is becoming an angry city.

As I approach the hospital, I recall my telephone conversation with my father. His increasing deafness facilitates remembrance. Short sentences. Loud clear enunciation.

'Dad, it's me. Tom. It's me, Dad. Is that you?'

'Ah, it's me. Nobody else lives here. Who did you think it was? Denis Thatcher? I'm all right. Been out in the garden. And you? Are you all right?'

'Yes. Fine. I want you to come down here. The day after tomorrow.'

'There's a race meeting on up here. Why not come up? Over the sticks at Uttoxeter. You like the jumps. Why not come up?'

'No. I want you to come to the hospital with me.'

'What's wrong with you?'

'It's not me. It's somebody else. He's dying. He's only twenty-eight.'

'That's bad. Half your age and nearly three times less than mine.'

'He's from our village.'

'What, this one? *Here*?'

'Yes. His name is Gerald. Gerald Moreston.'

'I know his dad. Got a garden centre. Remarried after his first wife died.'

'That's it — that's the family. His dad's not been to see him. Can you get down here?'

'Of course I can. I'll come on the eight-ten from Stafford.'

I gave him instructions to meet me at the hospital around eleven a.m. I wanted to repeat the directions from Euston but he stopped me by saying that if he got lost he had a tongue in his head and would ask.

I turn round the corner knowing that he will be waiting for me. And there he is, standing on the bottom steps of the hospital building, holding a plastic carrier bag in his hand. I know what the bag contains. His pyjamas, some packets of tea, a tin of salmon, a packet of bacon, a tin of ham. Even if he stays only overnight my father never visits empty-handed.

This open-handedness (open-heartedness?) would sometimes cause me irritation:

'Just because I'm not living at home, doesn't mean that I'm starving. I'm not a refugee, Dad.'

'I should hope not either. Did I say you was? Put that tin of corned beef and the tin of peaches in your bag as well.'

In the mid-sixties, I would take special friends – or lovers – home with me. Were there three? Four? Five? I can't remember. He can. He remembers all of them.

'What became of that Dougie? Douglas, that was his name.'

'Douglas?'

'Nice, quiet, fair-haired young man. Lived in Watford. Interested in amateur dramatics.'

'Oh yes. I remember. Don't know where he is now.'

'Probably too nice. Too quiet for you, our Tom.'

He would give these men-friends food too and cook meals for them. Always, on the journey back, they would marvel at his generosity and understanding. All the time, I never understood their reverence for this middle-aged widower coal-miner, who happened to be my father. I thought that all parents accepted their son's homosexuality in the same way as he did.

'Oh, our Tom always danced a lot on his own. It was ever on the cards how he'd be and to say that I'd want it otherwise wouldn't be fair to him. Nor to me either. Of course, he upsets me sometimes. He's not perfect. I don't know where he got his swearing from. Not here. But we have good times together and when he's in the mood he makes me laugh. And he makes me think. I make him think too, mind you. He taught me to read. Now I read as much as he does. He's always been slovenly about his clothes. And the way he cleans his flat is nothing to write home about...'

He says these things as he brings me and my male partner an early morning cup of tea. We sit up in the double put-u-up bed, our nakedness only half-covered by the sheets. He does not ask if we have slept well. He does not pretend that we are in that bed — his bed — merely for slumber.

I look at him now and know how much I took for granted. I stand here unobserved and study him. I suppose most people seem to shrink when they enter old age. Or could it be that old age enters them? Reducing them in size, preparing them for... for... I wonder if he has been waiting long. He waits but does not look to the left or to the right. He is not anxious as to whether I might be late or if he has the wrong address or if he has arrived too early. He has made an arrangement. He has checked the details over and over in his mind. He is on time and my accountability rests with me. I reflect that it has always been this way. I look at him now and in seconds I am twelve years of age. The time is five-twenty a.m. and it is his voice that I hear.

'Tom? Tom? Time to wake up now. Time to wake up. There's some tea and toast on the table. Don't doze off now that I've called. If you doze off it's fatal. We'll be late. Everything's ready. Make your way quiet downstairs. Don't wake your mam. It's warm down there. The fire is lit.'

We would have half an hour together before leaving the house, him for the pit and me for my grammar school. He would itemise things before we left, making an inventory of what he had to do and what he thought I had to. He would scrutinise my appearance.

'There's your blazer. Brushed it for you last night.

Blond hairs on the shoulders — must be Colin's because your hair is as black as a coot's feathers. I've polished your shoes again. Don't get kicking bits of wood around and scuffing the toes. Your mother's ironed a clean shirt. It's Wednesday, so I've put your white shorts and sports shirt ready. You do have sports on Wednesday afternoon, don't you?'

'Yes, Dad.'

'Ah, I thought you did. That's why your things are laid out.'

'I don't like football.' I drink some tea.

'No, I suppose you'd rather dance anywhere than play football.' We laugh together.

'Well, I don't like being on the coal face, Tom lad. I'd rather be another hour in bed or out in the garden in the daylight, but I'm not moaning. Have you done all your homework?'

'Yes, Dad. We only had English and Latin. I've done it.'

'That's good.'

'Yes, Dad.'

'Now then... Pit shoes, lamp, water-bottle, apple for me, apple for you, your sports things, put your books tidily in your satchel — you don't want dog-eared pages. Got your bus pass? Your train pass? Got my soap? Are we ready, then?'

At times, I would remonstrate with him — we were leaving too early. What was the point of waiting at the bus stop at the bottom of the road for fifteen or twenty minutes? Couldn't we cut the waiting time down to ten minutes? Or even five?

'I hate last minute touches. That's how mistakes are made. And what happens if we miss the bus? You would be late for school and I'd lose a day's pay. That cage waits for nobody you know. There's no hanging

about when it's time to go down. It wouldn't be fair to
the other men on the shift. And have you thought of
the bus driver?'

'The bus driver?' For the life of me, I couldn't see
how all of this could affect the bus crew.

'You can't expect somebody who is driving a bus to
get that vehicle dead on time at each and every stop,
can you? No, you can't — so pick up that satchel and
let's be off. Put your cap on your head, not in your
bag. I've got mine on.'

'Yours isn't red and gold. This cap makes me stand
out.'

'No it doesn't. You make yourself stand out. You
always have. Come on. Let's be off.'

We were always the first to be waiting at the stop.
Other miners would join us before the bus arrived and
my father would greet them as though he were starting
the day for them as well as me.

'Got your little friend with you, Richard?' They would
speak to my father and nod in my direction, acknowl-
edging my presence without wasting further words.
Even at that time, their observation was sharply close
to the truth. This man who was my father, also happened
to be a very good friend indeed. I suppose other people
in the village had recognised this, as we were seen
about the place in tandem far more than most fathers
and sons who lived there.

He's seen me. He smiles. He places his bag on the step
near to his feet. He makes a beckoning gesture towards
me.

'Don't stand there gazing like a spare light bulb. I've
been here for twenty minutes. Cross over by the
pedestrian crossing. People here drive like there's no
tomorrow. Like mad people, some of them. I've watched

them while I've been standing here.'

I offer to take the bag from him, but he gently pushes my hand away from the handle and says:

'No, no. I can manage. There's not much weight to it. I'm not on sticks yet. Not by a long chalk, I'm not.'

I suggest we have a cup of tea in the hospital cafeteria before going up to the ward. As usual, he wants to buy the teas, but I am firm and make him wait at a table while I get them.

'Well?'

This single word asks me what I want him to do. It asks me the purpose of our present rendezvous, and by the look in his tired eyes I feel he knows all before I explain anything. He has his best shirt and tie and wears the suit that he reserves for weddings or funerals of his friends and relatives. I speak quietly.

'He is dying. It's AIDS.'

'I'd worked that much out for myself. You're not telling me anything that I don't already know.'

'You know about this illness?'

'All about it. I made it my business to find out. It's killing you and yours badly, isn't it?'

'Mmm. Mmm. It is.' I lower my head.

'Well, I'm your father. That's why I'm here. Did you know him before the...?'

'The illness? No. The illness introduced me to him. I've visited regularly.'

'So you should. It's what I'd expect of you.'

'His father hasn't been to see him. I know that he wants his dad to visit him but he's not been down yet. That father must know what the situation is here. I don't understand how an only parent could be so cold and...'

'You don't know many fathers, do you? How could you? As you've only got one. Don't judge. Don't jump the gun. His dad might know only what he's read in some papers. Papers not fit to wipe your behind on — let alone inform anybody properly. Some people believe everything they read.' He raises his hand and shows the palm, just as Indian chiefs do in Western films. 'Don't judge his dad, I say. There's time. There's time for him to call.'

'Not much. Gerald's either semi-conscious or in a coma. I've seen this before, Dad. It's not long now. I was wondering. I was wondering if...'

'Oh. Ah. What were you wondering?'

'Would you like to talk to him? He might think that you're his da...'

'No. I can't take his father's place — but of course, I'll talk to the lad if you think it will do any good.'

'I've worked out a strategy as to what you might say.'

'You've done what?'

'A strategy... A plan of what you can say to him.'

'Not necessary. I'm not an actor. Never wanted to be one. That's more in your line.'

I am a little exasperated by his response but I admire his presentation. I pursue the subject no further.

As we walk through the hospital territory, it does not need a perceptive eye to see the evidence of poor funding. Paint uncurls itself from walls that should have been redecorated half a lifetime ago. The foyer is plastered with appeals and posters exhorting visitors for a donation to this unit, money required for a sorely needed wing, contributions for a machine which will save many lives... We pass through a crowded waiting room close to the casualty department. There has been an accident. People must wait longer. I am reminded of an air-raid shelter from my childhood. People wait for things to improve with the same kind of forbearance.

My thoughts return to the present.

'What will you say to him?' I address my father as the lift doors close. I press the button to the fourth floor. I panic a little and repeat the question with more urgency. 'What will you talk about?'

'I'll let the situation deal with that. I'll talk as the spirit moves me to.'

I cannot offer any further suggestions to this reply, which comes from an old man in his eightieth year, who has always been an avowed atheist.

I know the route to Gerald's. I know that I have to press a bell to gain entrance. I anticipate being in his presence and I am suffused with both pleasure and concern. We are at his bedside. We sit either side of him. The paraphernalia of medical care looks crude, awkward even. The drip-feed bottles of brightly coloured liquid look precarious and seem strangely alien to the man who lies on the bed before us.

Just behind my father is a respirator. Its mask reminds me, once more, of warfare. A nurse has told us that Gerald is semi-conscious. His eyes are closed, his breathing is faint, but both my father and I notice a small movement of Gerald's fingers. This fragile gesture lets us know that he is aware of a presence. I find that I can think of little to say. I realise that this is probably a farewell visit. I manage to mutter,

'It's me, Gerald. It's Tom.'

My father and I are looking at one another across the bed. He shakes his head slowly from side to side and then opens his mouth to say something to me but then seems to change his mind. His lips close. He averts his eyes from mine and looks down on Gerald. He reaches out and gently pats the back of Gerald's hand. He speaks. He does not look at me. He speaks to him.

'Never mind, old soldier. You are through the worst.

What's to come isn't as bad as what has gone before, these last few weeks. I only got down here just an hour or so and I feel as though I've travelled not just a hundred miles but a thousand. Coming to London is like visiting another world for me. I can't say it holds much wonder but it is good to see you again.'

I feel disorientated by this soliloquy. I am twelve years of age. I am in hospital after a road accident. A man, my father, is patting my hand and calling me 'old soldier'. I remember telling him this. I recall his laughter. Yet, this man is talking to someone else as if it were... How mean I am. I feel slightly jealous. My father talks on.

'I was over Cannock Chase yesterday. The autumn is a lovely time of year and our Johnny — he's my youngest brother — I say youngest, but he's on his pension — he drove me over there in his car. Of course, the Chase is not as big as it was when were young. You never had houses creeping up to its edge then. Somehow it seemed better for fields to give way to Chase land. More natural. People who build houses near canals or Chase seem to lay claim to bigger and bigger gardens. It's as if they haven't got enough land already. But there's still a lot of open country and there were a lot of people out enjoying it. The bilberries are in fruit and there were groups of people gathering them. I suppose you've always liked bilberry pie; everybody does from our neck of the woods.'

I recollect the deep purple stains on my white shirt and my discoloured finger-tips as though I were suffering from a disease of the heart.

'I thought that we'd nearly filled that pail. Have you been eating them, our Tom? We'll be here till midnight if you keep dipping into it.'

'No. No, I haven't.'

'If I had a mirror you would be able to see your face. Your face says that you are telling lies. Your lips are blue, so is your chin and your mother will go mad when she sees the state of that shirt. Now then. You pick by my side until we've got some more berries. Put them in the pail. Don't take them out. And don't lie. It's not in our family. If you tell lies, you'll live lies. Not good.'

There's a degree of animation and pleasurable expression in the aged face now. Is it from a sense of purpose or just the joy of sharing a parochial enthusiasm?

'...and near Brocton we saw a herd of deer. We got really close to them. Lovely creatures, deer. I've never understood how anybody could hunt and kill them. Call that sport? Ah, I know it's not. It's nothing short of murder. The idea of getting all dressed up to kill a creature like that is enough to turn your stomach over. I suppose if you work for most of your life beneath the ground, you tend to appreciate what is on top of it. There was a stag, a magnificent animal...'

He talks in this way as if he had known this dying man for most of his life. He talks as if this young man were — were related to him in some way.

A nurse indicates that there are other visitors. I look at my watch and see that we have been there for more than half-an-hour. The time has gone quickly. For some reason, I look for signs of distress in my father's face but see none. We both say a quiet goodbye to Gerald and I'm certain that both of us regard it as a final farewell.

Not until the lift doors close does my father begin to cry. He weeps in the same way as he did on the other three occasions. He wept quietly when the onset of war caused him to destroy his pigeons. He wept quietly for my mother's death, for my brother's death and now he does it for a stranger.

The descent seems all too fast. I press the ascend button so that his grief will not be made public. We speed upwards. When we get to the top floor again, he blinks and says,

'Are you operating a lift, our Tom, or playing with a yoyo?'

'I thought that you might not want people to see you upset.'

'Well, you thought wrong. I don't mind people seeing me as I am. Nor should you. Isn't that why we're both here? Press that G button and let's get out into the open air.'

On arriving home, I make a simple meal for both of us: grilled lamb chops, mashed potatoes and peas. He finishes all of his meal. I offer a choice of fruit, cake or cheese to follow. He shakes his head.

'No, no. That was just right. I've enjoyed that. I've enjoyed it a lot. I'll just take a look at your garden.'

We both study the small plot. As always, he centres his attention on the rose bushes. Some are in a second flowering and he marvels at this and then tells me not to cut the flowers and bring them indoors. I begin to argue about this. He shakes his head.

'They are no different from the deer.'

'The deer?'

'Well, they shouldn't be shoved in a compound or a big pen just so the likes of us can stare at them. What would it be like if you had that stag in this garden? He would hate it, wouldn't he? It's not his place. It's the same with flowers. They're not meant to be stuck on a polished sideboard or gracing a table.'

I laugh and say:

'I don't see how you can compare a stag with a

bunch of roses, Dad.'

'Don't you? Well, I've just done it, haven't I? Laugh if you like, but I tell you this. When you bury me, and I want you to bury me. No vicars. You bury me. When you bury me, there's to be no flowers.'

In a moment, I feel chilled by this prospect. Somehow I had always managed to believe that he was immortal or that I would go before him. In order to comfort myself, I say,

'Well, I don't have to think about that for years yet. Do I?'

'We all have to go when we are ready and I've had a good innings.'

I realise that he is preparing me for this time. He has stated what he expects of me.

It is seven p.m. and we are playing cribbage. We have done this so often throughout our lives that we can converse at the same time as we are scoring.

'Fifteen two, fifteen four and a pair of kings is six. I've put a pound of bacon in the fridge for you — should last you a few days. It's best back bacon, not that streaky stuff that disappears when you put it under the grill. There's a jar of beetroot, some decent tea and a tin of salmon that I've put in the cupboard for you and —'

'Three queens is six and a . . . No. No. There's nothing more, is there, Dad?'

'Not unless you're training to become a conjurer, our Tom. I'll shuffle the pack. You're always cack-handed with the cards. I'll go back on the eleven o'clock train from Euston tomorrow morning. There, I've a run as well. A good dozen there. See what's in your box.'

'You don't have to leave so early. Just two in this box?'

'Two is better than nothing at all. Eleven o'clock of a

morning is hardly early. Why, more than half the day has gone by that time.'

'One for a right jack. I don't know how Gerald's dad could stay away at such a time. For a parent to disown a child... Oh, and a pair of threes. That makes three does it?'

'Three. That's all. Don't crow. You've done it.'

'Done what.'

'You disowned a parent. You disowned your mother.'

'Never?'

We stop playing cards. We are level pegging.

'Think back. Think back a good bit. It doesn't seem too far back to me, but then I'm older than you are. Years get shorter as you get older. Think back. You were thirteen – at the grammar school. You had a Saturday job to give you a bit of extra pocket money. It was a doddle, that job was. Not more than a few hours and you were paid far more than some lads who did a morning and evening paper round every day of the week but Sunday. Perfect for the job, you were. All rigged out in your school blazer and cap and tie. Butter wouldn't have melted in your mouth, would it? Who would have thought that you were the bookie's runner? Now do you remember?'

'It was illegal but I never thought it was wrong. Nor did you.'

'No, I didn't. Some laws are too daft to laugh at, let alone respect, but that's not what I'm reminding you of, is it?'

He tilts his head on one side and then remains very still, his brows and eyes are quizzical. I become an adolescent, faced with a grown-up's question. My mother's voice is quiet but harsh. She addresses him and not me. It is he who is receiving her sense of injury, yet it is me who has delivered the wounds.

'It's not one person, but four that has stopped me on the High Street.' She was an excellent mimic. ' "Oh Esther, I'd never have guessed it. The news is safe with me, you know that. I suppose Tommy got his brains from his real mother. It was ever so good of you to take him on — him not being your own." Not my own? Not my *own*? I'm not toffee-nosed enough for him. That's what that red and gold uniform has led to. He's a scarlet boy that denies his own mother.'

'Nobody will believe his cock-and-bull stories, Esther. Don't let it get to you so badly.' He tried to assuage her anger. She turned to me.

'Well don't call me Mam or Mother anymore. As little lord almighty has decided I'm not good enough.'

'I'll call you Esther, then,' I said.

'Fine by me. I wouldn't want to be anyone else. I'm not ashamed of my name or my birthright. Not like you. Little snipe.'

And from that time onwards, I'd always addressed her by her Christian name until she died.

He shuffles the cards and urges me to cut them. As I turn up the card, he says,

'That's got to be in your favour. It does nothing for my hand. His dad will visit him. I know he will, so let's have no more carping about it. We don't know what has gone before.'

At nine forty-five p.m., we get ready to retire to bed. Neither of us has ever been addicted to late nights. The early morning has always been the best part of the day for both of us. Mornings for him begin at five-thirty and to share them with him constitutes a luxury for me.

When he is not here, my breakfast consists of two pots of tea and three cigarettes. At six a.m., he brings a cup of tea to my room and says,

'It's six o'clock. You're a bit late. Not a bad morning. A bit chill but not chill enough to keep that blackbird out of the garden. I've been listening to him. Beautiful. The cat's out there watching him. You would think that creature had never been fed. Your breakfast will be on the table in about twenty minutes.'

There is more food than I want but I eat all of it. I consume two rashers of bacon, two sausages, a fried egg, beetroot and toast. I congratulate him on the meal and tell him that no one has ever cooked breakfast for me but him. He grunts and makes an observation.

'Nowadays they give you something that's half-way between cake and a piece of bread with a bit of jam, and call it a meal. Cross Ann. That's what they call it.'

Later we glean the race meetings over the morning paper. We both make projected selections for our bets later in the day. I will not change my selection. I know that he always does. ('Do you know, Tom, I picked that winner out and for some reason I went off it.')

Just before ten a.m. there is a telephone call. My father is in the garden. I hear that Gerald is dead. I hear that his father visited, that his father sat with Gerald's friend. They were Gerald's last visitors. Do I relay this information to my father? Is it necessary? He seemed so sure of the event. Did my father and uncle Johnny visit that man? Was he confronted by those two mild but tough septuagenarians? I join my father, who is extracting ravenous slugs from the rhubarb and throwing them on to the path.

'Your uncle Johnny ate too much rhubarb, you know. That's what gave him his gall-stones. He's over the operation now.'

I am about to tell him details of the news from the hospital, but for some reason I talk about our forth-coming holiday in Lancaster. I've stayed there with him on two previous occasions. He loves the city and its environs. He enthuses,

'There's everything there for us two. Quick trips to the lakes, we've got Morecambe if we want the sea, the canals look good in any weather and there ought to be a race meeting at Cartmel in late October. We can stay with Keith. Is he better now...?'

I step out into a biting cold that causes me to catch my breath. It is mid-December and a raw east wind cuts through my clothing and goose-pimples my skin.

On Sundays, I take a walk with my friend and neighbour. It is always the same walk, around our local park. There is little deviation from our route; I suspect that a degree of routine and ritual gives comfort to the middle-aged. I realise that this is my father's birthday, and still I do not comprehend that heart attack that took him away from me on the third of October.

'I'll not be holidaying with you this year, our Tom. No more trips for us.'

I not only recall his words but also the inflection of his voice. I have buried him so I ought to accept that he is gone, but not a day goes by without me communicating with the idea of him in some way.

At sixty, my friend Martin is experiencing his first real romance, his first love affair. I enjoy hearing his appraisal of his lover, which is void of cynicism. There are few people in the park on account of the bitter cold. The grass is frozen hard and bereft of footballers. The ponds are ice-patched and only the bravest waterbirds explore their usual territory.

We pause near the wire enclosure that acts as a boundary for the herd of fallow deer which is grazing the unyielding ground. A large buck leaves the herd and comes right up to the wire fencing. We stare at the soft, brown eyes, the long slender neck. It eats a stalk of cabbage from Martin's hand. It remains standing there after its treat and seems to be looking at us in a knowing way.

'Beautiful,' Martin murmurs appreciatively.

I say,

'I'd like to put my arms about his neck and stroke his ears and tell him how much I love him.'

'I don't think that he would appreciate it very much,' says Martin, in a sad, reflective kind of way. 'Language isn't always spoken and some truths do not need demonstration.'

As we walk away from the compound, I glance back over my shoulder and see that the animal is still watching us. I feel... I feel... I feel like an orphan, and trail behind my friend as he leads me out of the park.

The Burning-Glass

FRANCIS KING

◆

'Thou shalt not kill.'

◆

My father was loosening his Leander Club tie as, charcoal pinstripe jacket already removed, he stepped out through the French windows into the garden. All that summer of 1939 we had seemed to be living under a gigantic burning-glass. As he approached us, where we lolled out in deckchairs, I inwardly shrank from the peppery smell of his sweat. He was a man who sweated a lot, so that even in winter his forehead and nose would glisten and that peppery smell would seep out of him after he had done nothing more strenuous than sweep up leaves or mend a fuse.

'This'll tickle you all,' he said, not realising that we were all far too hot and lethargic to wish to be tickled. 'On the way home I dropped in on Lucy.' Lucy was his unmarried, older sister, a gynaecologist, who shared a flat with Ruth, a physiotherapist. 'She told me an absolutely priceless story about Ruth.' He dragged a deckchair out of the sunlight into the shade beside us. With a groan and a sigh he lowered himself into it. Ruth, like Lucy, was a pacifist. 'It seems that she was at Speakers Corner last Sunday, giving her support to that Donald Soapbox creature, who was spouting there. There was some woman present – a sensible body by the sound of it – who kept heckling him. Ruth told her to shut her trap or to put a sock in it or something equally inelegant, and the woman then lost her rag and answered back in kind. In no time at all, the two of them were screaming abuse at each other. And then our Ruth, our peace-at-all-price Ruth, disciple of John

Muddleton Merry and the Great Mahatma, socked the other woman, socked her not once but twice, knocked off her hat and began to pull her hair. So she got herself arrested — aggravated assault, was it? — something like that. And had to pay a whopping fine. Or, rather, Lucy had to pay it, since Ruth, as we all know, gives so much money to charity that Lucy's only charity has now become Ruth.' My father laughed. 'Isn't that just marvellous? I love the idea of a pacifist being had up for assault.' He laughed again. 'Don't you love it, Deirdre?'

My mother, who had been gazing at him with a characteristically rueful, bemused expression over the top of one of the detective stories which were now her staple reading ('I'm afraid I'm letting my mind go,' this former teacher of English would often sigh as she asked me to bring her back yet another from Mudie's Library), twitched her mouth in an effort at a smile. 'Yes,' she said. 'Yes. Marvellous!' She began to fan her face with the book. 'It's so hot. Why does it have to be so hot?'

I got up from my chair and began to wander across the lawn towards the house. I somehow knew that my father would be scowling at my back. At any moment he would be shouting after me: 'Doesn't anything ever amuse you?'

But fortunately my sister, Ivy, then distracted him. 'I can't see what Lucy sees in Ruth. I mean, they seem so incompatible. What *do* they have in common?'

Yes, people could be as innocent as that then.

I went up to my little room under the eaves of the house, crossed over to the window and stared down. My father had now got up from his deckchair and was leaning over my mother. He put out a hand and eased her book away from her. He turned a page, read out something from it, and then laughed. He often mocked at this addiction of hers — 'Here we all are, preparing for Armageddon, and there you are interested in nothing but mayhem in vicarages, country houses and gentlemen's clubs.'

I thought again of Ruth's conviction for assault.

Bloody fool!

Have you never been inconsistent? You're always talking about honesty but only yesterday — no, the day before — you showed me the change the girl at the Gaumont had handed you and said: 'Look what she's given me! Ten shillings too much!' You didn't go back. You just walked on. How is a man who calls himself honest but goes off with change not due to him any more consistent than a pacifist who commits assault?

Answer that!

But how could he answer that when, as so often, I'd lacked the courage to put the question?

Instead of putting the question, I'd merely run away.

As we walked along the towpath my father detonated one of his puns, as noisome and as unfunny as a fart, burst into laughter, and then threw his arm around my shoulder and briefly hugged me to him. There were often such moments, islanded in a sea of disapproval, irritation and sarcasm, when I thought, both astonished and guilty: He's fond of me, he's actually fond of me! Strangely, although it was obvious that he was far fonder of my elder brother, Giles, I had never seen him put his arm round Giles and hug him in that same fashion. Perhaps Giles's bulk made it more difficult to do so. I came up only to my father's shoulder.

My father breathed deeply three or four times, in through the nose, out through the mouth. ('Fill up your lungs! Fill up your lungs!' he would sometimes

admonish one or other of us. 'You don't know how to
breathe.') Then he squinted at an eight scissoring its
way up the river. 'Dreadfully ragged,' he said.

When I coxed, did I sound as girlishly shrill as that
diminutive figure, a pink-and-white cap making it
difficult to discern his features, perched up in the
stern? I hated coxing. I coxed only to please my father,
a former Oxford Blue, who now coached a crew from
his stockbroking firm, with the addition of myself.

'There's going to be a war,' my father said apropos
of nothing.

'Do you think so?' I still believed that war could be
averted.

'I'm sure of it. And it's not going to be any more of a
picnic than the last one.' My father had won a DSO in
the trenches. 'I wish you and Giles were five years
younger.'

Oh but, father, I'm not going to fight in this war.

Instead of saying that, I merely stared out over the
river at the gardens of Fulham Palace. Suddenly I was
once more aware of that peppery smell.

'What's the betting one of them is late? If I can be on
time, then why can't all of them? He quickened his
pace as though to ensure for himself the satisfaction
that at least one of the crew arrived after we did.

I unloaded from the back of Lucy's box-like Morris,
dating from the twenties, the platform which I had
constructed, using a folding step-ladder as its base.
Leah, a fellow art student, whose sturdy bare legs,
strong bare arms and thick black hair filled me with a
palpitating excitement, hauled out the copies of *Peace
News* which she had made into two untidy bundles
held together by lengths of hairy green string. The
string had come from a ball used by Ruth to tie up

plants in the narrow tongue of garden which stuck out from the rear of the cramped basement flat which she and Lucy shared.

'Are you sure you can manage that, Noel?' Ruth always asked that question of me, without ever actually providing any assistance. 'Would you like a hand, Leah?' She always also asked that question of Leah, without ever actually providing any assistance to her either. Lucy herself never once made such offers. Perhaps, as speaker, she felt that she was doing enough for the cause already.

'I do think it's clever of you to have made that platform,' Leah said over her shoulder as she strode out ahead of me. Lucy had been less complimentary about my handiwork. 'It seems awfully rickety. I hope it's not going to collapse under me. I'd look a real chump.'

Leah favoured a porridgey impasto, grey, beige and white, for the huge non-representational oils which she dashed off with so much speed. Lucy had bought one of them as a birthday present for Ruth, and it now hung, slightly askew, like so much else in their lives, between their two beds. She had never bought one of my meticulous watercolours. That hurt me.

Perhaps because of the heat, the crowd at Speakers Corner was large but unusually lethargic. Sweating people, some of them trailing cowed dogs or fractious children, drifted from group to group. There was little of the usual heckling until Lucy, dressed in a crisp white linen dress, with a belt woven of small green, red and yellow beads, began to speak. I had made a wooden railing for the platform and she gripped this in both her strong, square hands. Her voice, so low in conversation, had a remarkable carrying power on these occasions. What she said, about the immorality of killing, about the devastation of air raids, and about the futility of imagining that a war could ever solve anything at all, I had heard often enough before. But once again I thrilled to it, as did Ruth and Leah. Ruth and I were stationed behind the platform; Leah beside it, with one of the bundles of *Peace News* on the ground at her feet and the other, its string removed, over an arm. Round her neck she wore a leather purse on a strap.

At that period of simultaneous dread of the war which most people now regarded as inevitable and guilt at yet another ignoble postponement of it, any pacifist could be sure of a rough reception at Speakers Corner. But the rougher the reception, the more Lucy came to resemble some medieval saint, her eyes closed in ecstasy and a seraphic smile on her lips even as her torturers inflict the most refined atrocities on her.

The chief of the hecklers was, as so often, a plump middle-aged man in a bowler hat, rakishly tipped over a sparse, sandy eyebrow which looked as if he had drawn it there in pencil; a grey pinstripe suit, the trousers so short that they revealed the grey woollen socks which he wore even on a day as hot as this; and a grey-and-white striped shirt surmounted by a stiff collar into which the hard, unmoving little knot of his tie seemed to have been screwed. Every Sunday afternoon he was there; always unaccompanied, always in that same garb, and always propping himself negligently sideways on an unfurled umbrella, its black cotton bleached at its struts. Sometimes he would content himself with a derisive 'Oh, I say, I say, I say!' in what he saw as an exquisitely funny imitation of Lucy's lah-di-dah voice. Sometimes he would shout out something like 'That's rich, that really is rich!', 'You can't expect anyone to swallow that!', 'Trust you to make a meal of that argument!', 'Well, that finally takes the biscuit!' or 'Aren't you rather over-egging the cake?' It was Ruth who first pointed out how so many of his metaphors seemed to derive from food. Mightn't he be a cook? she sometimes surmised. But I preferred to think of him as a bank clerk, swallowing back all the aggression which he felt against tiresome customers weekday after weekday, only to void it, an explosive, bitter vomit, on Saturday and Sunday. There was only one mystery: why, when there were so many other speakers on such a variety of topics — naturism, Buddhism, Marxism, vegetarianism, spiritualism — did he always choose Lucy for his target?

That day he was particularly vehement. 'You ought to be locked up!' 'If you love your chum Adolf so much, why don't you take yourself off to live with him in Germany?' 'Haven't you any shame?'

A small, wizened woman, standing beside him, her near-toothless jaws chomping — I imagined her, for some reason, as running a small sweet-shop or drapery store — would from time to time vehemently applaud these remarks: 'Yes! Yes!... That's right!... That's the whole point!... Answer that one!' Might it have been she whom Ruth had assaulted? I had been too embarrassed to ask Ruth about that incident or even to refer to it.

Lucy spoke of turning the other cheek, as she often did.

The heckler let out a derisive cackle of laughter. 'Just listen to that!' He turned to the people on either side and behind him. 'Turn the other cheek! Haven't you realised, darling, that if someone slaps one of your cheeks and you then present him with the other, then the likelihood is that he'll slap that one too?'

Most of the others greeted this observation with

approving jeers and hoots of laughter.

'Yes, of course I've realised. *Darling,*' Lucy added, leaning forward on the platform. (Oh God, don't let it collapse, don't let it collapse!) 'But that doesn't alter what I was saying. Not one bit. You get one slap and you turn the other cheek. You get a slap on that cheek, and you turn the original one. And so on. And on. Eventually it will work. Eventually.'

'Sounds a mug's game to me,' the near-toothless woman cried out. One could imagine her husband returning drunk from the pub and giving her a cuff. She would certainly not turn the other cheek, she would go for him, spitting and scratching like some famished alley cat.

'I daresay that, when Christ preached the Sermon on the Mount, there were a lot of people who thought him a mug.' The reference was too arcane, the sarcasm too lofty for Lucy's riposte to impress such an audience.

When Lucy had clambered down from the platform – Ruth and I both held out hands to support her but it was only Ruth's that she took – she had that dazed, exalted look which she always had after one of her speeches. She drew a lace-edged handkerchief out of a pocket and began to mop her wide, low forehead.

The crowd was beginning to drift away.

'*Peace News! Peace News!*' Leah began to call out, in that loud, clear voice so different from her usual soft, husky one.

'You were marvellous,' Ruth told Lucy. 'As always. That goes without saying.'

'*Peace News!*'

As I folded the platform, I caught a forefinger in a hinge. Ouch! I pulled a face.

'Have you hurt yourself?' Leah sounded genuinely concerned.

'No, no. Not really.'

The heckler, who had been chatting to the near-toothless woman, now approached Leah. He pointed with his umbrella at the copy of *Peace News* which she was holding out to the indifferent people hurrying past her.

'I'm truly amazed that you should be selling that rag.'

'Are you? Why?'

'Well, it's easy to tell from your looks that you're one of the long-nosed fraternity. And if Hitler were to come over here, you'd be one of the first to suffer, now wouldn't you? I shouldn't care to be one of your lot if Hitler were to come.'

Slow in her responses even in the course of an ordinary conversation, Leah at first merely blushed, frowned and shifted as though her body were itching in its clothes. But I knew that really she was furious. 'Well...' she eventually said. Then: 'Do you have to talk to people in that — that very rude way?'

It was then that I intervened. I was even more furious than she was. I hated that voice which, snootily drawling, did not even have the courage of its own commonness; I hated that pudgy, pink face; above all, I hated that bowler hat tilted over one sparse, sandy eyebrow. I advanced on him. I could understand how Ruth had committed her assault.

It was, however, in a quiet, reasonable voice that I forced myself to speak. 'Yes, you're right. My friend is Jewish. So there's absolutely no self-interest in her pacifism, quite the reverse. If one holds a belief which, so far from benefiting oneself, is likely to do one harm, isn't that an indication of how sincere one is? Yes?'

The man stared at me, umbrella at half mast, as though he were about either to poke me or strike me with it. Then, in a strident, crude voice — now it certainly had the courage of its commonness — he said: 'Oh fuck off, you self-righteous little prick!' He turned on his heel and strode off.

'Charming! Charming, I must say!' Ruth called after him.

'Did he say prick or prig?' Lucy asked.

'Prick, dear. *Prick!*'

Then we all burst into laughter.

Later that afternoon the four of us sat out in the garden, sipping at the iced lemon barley water which Ruth had twice told us that she herself had prepared. One of her patients — 'absolutely *twisted* with spondylitis, like a tree really, poor creature' — had given her the recipe.

'When are you going to tell your father?' It was a question which Lucy often put to me. Since I could not answer it, it always irritated me.

I shrugged.

'Sooner or later, you'll have to tell him,' Ruth said. 'If war comes, then conscription's certain to come with it.'

'Your brother's in the Terriers, isn't he?' Leah said. She had never met any of my family.

'Well, kind of. He's training as a pilot.'

Oh, why couldn't they leave the whole subject alone? Why couldn't they mind their own business?

'If you liked, I could tell him,' Lucy volunteered, discreetly spitting out a lemon-pip into her palm and then dropping it to the ground.

She had made this offer before. Oh, no, no, *no!*

I said: 'No, I must tell him.'

'Yes, you *must,*' Ruth said.

'The longer you delay it, the worse it will be,' Leah opined.

Why did she have to gang up with the others?

'It's a question of choosing the right moment.'

'You've been waiting for the right moment for an awfully long time,' Lucy said.

The moment finally came some months after the outbreak of war. It came because, on the evening before my brother left home to join the Air Force, we had a party for him, and in a mood compounded in equal measure of isolation, guilt and despondency, I had managed to drink too much.

There were many girls at the party, since Giles had many girlfriends; and there were also cronies of my father, sleek men in well-cut suits and hand-made shoes, with jovially booming voices, and their elegant, self-effacing wives. My sister Ivy's boyfriend, a handsome, vacuous lieutenant in the Coldstream, soon to be killed in an accident on Salisbury Plain, was there; but Leah, although I had invited her, had failed either to put in an appearance or to excuse herself for not doing so.

Soon after eleven, the 'grown-ups' (as I still thought of them) began to drift off; and it was then that Giles had suggested, 'How about going on to Skindles?' Eventually all the young people without cars were crowding into the cars of those with them. 'It's all right if I take the old bus, isn't it, Dad?' Giles said. The 'old bus' was an Armstrong Siddeley. 'Yes, go ahead, go ahead!' Ivy's boyfriend had a long, low, open, powder-blue Lagonda with crimson upholstery.

I made no move to accompany them; and none of them, not even Giles or Ivy, urged me to do so.

Our maid, Betty, and the hired waiters began to clear up the mess. My father sank into a chair and my mother into another.

'Well, that was a very successful occasion,' my **father** said.

'Even, if rather a sad one.'

'Sad?'

'Well, Giles going off to the war tomorrow.'

My father laughed. 'Well, you *are* a gloomy one! He's not going all that far, you know. In fact, only as far as Norfolk.'

That did not console my mother. She looked despondent, as she got up off the chair into which she had so recently sunk, picked up her latest detective story off the top of the piano, and said: 'Well, I'm off to Bedfordshire.'

'Oughtn't you to...?' My father's voice was low as he indicated the two members of the temporary staff who were loading a trolley with glasses.

'Oh, I can leave everything to Betty.' My mother usually did leave everything to do with the household to Betty, who had been with us for as long as I could remember.

'Another swig?'

'No thanks.' I placed my glass on the floor beside me. I'd already had at least one swig too many.

'Can't do you any harm.' My father was in a jovial mood. 'It's not as though you had any classes tomorrow.' I had just gained my diploma at the Byam Shaw School.

'No thanks.'

'What happened to your girlfriend?'

I never thought of Leah as my girlfriend. She had too many boyfriends for that.

'She didn't come.'

'Yes, I know that, I know that. The question is — why didn't she come?'

'Search me.'

'Not an altogether reliable young miss. Eh?'

I did not answer.

Ruminatively my father sipped at his neat whisky and sipped again.

Then he said: 'Well, I suppose you'll be getting your own call-up soon. Any day now. And then it'll be your turn for a farewell party.'

'No.'

I amazed myself as much as I puzzled him with the monosyllable.

He stared at me. 'What do you mean — No?'

'No.'

'I don't get you.'

'When I get my call-up papers, I'm planning to register as a conscientious objector.'

'*What*?... Bloody hell!'

He was not as amazed as he pretended to be or as he would have been if my brother and not I had made that confession.

I forced myself to look at him, as into a painfully dazzling searchlight. I nodded my head. 'I've thought a lot about it.'

Suddenly he exploded: 'This is Lucy's fault!'

'I told you, Daddy — I've thought a lot about it.'

'She's got an excuse of a kind. You haven't.'

'What do you mean?'

'Well, her fiancé being killed in the last show. Though I'm convinced that, if he'd come back, he'd have changed his mind about her.'

'I don't think her pacifism has anything to do with that. She's far too rational, unemotional.'

He seemed not to have heard me. He gulped at his drink. 'How am I going to explain this? Tell me that! How am I going to explain this?'

'Explain it? Explain it to whom?'

'To everyone!'

Of course he meant, to those sleek, loud-voiced cronies of his and their elegant, self-effacing wives.

'I'm sorry, Daddy. But there it is'

'There it bloody well is! Fucking hell!'

After I had registered as a conscientious objector, many weeks passed before my tribunal. During that period, I suffered a paralysis of will, such as I had never known before and have never known since. For much of the day I lay out on my bed, sometimes listening to music on my portable gramophone, sometimes reading one of the detective stories which I brought back for my mother from Mudie's, and sometimes merely staring up at the ceiling. From time to time I used to drag myself out to visit Lucy and Ruth. At weekends I also still accompanied them to Speakers Corner. The heckler had disappeared — evacuated, called up, too busy? — but in his place I was from time to time conscious of two men in dark suits and grey trilby hats who, Lucy assured me, must be from M15. Leah was no longer with us. Having accompanied her doctor father and her mother to Wales ('Trust them to skedaddle to the safest place they could find,' my father commented), she was teaching art in a school for mentally retarded children. From time to time she wrote me letters which appeared to be composed of lengthy extracts from her diary, totally devoid of any affection for me or, indeed, of any interest in my doings.

'Why don't you get on with your painting?' my mother asked.

'Because it's no good.'

'But you've done some lovely things. You've so much talent. Everyone says that.'

'Only your chums. Who want to be kind or polite.'

'Why do you have to be so cynical, darling?'

My father was far less tolerant. He would come home exhausted either from his office — where, he would often proclaim, he was doing the work of three other people in addition to his own — or from his duties as an Air Raid Warden. 'So what you have you done for the war effort today?' he would ask me over supper.

'Oh, Jack, do leave the boy alone!'

'I'm only asking. I'm interested.'

On one such evening, he suddenly leaned across the table, his face grey with fatigue and ugly with resentment: 'Why don't you get yourself a job?' He might have been asking 'Why don't you get lost?' or 'Why don't you drown yourself?'

'Oh, Jack, you know he's waiting for his tribunal.'

'Just as the rest of us are waiting for a possible invasion.'

'Oh, Jack!'

But even my mother, so impractical and seemingly so detached from the world drama exploding all around her, was now putting in several hours each week with the St John's Ambulance Brigade.

Two days later I roused myself to call in at an academic agency, to ask if there was any temporary work available for an art master. I was told that, yes, certainly there was — 'They're digging seventy- and even eighty-year-olds out of mothballs,' I was told by a pale, wrinkled, wizened man who looked as if he had just been dug out of mothballs himself.

I wrote off a number of letters of application; but they received either no answers or else rejections discouraging in their polite formality.

'I can't describe to you the things I saw last night. Horrific. There was this old girl, one of your true East Enders... No...' My father broke off. 'Better not to dwell on it.... I don't seem to have any appetite. What

I think I need is a drink!'

'Oh, not at breakfast, Jack!'

But my father lurched up from the table and fetched himself half a tumbler of whisky. It was during those days that he began the heavy drinking that was eventually to cause him to die of liver failure several years later.

Betty, still with us, came in with the post. No longer bothering to place it on a silver salver, just as she no longer bothered to address my mother as 'Madam' or my father as 'Sir', she merely extended it in a hand: 'I forgot to bring these in, I was having so much trouble with that stove.' The hand was streaked with coke dust, and there was a smear of it on her forehead.

'For you.' My father spun the thick letter across the table towards me. 'From your girlfriend. And this!' He spun another at me. 'Perhaps it's from that agency of yours — Grabbitall and Thingummybob.' Having opened two bills and gulped at his whisky, he eventually looked up: 'Well, is it from the agency?'

'No.'

'An answer to one of your applications then?'

What business was it of his?

'Yes.'

'Any luck?'

I shook my head, humiliatingly conscious that my hand was trembling as I pushed the letter back into its envelope.

'I don't understand it,' my mother said. 'We keep hearing of this manpower shortage and yet you can't get a job — in spite of all those letters.'

'I can understand it.' Again my father gulped at his whisky. His face, so grey when he had first come into the room, was now unnaturally flushed. I suddenly noticed that he had not yet shaved. In the past, he had often ticked me off for coming down to breakfast without shaving.

'What do you mean?'

I wished my mother had not asked the question. I felt a totally unreasonable fury against her for having done so.

'Well, look at it this way. Suppose you were the headmaster of a school and you knew that at any time, day or night, there might be an air raid. Well, mightn't you hesitate about employing a conchie?'

My father now often used that word. Each time that he did so, with a scornful distaste, I felt as if he had spat on me.

'I don't see why,' my mother said, frowning in genuine puzzlement.

'Well, there'd always be the possibility that the conchie would rush into the air raid shelter ahead of the pupils. He might even knock them down in doing so.'

'Oh, I don't think...' my mother began.

She looked at me, eyes wide and lips parted. Her hand, holding a piece of toast, was half raised to her mouth. She was imploring me: Say nothing.

I said nothing.

Later, after my father had set off for his office, my mother knocked on the door of my little room.

'Don't be upset by Daddy. He's living under a terrible strain at present. The office. His ARP work. And of course his worry over Giles.'

By then the Battle of Britain had started. Giles was a fighter pilot.

'Yes, I know, I know.'

Suddenly she sat down on a corner of my unmade bed. I was lying on it, my hands clasped behind my head. 'Darling, I'm being awfully stupid. But explain to me. I've never really understood. This — this pacifism of yours... Do you mind my asking this?'

'Not at all.'

'Is it — is it something religious?'

'No.' I spoke up to the ceiling. 'I don't really think so. I'm not sure that I even believe in the existence of God. At least, there are times that I don't.' I felt no resentment at her question, since there was, I knew, no malice in it, only a hurt, bewildered wish to understand. 'It's just that I couldn't kill anyone. I just couldn't. Even if someone were going to kill me — even if a German entered the room at this moment to kill me — I somehow couldn't... absolutely couldn't....'

'I see.'

But of course she couldn't see.

She placed a hand over mine. 'I think you'll feel better when your tribunal is over. It's the waiting that's... demoralising.'

I had come up for the weekend from the Cambridgeshire farm at which I had now been working for several weeks as a cowhand. I had one weekend in every four off.

For that same weekend Giles had been allowed out of hospital. Having been shot down in his Hurricane over the Channel and then been miraculously rescued, he was one of what were called 'McIndoe's guinea-pigs' in the burns unit at East Grinstead.

As always with the mutilated, the disabled or the deformed, I found that the problem was: To look or not to look? If I forced myself to look at that skull over which the skin was here stretched unnaturally taut and there wrinkled like soiled tissue paper about to peel off, would not Giles be aware of my horror, however much I attempted to conceal it? But if I did not look, would he not say to himself: 'He can't bear to look at me. That shows what a sight I am'?

'What's the news of Marianne?' my mother asked him.

'She's still in Portsmouth. Still in the WRENS.'

'I mean — have you seen her recently?'

How could she be so maladroit? How could she, how could she?

'No. Not recently.' He answered in a totally even voice. 'We've rather — drifted apart.'

'Oh, dear!' My mother could not conceal her shock and pity.

'We never had much in common.'

Giles and I had never had much in common either. But now he was at pains to ask me about myself. Was the work on the farm terribly boring, terribly exhausting? What exactly was it that I did? Had I made any interesting friends? What sort of accommodation did I have? I had never known him so gentle, sweet and friendly. In the past he had so often ragged me, bullied me or merely ignored me.

He reminded me of some giant bird. The face was bird-like: the nose small and hooked; the almost lidless eyes constantly blinking, blinking, blinking; a sparse coxcomb of hair sticking up from the crown of the otherwise bald head.

Sorrowfully my mother waited on him; even more sorrowfully my father also did so. I guessed that Giles hated this attention — after all, he was perfectly capable of looking after himself; but with a calm forbearance he submitted to it.

On the Sunday afternoon my father decided that he would accompany Giles on the train to East Grinstead.

The next day he would be having yet another skin-graft, his eleventh.

'Your father's taken Giles's accident very badly.'

Accident! It was a strange word for what had happened to him.

'Yes. Yes, I'm afraid he has.'

'Once he's passed fit, he wants to return to his squadron. I can't understand it.' My mother's upper lip trembled as though she were about to sneeze, tears formed along her lower eyelids.

'Oh, Mummy, don't, don't!'

'It's easy enough for you to say don't, don't!'

She had never before spoken to me with that harsh, contemptuous bitterness.

Because of a cancelled train, it was past eleven when my father returned. He had had to stand in the corridor most of the way, and he had had nothing to eat since luncheon. Entering the sitting-room, he was oddly hunched over to one side, a hand pressed against his right ribs, as though he had a fracture there. His face was as grey as I had ever seen it.

My mother had already gone upstairs − 'I think I'll prepare for Bedfordshire and then read in bed until your father gets back.'

'Where's your mother?'

I told him.

He began to speak of the trials of his journey, as though I were to blame for them. Then he crossed over to the drinks cabinet. 'What a world! What a world!' I realised that, even if he had found nothing to eat on the train, he had somehow miraculously found something to drink. Or could it be that he secretly carried a flask around with him? 'Christ!' He turned round, a half-full glass of whisky in one hand.

Suddenly I was overwhelmed by his pathos. He was like some huge, heroic statue suddenly beginning to crumble. I realised that I not only hated him, I also loved him.

'Shall I get you a sandwich?'

He gazed at me, stunned. I had never offered to do anything of that kind for him before. 'A sandwich?' He might have been trying out a foreign word.

'There's some cheese. There's also some ham left over from supper.'

He nodded. 'Thanks. Thanks.' Then, in a ludicrous approximation to an American accent, he added: 'That would be dandy. That's mighty kind of you.'

Clumsily I made the sandwiches, cutting the bread too thick and using up far too much of what was left of our week's ration of butter.

My father bit into one of the sandwiches and chewed for a while in silence. I sat opposite him, watching.

Then he burst out: 'What a thing to have happened! I never thought that a thing like that could have happened to my Giles. He was so – so bloody handsome. And now! And that bitch of a girl has dropped him. Oh, Christ, Christ!'

Suddenly, without any effort at concealment, he was crying. His mouth was half open, screwed up to one side, and a soggy fragment of the sandwich slipped out of it and stuck to his chin. He made no attempt to wipe it away. Huge tears ran down his cheeks.

I jumped off my chair and hurried over to him. I stooped, put an arm round his shoulders, then put a cheek to his. 'Daddy! Don't! Don't! Please!'

Suddenly I felt an extraordinarily violent shove. I all but fell over. 'Oh, get away! Leave me! Leave me alone!' Then he swivelled round in the chair. There was no grief now in his expression, only a malevolent fury. 'Do you know what I was thinking in the corridor of that bloody train throughout that bloody journey? I was thinking: Why him? Why, why, why? If it had to be someone, why couldn't it have been you? And then I answered myself. Because it's the best who always carry the can. And it's the sneaks, the cowards, the shits...'

I snatched at the knife on the plate beside the sandwich. I raised the knife. I lunged out with it. I stabbed. I stabbed a second time. I stabbed repeatedly.

My father was wearing a hairy Harris tweed jacket. The blade of the knife buckled and buckled again and again, until it was twisted up around my hand.

My father jumped to his feet. He snatched the knife from me.

He raised a fist, preparatory to hitting me. Then lowered it. Burst into laughter.

'You feeble little idiot! You can't kill a man. You haven't the guts or the strength or the savvy to kill anyone or anything.'

Later my mother came downstairs in dressing-gown, hairnet and slippers. She had finished one detective story and was fetching another.

She stared at me, where I sat slumped in an armchair before the dying fire.

'Your father came up in such an odd mood. Did you say or do something to upset him?'

'No. Nothing. Nothing at all.'

◆

If a Man Answers

DAVID B. FEINBERG

◆

'Thou shalt not commit adultery.'

◆

K_{en}

'Hello,' said Ken in a voice about an octave lower than his normal range. Ken found that men were much more likely to respond when he spoke in a deep, resonant voice. He had developed an entirely distinct persona for phone sex. He suppressed his normal nasal twang that brought to mind Gilda Radner impersonating a Jewish American Princess. It was the old Marilyn Monroe trick, but not quite so breathy. His voice was virtually unrecognisable.

'Hello.'

'My name's Rick, what's yours?' Even though it was a one-on-one phone sex line, Ken didn't want to risk the wrong person finding out. He *did* have a lover. If Liverlips ever found out, there would be hell to pay. Ken had experimented with other nommes de latex. Rod was the stud, first-runner-up-in-the-Mister-New-York-Leather-Contest (how he adored beauty contests). Martin was the tight-assed-anal-retentive-accountant-in-heat-about-to-explode. Rick was the straight-guy-next-door-who-didn't-mind-getting-sucked-off-by-a-guy-when-his-wife-was-away-in-another-city-visiting-her-mother-for-an-operation.

'Bill.'

'How are you tonight?' Ken didn't use the group line any more. On the one hand, you could meet up to seven different people on the group line. Using the one-on-one line was like going to the cavernous Palladium at 10 p.m. on a Saturday and finding only one other guy, standing in the shadows, a drink in his hand. But the group line had its hazards too. Ken was tired of listening to crazy Artie rant and rave. Artie, a sixty-one-year-old from Westchester who claimed he looked like thirty-five, was always trampling on the group line, encouraging people who had no interest in one another to meet, playing yenta to the global village, and then cursing everyone out while bragging about the size of his legendary dick. If it wasn't Artie, there was always some other insistent crank with a bizarre kink unique to perhaps ten people on the planet Earth, interrupting the conversational flow every twenty seconds: 'Anyone into chocolate enemas?' 'Anyone into tattooed foreskins?' 'Anyone into fisting in evening gloves?'

'Pretty horny.'

'Same here. Can I call you?' Ken liked the sound of his voice. Hurry, the meter's ticking. There were times on the group line when he would find an appealing someone who was unable to give out his number, which was more or less like going to the baths a hundred million years ago with a locker and meeting a hot stud who also had a locker, when there were no empty rooms to 'borrow' and neither had the predilection for the orgy room, where it was impossible to contain sex to just the two of them. The one-on-one line was his best bet.

'Sorry, I can't give out the number. I'm staying with a friend.'

'I can't either. I have a roommate.' Liverlips. Asleep on the couch in the study. Said he had some kind of bug, didn't want to risk giving it to Ken. Although for the life of him, he couldn't imagine how, since they haven't had sex in six months. He's so fucking cold.

'Where do you live?'

'Manhattan. You?' Stay general, vague. Never give out any more information than necessary. The more you tell the more likely you're not going to fit his psychological grid. At least, get to know him first. Find out how well he fits your own criteria. Any damaging personal details can come later.

'Same.'

It didn't really matter where he lived. It was impossible to invite Bill over with his 'roommate'. He certainly couldn't go out to Bill's. Pets were the perennial excuse. His friend David had a pair of exhausted Weimaraners, constantly woken from a sound sleep for 'a walk', the alibis of adultery. But Ken couldn't very well go out to walk the goldfish. And he couldn't give the old line about running low on fags, going out for a pack of Marlboros. That's the trouble with lovers: they knew you so well, they could practically read your mind. After ten years together, Ken had a hunch that Liverlips probably knew he didn't smoke. And he could hardly say he was going out for a late night stroll in the park, not after he got rolled in the Rambles back in '82. One guy did him, pants down at the ankles, while the other fished out his wallet. Thank god he didn't take the keys too. It would have been cheaper to rent a whore. Well, let's get down to business. 'What are you into?'

'I'm into body contact, oil and massage, tit play, that sort of thing. Safe stuff.'

'Sounds good.' Pretty vanilla. That's fine with me.

'You like to fuck?'

'Depends on the guy.' Like maybe if Arnold Schwartzenegger was gay, he could get into it. In other words, not really. Did he go along? Ken didn't want to be patronising. He could always pretend to stick some ten-inch dildo up his ass.

'So what do you look like?'

'I'm about five-ten, one sixty-five, with brown hair and blue eyes.' Ken always wanted blue eyes, and a few more inches. 'I go to the gym maybe four times a week.' OK, so it's more like once every two weeks. 'I've got a slim muscular build. I'm sure you'd like it.' Liverlips didn't anymore.

'I'm six-two, two hundred pounds, with short blond hair and a goatee.'

Ow! Another fashion victim.

'I've got a couple of earrings in my right ear and a tit ring.'

Body mutilation. Watch out. Still, that word 'tit'. Somehow, just saying it got a rise out of Ken. Stimulus, response. Press the nipple-lever and be rewarded with an erection. 'Wow, I go crazy for tits.'

'You'd like mine.'

They'd have to be better than Liverlip's. His are buried under flesh. He's gained as much weight in the past six months as Liz Taylor did to play Martha in *Who's Afraid of Virginia Woolf?* Ken might not go to the gym as often as he should, but at least he'd been able to keep the middle spread from spreading down his thighs. 'And what would you like me to do to them?'

'Suck 'em, twist 'em, lick 'em, bite 'em, whatever you want, so long as you've got one hand on my dick at the same time.'

Ken felt he should be wearing rubber gloves. God, did he have to have safe sex on the telephone? Did he have to whitewash his fantasies too? Wasn't it enough that he used Lysol on the receiver after he was finished?

'So what are you wearing now?' Let's get visual.

'Just a jock strap.'

'Why don't you take it off?' The oldest fantasy in the world. The stripper. He slowly takes it off, bit by bit, while Ken watches, stroking himself.

'Why don't you lick it off for me?'

Now it's getting exciting. Hard to do over the phone wires, but Ken would try his best. 'What's your dick like?'

'Wouldn't you like to know.'

'I think I can feel something snaking out of your strap.' Ken couldn't believe he was having phone sex with Liverlips practically in the next room. He wondered if he'd be jerking off with some stranger if he hadn't had a few drinks before. OK, seven cocktails, mixed. Not that he was slurring his words or anything. Ken held his liquor well. Liverlips was out on the couch after three, a slobbering fool. Still, it was sort of risky with his lover in the study. Well, screw him. Liverlips was a horror show. Once he even counted the condoms after returning from a business trip. Miss Priss deserves what she gets. It's a wonder she doesn't mark the phallic container of Foreplay with lipstick.

'I'm not going to let you touch it for a while. Why don't you slip out of your boxers and let that thick eight-inch dick pop out to attention?'

Flatterer. Ken was wearing jockeys and it wasn't an inch over six, but he might as well play along. 'I'd like to lick the bulge through your dirty jockstrap.'

'Lie down on your back. I'm towering over you. Look up at my tits.'

'I'm scratching them with my toes. Do you like that?' Ken was getting into this. Fuck, Ken was so horny, it was either the sperm-line or an inanimate object. Even the cat knew he was on heat. Earlier that evening, Felix had abruptly jumped out of his lap in alarm, and been skittish ever since. It was time for release. Well, he had the security of knowing that Liverlips wouldn't pick up the extension to order a midnight pepperoni pizza from Ray's and catch him in the act. His lover had a separate line for tax purposes. Life with a consultant had its advantages.

'I'm standing over you with my big fat dick six inches above your face, and my low hanging balls even closer. You want to lick it, don't you? Maybe I'll let you. You have to beg.'

Liverlips wouldn't dare try this on Ken. He was the Ice Goddess of Great Neck, Long Island. He had all the sexual appeal of a bruised banana. His fantasies were all so predictable. After a decade Ken knew them all by heart: the fireman, the lifeguard, the support-hose stocking salesman. Were they ever in a rut. In a way, with his lover in the den, it was risky, even exciting. 'I want it. I want it real bad. I want to lick the vein on the underside.'

'I'm not giving it to you just yet. Turn over. I want you to get nice and relaxed for me. You like massage?'

Who was this man and how did he know all of Ken's buttons? He wanted to get naked with him. 'Who doesn't?' Christ, he could almost hear Liverlips speaking to him. Was this guilt or what? Maybe he had had a bit too much. It couldn't be Liverlips. He would never call a jerkoff line: he was too repressed. Ken would be more likely to be talking to Mamie Eisenhower on the TOOL line than Liverlips.

'I've got you on my bed lying on your stomach. I'm rubbing oil on your shoulders, into your neck. All of your tension is at your neck. I'm getting you relaxed. You feel it? Your dick gets hard, then relaxes. You're so relaxed you're almost falling asleep. I reach over and pinch your left tit. A surge of energy goes through your cock. I rub oil into your back, down your spine. I run my thumbs up your spine. You like that, don't you? Do you want me to do more?'

Conscious thought was almost gone. What could Ken say but 'Yes'.

'I'm rubbing oil into your tight hard ass. You've got a football player's ass, two hard globes of muscle and flesh. I slip my forefinger up your ass, it contracts, I feel up to the first knuckle, just touch-typing my way up your love canal. I take it out and sniff it. It smells good. I continue rubbing your tight buns. I work my way down your left thigh and calf. I work down to your ankle. I lift your foot and rub your individual toes. You feel like you're floating on air. I press the heel of my hand into the sole of your foot. I work my way up your right leg. I press all of my weight on your ass with the heels of my hands. I work my way up your spine again. I pound your back with the sides of my hands in a gentle rapid drumming. I work on your neck again. It is less tense. There are still a few knots to untangle. I feel your tight biceps and triceps. I work down to your hands and rub your fingers individually. I go back to your neck again. I turn you over like a beached stud whale. Your dick is thick and soft. Wetness oozes from the head on to your tight stomach. I pour some oil on your chest and start working it in. You have just enough hair to get me excited.'

Slow down. At this rate, they'd be finished in no time. 'Oh yeah, don't stop.'

'I lick my thumbs and then circle your tits with them. Then I press on them with my thumbs. Then I scratch your left nipple with my thumbnail, gently. Your dick stirs to life. How are you doing?'

Did he have to ask? 'Oh man, real good.'

'Do you want me to stop for a while?'

Fucking tease. 'Please, don't stop.'

'I cover your right nipple with my lips. I start gently

sucking. I pinch your left nipple, and work my hand down to your dick. It's rock hard.'

Ken traced his movements on his body. Ever since he shaved his balls last February, the sensation was somewhat dulled. Ken was getting into it. It was beginning to feel like sex. Ken wanted some sort of panty shield for the mouthpiece, a condom for the receiver. A withholding WASP, Ken usually refrained from shooting online. With phone sex, the male of the species was finally able to convincingly fake orgasm.

'I'm really close.'

'Stop.'

'I've got my tongue down your throat. I'm spitting. A strand of spit from my mouth to you. I'm sucking your tongue. It tastes good. It's hot.'

'I can't hold it any longer.'

'I'm going to shoot.'

'That was the best.'

'You're a very visual person.' Where was a towel when you needed one?

'That was great. Maybe we can get together some-time?'

Sure, if Ken could sterilise him first. Heat him up to flash point. Get rid of those germs! Why didn't his microwave have a setting for humans? Was it possible to eliminate all germs and bacteria from the human form? Ken doubted it. Now the guilt came. He wouldn't exactly call it cheating on a physical basis, yet, somehow, he felt he'd betrayed his lover. 'I don't think so. I'm kind of involved with this guy I'm seeing now.'

'That's cool. I have a lover I've been trying to break up with for the past two years. You know how it is. Manhattan apartments.'

'And the AIDS crisis.' That should get him off the

line. The A-word an instant turn-off in any encounter. Ken felt suddenly tired.

'Yeah.'

'Well, thanks.' At least he didn't have to worry about catching a cab home at three in the morning. Christ, he couldn't even shower now. That would wake up his lover. He was suddenly suffused with tenderness for his lover, who had put up with all of his shit for the past ten years.

'Sleep tight.'

'Pleasant dreams.' Ken decided he should really give it another shot with his lover. He wasn't all that bad. Shit. When would he get the courage to tell him his test results? He couldn't go through this alone. Even if they stopped having sex, what difference would it make? They hadn't had sex for years. OK, maybe months. Ken would talk to him tomorrow. Over coffee. They'd straighten things out. They'd finally communicate. It had been such a long time. Fucking shitty world they lived in.

Paul

'Hello.'

Sounds nice. A deep, resonant voice. Not like Sparky, his whiny lover. 'Hello.'

'My name's Rick, what's yours?'

Sure, Rick. Rhymes with dick. What name would he use today? A dollar bill was on the night table. 'Bill.'

'How are you tonight?'

Oh, he was just bored and felt like dialing the sex line. He took another surreptitious toke on the joint. His voice was nice and raspy. No dope for Sparky. Some fucking health nut. What was the point? Nobody he knew was going to die of a heart attack at seventy-two. This fucking virus was playing Russian roulette with his friends and lovers, wiping them off the face of this earth at random. Who needed to worry about high cholesterol or secondary smoke? 'Pretty horny.'

'Same here. Can I call you?'

It was all pretty standard to start out, like the opening of a game of chess. Pawn to Queen-two. Knight to King's Bishop. Castle. Suck, fuck, shoot your load, and hang up the phone as you searched for the Kleenex to wipe up with. 'Sorry, I can't give out the number. I'm staying with a friend.'

'I can't either. I have a roommate.'

The social etiquette of phone lines required such strict adherence to the basic script, just like an async eight-bit telecommunications protocol. One false blip and you're offline. It was just like in Goffman's book *The Presentation of Self in Everyday Life*. Very little new information was communicated. Language itself was 50 per cent redundant, which is what made two-dimensional crossword puzzles possible. 'Where do you live?'

'Manhattan. You?'

Apartments were so fucking expensive in New York. Paul would have moved out six months ago, except for the rumors that the building was going co-op. He'd split the profits with his ex and then split. Things had been strained with Sparky for some time. 'Same.'

'So, what are you into?'

'I'm into body contact, oil and massage, tit play, that sort of thing. Safe stuff.' Sometimes he lost them at this point. Paul didn't like the group lines: the humiliation was too public. Why am I a homosexual? Because I crave rejection, he kidded himself. If Paul was dissatisfied with the current match, it was easy enough to reject him and move on to someone else. Simply press the number sign for the next contestant. He felt like he was on an endless episode of the dating game, no doubt with corporate sponsorship by Trojan condoms and Astroglide lubricant. There seemed to be an infinite supply of horny men in New York. Except, of course, when he was truly desperate. There were times, desperate times, when he'd call the group line and it would be silent. No one at all horny at 5:30 a.m. on Tuesday morning. Paul would practice Shakespearian monologues just to see if anyone was there; he would read the phone book; he would act as if his dearly departed therapist were still alive to hear his complaints and he would tell them into the receiver. There was no one to complain to: the monitor was asleep, no doubt. He would play Julie London singing 'Cry Me a River' into the receiver and then hang up.

'Sounds good.'

'You like to fuck?' Just testing the waters. He'd play along if necessary. How much collusion was necessary for good sex? Paul didn't want to reveal himself to an absolute stranger. Yet, why not? He'd never see him or call him. Where could he possibly meet him? At the bar on Second Avenue, with a green carnation? How could he elude his boyfriend? But what was the problem? He felt that they had broken up months ago, they just hadn't hashed it out verbally. He could have a little on the side. It was time to start dating again, he knew. But Paul was scared. Oh, fucking viruses. Life was such a bummer.

'Depends on the guy.'

Pretty evasive. Was that a yes or no? Paul wished he'd be quick about it. It was like a cab. It was only with the most extreme self-control that Paul was able to ride cabs to the airport without being transfixed by the meter, unable to remove my eyes from it, ticking away in my wallet. Thirty-five dollars to JFK two weeks ago, with tip and toll. He'd never do that again. He'd sooner walk. 'So what do you look like?'

'I'm about five-ten, one sixty-five, with brown hair and blue eyes. I go to the gym maybe four times a week. I've got a slim muscular build. I'm sure you'd like it.'

Who had time to go to the gym? Paul had a goddam beeper in case the new software installation failed. He was working realtime now, not in virtual. Those thirty-six-hour test periods took it out of him completely. Paul really had to stop consulting. Relax. Take a vacation once in a while. Health insurance was such a bitch. Every three months he had to scramble to make the payment to Blue Cross, he'd been working on a manual on C compilers for the past year, he didn't have time, and the publisher was chomping at the bit for the second draft. It was set for next spring. 'I'm six-two, two hundred pounds, with short blond hair and a goatee.' Paul would never grow a goatee, but Rick sounded like a trendoid. 'I've got a couple earrings in my right ear and a tit ring.'

'Wow, I go crazy for tits.'

'You'd like mine.' His ex used to. He didn't know what went wrong. He got his lover flowers for his birthday, sent them to his office, and Sparky called him right back, screamed at Paul for 'outing' him. Paul signed with an initial. So they were pansies? Fucker can't take a joke. Sparky forgot Paul's birthday. Paul had it all programmed on his laptop. Just check the calendar function every morning for anniversaries and birthdays. An alarm even went off on special occasions. Last year for their anniversary they just rented some porno and ordered in. *Asshole Buddies*, Paul thought it was. Porno movies were like Marx Brothers flicks, how could anyone remember the titles? Exactly what is Duck

Soup anyway?

'And what would you like me to do to them?'

'Suck 'em, twist 'em, lick 'em, bite 'em, whatever you want, so long as you've got one hand on my dick at the same time.' Paul hated talking dirty, but if it got him off. Christ. He hated when they shot and then hung up, the receiver clunking into its slot. Still not hard. Spit won't do. Paul could use some lube now. In the bedroom. He'd like to go to the bathroom and lift some hand lotion. He'd even settle for Crisco.

'So what are you wearing now?'

This guy was so imaginative, he had to be from Jersey. 'Just a jock strap.' That should get him hard. He's probably the type that stays until closing at the Spike, leaning against the wall by the piss factory, right under the military red bulb dot matrix clock. Paul bet he'd look good in a harness.

'Why don't you take it off?'

'Why don't you lick it off for me?' For godsakes, the dirtier Paul talked, the hotter he got. Paul didn't understand. His voice was deep. It was a turn on. He talked nice and slow. Paul felt he was doing all of the work. They didn't have to rush. It's only fifteen cents a minute, with forty for the first. Paul could deduct it anyway. Pretend it was a modem link, and he was sending a three-hundred page document to Tanzania. Nobody checked that closely. If Paul ever got audited, he was screwed anyway. What was one more white lie after a thousand of them?

'What's your dick like?'

'Wouldn't you like to know.' Everyone was a size queen. Paul was into quantifiable figures himself, but of a more theoretical nature. What was the minimal path a traveling salesperson must make to visit all of his sites? An incredibly complex problem, much more than one would expect. Algorithms were available to approximate, make a rough guesstimate. But Paul wanted the exact answer, however irrational, however many digits past the decimal point were necessary.

'I think I can feel something snaking out of your strap.'

'I'm not going to let you touch it for a while. Why don't you slip out of your boxers and let that thick eight-inch dick pop out to attention?' How did that slip out? God, that was his favorite. Some queens like dicks so big one couldn't do anything with them. Rearrange the furniture. Divine water. Clean shotgun barrels. The really big ones that never got hard. Probably from some growth hormone they took when they were kids. Paul wished he could get a hold of it. Eight inches was the ideal. Oh, fuck, everyone has eight inches on the phone lines anyway, why try to tell the truth. He read about a survey where the average American hetero male thinks an average dick is ten inches, and the average American hetero female thinks it's four. Kinsey said it was six. Fags know better. They do their own extensive research, one-on-one.

'I'd like to lick the bulge through your dirty jockstrap.'

'Lie down on your back. I'm towering over you. Look up at my tits.' Was Paul supposed to lick his finger after he stuck it up his ass? Was it OK just to smell it? He considered the consequences of having a crossed connection with a nun, a policeman, and his mother. None of these possibilities got him hard. Since deregulation, service on New York Telephone was not the best.

'I'm scratching them with my toes. Do you like that?'

'I'm standing over you with my big fat dick six inches above your face, and my low hanging balls even closer. You want to lick it, don't you? Maybe I'll let you. You have to beg.' Where did this master voice come from? Not exactly p.c. these days? He swore he'd stop this dominance trip. He'd never tried it on Sparky. But let's face it, Paul wasn't good on resolutions. Paul had been calling the TOOL line for too much. He supposed that eventually he would get the phone company to block the 550 numbers. He was waiting until the monthly bill hit an even $100. But then, how would he ever know what the weather was at forty cents a minute? Paul's apartment had a view of a bricked air shaft. From the bathroom, he could see the neighbor's smoked glass shower. Suppose Paul wanted to find a government job at $3.50 a call? If Barbara Stanwyck had discovered the joys of phone sex in *Sorry, Wrong Number* he doubted she would have nagged her husband into killing her.

'I want it. I want it real bad. I want to lick the vein on the underside.'

Every week he promised himself to only use the phone sex line once a month. That usually lasted until Tuesday. Nondenominational, his weeks started on Monday. He told himself he would make the time and go to the gym three times a week, using the stairmaster for half an hour. Whenever he thought of the stairmaster he imagined a machine dressed in Nazi regalia, all black leather, admonishing him, 'You are not stepping fast enough. You must go faster.' Well at least he never went down on anybody in the steam room. But how many unsolicited backrubs had he perpetrated? How many embarrassing stares had he committed? How many friends had turned to strangers after his careless caress? He would vow to quit the steam routine, and usually he'd be back within a week. Even after he caught crabs. He'd swear he wouldn't sit without a towel, and limit his saunas to ten minutes. Paul was drowning in his own regrets. He had no self-control. A pint of Häagen-Dazs never made it through the night in his freezer. Paul would ravage his way to the bottom of the carton at three in the morning, lit by the refrigerator bulb. A bag of M&Ms would be gone in the blink of an eye. Only broccoli, like so many men in the distant past, would go limp on him after weeks in the crisper. 'I'm not giving it to you just yet. Turn over. I want you to get nice and relaxed for me. You like massage?'

'Who doesn't?'

'I've got you on my bed lying on your stomach. I'm rubbing oil on your shoulders, into your neck... I run my thumbs up your spine. You like that, don't you? Do you want me to do more?' Paul closed his eyes and saw nebulous spirals of equations describing muscular planes, the physiognomy of desire. Christ, computers were always on his mind, mathematical postulates, unproven theorems. The four-color map theorem was finally proven a few years ago on a computer, not very elegantly, just an enumeration of all of the possible typologies of maps, a set of exhaustive possibilities. He imagined the orgiastic possibilities of all of the voices on the fiber optic network of lust.

'Yes.'

'I'm rubbing oil into your tight hard ass. You've got a football player's ass, two hard globes of muscle and flesh... I pour some oil on your chest and start working it in. You have just enough hair to get me excited.' The minimum for adultery was three, thought Paul, two lovers in a relationship and two outside of one, where the sets intersect in the guilty party. Did both have to come? Did they both even have to been in the same room? Paul wondered whether phone sex constituted a violation of his relationship. To what degree was he cheating on his lover? Conceivably, he could be having this conversation with himself, having scripted the other's dialog into a tape recorder. In this sense, it was masturbatory. Ken would have forgotten the entire exchange. One can barely tickle oneself. Only the most self-absorbed narcissistic homosexual could stimulate himself. But wasn't that what Sparky accused him of that last argument? It was the Turing problem all over again. Imagine you are in a room with a terminal. You type a question. A response appears on your screen. You have an interactive conversation. If you can't tell whether the responses are being typed by another person in the next room, or a computer, then the computer can be said to possess artificial intelligence. Poor Turing. Another fag in distress. Alan Turing whose ultimate destiny was a poisoned apple.

'Oh yeah, don't stop.'

'I lick my thumbs and then circle your tits with them. Then I press on them with my thumbs. Then I scratch your left nipple with my thumbnail, gently. Your dick stirs to life. How are you doing?' Christ, it was all a risk these day, and they were all unacceptable. Fred went to San Francisco and had his left tit pierced at the Gauntlet. He came down with hepatitis after the tit ring. OK, so maybe it *was* seafood. Sure. Some sailor he picked up at the Stud.

'Oh man, real good.'

'Do you want me to stop for a while?'

'Please, don't stop.'

'I cover your right nipple with my lips. I start gently sucking. I pinch your left nipple, and work my hand down to your dick. It's rock hard.'

'I'm really close.'

'Stop.'

'I've got my tongue down your throat. I'm spitting.

A strand of spit from my mouth to you. I'm sucking your tongue. It tastes good. It's hot.'

'I can't hold it any longer.'

Every equation held forth the possibility of singularities. An orgasm was the sexual equivalent of dividing by zero, approaching that point of infinite slope where derivatives are useless. His hyperbolic ejaculations reached their asymptotes as he climaxed. 'I'm going to shoot.'

Paul rarely made a noise when he came. A history of sex in bathrooms, back seats of cars, museum roofs, backrooms, elevators stuck between floors, public gardens, empty subway cars stuck in tunnels, parks, and so on had taught him the lesson of discretion. No handkerchiefs were necessary to muffle his cries.

'That was the best.' Why did he feel guilty? Adultery was of the soul, not the body. Was sex all in the mind? Was it always a form of masturbation, sometimes with someone else present? No, that was the thing: they had exchanged something more intimate than fluids. They had exchanged confidences.

'You're a very visual person.'

'That was great. Maybe we can get together sometime?' Paul was amazed. Out of all the randomness in the universe, the electronic sea of phone cords and remote attachments, all of the connections, n factorial over j factorial, out of the infinite number of connections, it was possible for Paul to connect.

'I don't think so. I'm kind of involved with this guy I'm seeing now.'

'That's cool. I have a lover I've been trying to break up with for the past two years. You know how it is. Manhattan apartments.' Of course, Paul was always looking at men, appraisingly, on the beach, in the bars, at the gym, in the steamroom. But still, up until now, it was only innocent, unconnected with intention. He felt guiltier than if he had defiled the lover's bed. Why was he guilty? No bodily fluids were exchanged. That embarrassing silence after coming. Sometimes people hung up immediately. Did this constitute adultery? The post-coital conversation? The intimacy he lacked, never would regain with his lover? Paul was already thinking of Sparky in terms of an ex-lover. Something had clicked in his head. It couldn't be adultery, if they weren't even sleeping together. That's when it hit him. It was over. The relationship was over.

'And the AIDS crisis.'

'Yeah.'

'Well, thanks.'

'Sleep tight.'

'Pleasant dreams.'

Paul waited a moment and hung up the phone, turned off the light. He had made up his mind. Things had soured past repair. He didn't know it was possible to start over with someone new. But it was time to leave. The inertia of their relationship shouldn't be an excuse. Even the health crisis. Paul felt reaffirmed. There were people he could connect with, communicate with. He would start anew. Take things from scratch. Firm with resolve, Paul turned over and went to sleep on the sofa. He would leave Kenneth S. Parkington tomorrow.

◆

Revival Week

NOEL VIRTUE

◆

'Thou shalt not steal.'

◆

*B*ack in the dark ages, when I was a sticky-beaked larrikin of thirteen and as busy as a bee with a bumful of honey, the Reverend Fulk and his Gospel Crusade of Hope came to town. It was the 1950s. According to some the country had been swarming with evangelists and faith healers. And missionaries on furlough. The war was over. A lot of people had wanted to get their souls sorted. It was a new age.

Mum and Dad and I lived in a township called Sandspit Crossing. We had only just moved into a new Beazley home that Dad had got built. It even had an inside dunny. For years Mum had been pretty narked at having to go outside to commune with nature at the old house. It had only been a creosoted shack with the outside toilet five hundred yards from the back door and overrun by Wetas and spiders and other insects that had no right to live, even under the wooden seat. It'd been hell in winter.

Mum loved the new house. She was the green envy of the neighbours. Though she still harped on about getting modern all the time. She'd been trying for months without success to get on to a radio quiz show called *Try Your Luck*. She wanted to have a go at winning a brand new automatic washing machine that was the big prize. Despite the fact that two doors along our street the Barkers had bought one and old Gran Barker had caught her tits in the wringer one washday and was in hospital for a week.

Sandspit Crossing was a backblocks settlement of jerry-built shacks and a main street. We'd always called the place a township. That sounded better. It was in the far north of the North Island and wasn't even on the map. The main drag was called Hinemoa Street. There was a public house called the Golden Hope, a Four Square Grocery, a Post Office and General Goods where you could buy anything from a pair of black gumboots to a Berlei bra or health stamps. There was the local flea pit of a theatre called the Majestic where Maoris came from miles around every Saturday night on horseback to watch Westerns and James Cagney double bills, a Milk Bar, and a few other places which were either falling down or empty. There were a couple of factories. One belonged to the Dairy Board. Dad worked in the other. There wasn't much else. There was no church. Most of the time it was a quiet sort of a place except on Saturday nights when the pub closed and drunks wandered all over the main street like Brown's cows. I used to nick out and throw stones at them while Mum was soaking her corns in the bath.

My Dad was a woodworker. He could do anything with timber. He often cracked on that he had brown fingers but no one understood what he meant. His jokes usually fell flat. The story went that he had got out of going overseas to the war as some goofy four-eyed clerk down in Wellington had mucked up his papers with someone else's and Dad was supposed to have been suffering from TB. He stayed in the country and worked in an office which he'd hated, according to Mum. He and Mum never did find out what happened to the other bloke. No one told them when the mistake was discovered. They'd planned to send Dad off after that but for some reason they never got around to it, so he said he'd missed the war but the war hadn't missed him. Mum sometimes half-joked that the other poor bugger had probably died a real crook death in Timbuktu so that Dad might live and it'd been a real miracle.

I was a bit of a nosy parker in those days. I wanted to know about everyone and everything. When I saw the posters going up on the telegraph poles around town, announcing that the Reverend Fulk was coming, I pestered everybody about who he was and why he was coming to Sandspit and what he might do if he was out to save people from wicked sin. Wicked sin sounded pretty exciting. I hadn't known much about it at thirteen. A few days later there were even bigger posters put up along Hinemoa Street. Reverend Fulk was bringing the whole caboodle. There was to be a choir of ten called The Heavenly Hopers, some people called Counsellors, two negro gospel singers from America and a cage of white doves which were to be let loose once the Reverend had finished his soul gathering. Mum reckoned it all sounded like a circus was coming to town. We'd never had a real circus visit Sandspit. There had been one before the war, Mum told me, before she had married Dad. There'd been clowns, a trapeze artist, two white horses and a camel that had belched to music. She couldn't remember what else. Dad had taken her to have a look but she'd told me on the quiet that they'd been too busy getting to know each other carnally and it'd been as rough as guts anyway. She'd reckoned the Gospel Crusade of Hope might be almost as good as that circus. She had laughed like billyoh when she'd said that. Mum hadn't any time for Bible bashing. She'd thought religion was codswallop. Yet her and Dad had always laughed like loonies about everything and hadn't taken life too seriously up until then. They never kept anything from me. They were beaut. They're both dead now.

Mum slaved flat stick looking after Dad and me all the years I was growing up. She used to make all our clothes. She made all my shirts by hand and knitted socks and made my undies out of old sheets that Dad had ripped with his toenails. Up until I was ten she had run up shorts on the Singer out of potato sacks that weren't stained. Then she stopped for some reason and for my thirteenth birthday I'd been given a pair of real serge shorts that had a leather belt with a tin buckle depicting a cowboy riding a bronco. I was so proud of that belt. I belted all over town showing off and skiting that we'd got rich. I don't think anyone believed me.

Because I was a one-off and had no brothers or sisters I spent a lot of time with old folk after school and at weekends. Mum had nagged me into that but I never minded. They were those who were also mostly on their own Mum said and grateful for the company of a thirteen-year-old boy. I didn't have many friends my own age so it wasn't too much of a sacrifice. My favourite was Miss Maidstone. She was in charge of the local library. I loved reading so I spent a lot of time over at the library. Miss Maidstone and I had become such good mates she'd yack away at me for hours about things I've mostly forgotten. Miss Maidstone had never married. She wore her hair in a tight bun and had a real hairy moustache she never shaved off and was as strong as a Canterbury sheep farmer. I was in love with her nut brownies. She was forever baking biscuits and making preserves and cooking meat pies. She did seem to like me quite a lot and never stopped flapping her gums when I was around. Everyone said she was lonely and needed a good bloke but I never had any inkling of that.

There was Mr Ritter the butcher. He lived on his
own too, behind his shop. He stuffed and mounted
dead possums during his spare time in his backyard
shed and sold them to a shop down in Wellington. I
never did find out where he got the dead possums
from. Mr Ritter had been an undertaker in Invercargill.
When his wife died young from a crummy heart he
had come north and given up the undertaking. He was
the only butcher in town and did a roaring trade in
home-made sausages and something called egg stuffing.
Mr Ritter was six foot four inches tall in his bare feet
and was so buck-toothed he could have eaten an apple
through a picket fence. He was even more lonely than
Miss Maidstone, according to Mum. I used to help him
bag up sawdust at the small factory where my Dad
worked and help him drag the bags back to his shop
and after he would tell me stories about pirates and
American Indians. He'd read a lot of books and been
overseas. I'd always hoped that he and Miss Maidstone
might get together one day and get hitched but Miss
Maidstone told me when I used to kid her about it that
Mr Ritter was a gutless wonder and she reckoned his
hair looked like it had been grown on a wild boar's
bum.

Miss Maidstone was my friend and ears for the years
when no one else listened because I was too young.
She drank whisky and wore men's trousers and laughed
a lot. She smoked a pipe and for the last two weeks
every April she went off to Whangarei on her Harley
motorbike to visit her sister who had once been a
Catholic nun in New Guinea. Sometimes we played
footy in her backyard after school, but only after she'd
closed the library where no one ever went. She loved
sport. She died of blood poisoning ten years ago after
cutting her hand on a rusty tin. She didn't do anything

about it as she'd hated doctors and so she'd died. She'd got pretty old and dithery by then. And forgetful.

Mr Ritter's still alive. He's been living in a Home in Whangarei. He can't look after himself anymore. Up until a couple of years back I used to go down on the coach to see him from where I now live but he'd started to forget who I was. Mr Ritter had become a bit of a dickwhacker. The doctors called it senile dementia. He kept asking me to take him bags of blackballs and bunches of Canna lilies when I visited and told everyone that I was his young wife. He'd kissed me on the hand and one time he put his hand right on my crutch and squeezed and looked surprised. He called me Mabel which'd been his wife's name. No one else ever visited him. In the end the doctors told me to stay away as I got him too excited.

I used to go over to the Bidwell sisters' place a fair bit. Maudie, Dorothy and Bessie Bidwell lived in an old ramshackle house that had once been a farmhouse up until the big Depression of the 30s made changes. They owned five acres of land which was mostly covered by gorse shrub. The week before the Gospel Crusade was due to show up they had a whole acre cleared and laid down with the best sawdust. That was where the marquee was to be erected for the Revival. The Bidwell sisters had been missionaries most of their life. They'd been in Africa and China and Rarotonga but had been retired for years after Bessie broke her pelvis falling off a horse and Dorothy had had a nervous breakdown. Some said they were stinking rich but I never saw any sign of it. They were pretty kind sorts. They always gave me a big feed whenever I nicked over to see them after school or sometimes on Saturdays if there was nothing worth seeing at the pictures. They held their own church services in their front room on Sundays, grew their own vegies and fruit and kept chooks. They sold the eggs to the Four Square. It was they who had invited Reverend Fulk to Sandspit. They'd been forever going on at townsfolk like a trio of parrots about Jesus and that Sandspit was chocka with sinners ripe for saving. Mum couldn't stand them. She'd cross to the other side of the street if she spotted them coming towards her. They'd hoped I was going to find salvation at the Crusade. As well as Mum and Dad and everyone else around town who drew breath.

The week before the Crusade began had also been the first week of the school holidays. I was sent to school miles away in an old bomb of a bus. There were only seven kids at Sandspit who went out of town to that school, including me. There was a school in Sandspit but it was ruled over by Methodists from Whangarei so I wasn't allowed to go there. My best mate who went to school on the bus with me was called Roy Gonda. Roy Gonda's parents were from Hungary. He'd been the same age as me but older by two weeks. He grinned a lot.

Mum was never all that friendly to him and reckoned he had so many bad spots that his face was beginning to look like an abandoned quarry but back then he'd been my mate and couldn't have done wrong in my book. Roy had two hundred butterfly marbles, a real shrunken head from South America that he'd got from a comic advertisement, a twenty-six inch bike that had gears, ten wind-up tin toys and the biggest Meccano set I'd ever seen. His Mum and Dad were pretty well-off and owned the local Men's and Ladies' Outfitters. They had a hi-fi in their front room. Mum didn't like Mr and Mrs Gonda either because they were foreigners and had more money than we did. But she never stopped me being mates with Roy. She reckoned that as a family they were far too toffee-nosed and didn't try to fit into the New Zealand way but she thought they were honest sorts. I only saw Roy during the week and never during the school hols. He was sent down to somewhere just outside Wellington to stay with his Gran who had a real queer name and kept goats. She was well-off too. Roy was all right. He let me play with his marbles and sometimes I'd borrow his bike. Though he was a real hot-head about sex. We used to take off all our clothes in the pup tent his Dad had put up in their backyard. We'd sit in there showing off our dongs to each other and giggling quite a bit but I hadn't been ready to find it all that interesting. We were just doing what other boys at school said they did and because Roy had done the same thing with Raewyn Scudder whose Mum had a goitre and Roy had reckoned it had been really exciting. According to him, Raewyn had let him touch her after she'd pulled down her bloomers. Roy never stopped talking about that. He thought he'd got her pregnant because he'd touched her with his wet fingers. I half believed him for a while because both of us knew bugger all about sex.

Dad had spent most of his free time down at the Golden Hope Hotel after work. It was the only pub for miles. He boozed there with his mates who were all bludgers, according to Mum, and on the dole because they'd let themselves go to the pack living in Sandspit. Dad shouted his mates drinks and Mum shouted at Dad when he came home so stuffed from boozing he could hardly stand up. He'd lean against the paling fence outside the house and sing dirty songs at the top of his voice until Mum came out with the broom and chased him indoors, yelling blue murder, trying not to laugh because of the neighbours.

'You only think of your belly and what hangs on the end of it!' she'd yell at him every time he came rolling inside as blotto as a drunk could get. Then she'd laugh out loud as soon as the front door was shut. I think he must have been a bit of an alcoholic but no one ever said anything. Mum sure didn't. Dad didn't give a bugger about anything. He was a real hard shot. He always made it up to Mum after he'd been home an hour and had sobered up. They'd push off to bed for a naughty while I was allowed to stay up and listen to *Night Beat* on the radio, turning the volume up loud so I couldn't hear them and picking fluff off the carpet until Dad yelled out to me to knock it on the head and get off to bed too.

I never really found out why Mum had started hating Bible bashing. She'd told me and Dad loads of times that Bible bashers were the cause of more family bust-ups than adultery. It must have been to do with her past, the only thing she wouldn't talk about. Her own family had been Baptists. There were no photographs in the house of her own Mum and Dad. Just her Grandad who'd been part Maori and a hard shot like Dad according to her. I overheard her once telling one of the neighbours that her parents had not been all there in the mental department and that Dad had saved her skin and married her before she'd gone bonkers. She had grown up down in Auckland. She never spoke about that either. Both her and Dad hated cities.

By the time the big marquee had been put on the Bidwell sisters' land Mum and Dad were fed up to the back teeth about hearing of salvation and sinners-who-were-about-to-be-redeemed so that Dad was downing the Dominion beer as though there was no next week and Mum was in such a ratstink mood she was yelling at Dad twice as much as she usually did. I don't know to this day why she'd got herself so riled up but all I could care about was the excitement in the town. Everyone was flapping gums about the Reverend Fulk arriving. It sort of reached fever pitch right up until all hell broke loose and things fell apart like a fart having a fit.

I didn't see the Crusade arrive. Mum was making up a new frock that day out of some material Aunt Huldah had sent her and I had to be her model and pin cushion. Aunt Huldah was Mum's older sister who ran an old folks home down in Havelock North. She was always sending up stuff. She sent a whole box of condoms once for Dad's birthday and Mum was livid about that. I only found out what they were by pinching one when she wasn't looking and taking it along to show Miss Maidstone. I'd thought they were balloons. Mum reckoned everything Aunt Huldah sent she stole from shops but we never heard anything to prove it.

Anyway, the Reverend arrived in a Model T Ford painted white with a huge trailer and the rest of the Crusaders came behind in a decorated bus. According to Miss Maidstone who'd gone along to have a gizzo it was pretty exciting. She'd even had her hair done at the Hair and Beauty Parlour so she would look good at the opening meeting of the Revival. She didn't want to get saved but wild horses wouldn't have stopped her from being there to see who did. She even claimed that some bloke was laying on bets as to who might get saved. She was raring to go when I nicked down to see her the next morning. Mum had said she didn't mind me going to the meetings if I was going with Miss Maidstone. But I wasn't on any account to go up front to get saved and not to let anyone force me to either. She and Dad were having nothing to do with the Revival. Dad had told us he was taking to the grog the whole time the Revival went on. There was a load of his mates going to whoop it up at the Golden Hope every night and Mum even cracked on that she might join them which caused Dad to go about with a bit of a hang-dog look. He preferred being alone with his mates while he downed the Dominion. Women weren't welcome. He drank Dominion beer by the gallon and swore by it.

Well, on the first night of the Revival it seemed like the whole town had showed up. People were squashed into the marquee like stunned mullets. It was still stifling hot and everyone was wheezing and coughing and sweating. The day had been a real scorcher. Miss Maidstone and I managed to get a good seat near the front on the side where she said the Reverend mightn't point at us. He was well known, she'd told me, for his hellfire and brimstone preaching and getting everyone het up and writhing in guilt. The Reverend had been making a real name for himself all over New Zealand.

There was a choir right at the back of the makeshift stage. They were warming up their voices when we got there and pushed our way in. A huge sign made of canvas had been put across the middle of Hinemoa Street. The sign read BE SURE YOUR SINS WILL FIND YOU OUT and below that was written COME AND MEET YOUR JESUS CHRIST.

I can't remember too much about that meeting now except the Reverend shouting a lot and pointing his finger and the two negro singers from America sang so smoothly they kept getting clapped back on stage and some folk were getting to their feet and shouting hallelujah every five minutes, and an old bloke called Charlie Gregg who Miss Maidstone said was a Commo fell down and had a sort of fit before he stood up and got saved. There were so many went up front when the call came I wanted to hide under the seats. I was scared stiff someone might point the finger at me. Miss Maidstone had held on to me like a vice so I was all right in the end. Part of the way through she kept trying hard not to laugh. But then she went real quiet and sat very still and I was worried sick she'd get up and go down front. But she didn't.

It was after that first night when all the strange ponk started to happen. The first event was the Reverend announcing that all the collection money from the last two Revivals he'd undertaken elsewhere had been stolen from the marquee. The news spread over Sandspit like a bushfire. There was a special meeting called for the afternoon after the money had been discovered missing. It wasn't held in the marquee but right on the main street outside the pub. I'd run on down there when one of the neighbours came over to tell Mum what was about to happen. The Reverend was being nice when I got there, surrounded by his cronies and just talking calmly about thievery in general but then he started putting the boot in and acting as if his head was stuffed full of dynamite. There'd been a heck of a lot of people gathered nearby. They all listened to him raving on and after a bit some bloke yelled out for the Reverend to shut his gob and to bloody well go and take a long walk off a short plank. Others joined in and in the end the Reverend said he was sorry for all us sinners and marched off back to where he was staying at the Bidwell sisters'. Once he'd gone blokes stood about grumbling as if they'd really got the pricker and hated the Reverend's guts. Only one or two in the crowd stuck up for him.

The next day the big sign that had hung across Hinemoa Street had been taken down and another one put up in its place. The new sign read THOU SHALT NOT STEAL and underneath had been added JESUS IS WATCHING YOU!

Dad had come home and said there'd been a noisy gathering at the pub. The police had no clues as to who had taken the money and they'd reckoned that a collection should be organised to replace the Reverend's missing money. Dad had been dead set against the idea and the vote they took had been ten for to ten against with some blokes refusing to vote at all, so nothing was done. There were a lot of folk in town who didn't like having religion rammed down their throats and serve the Reverend right for coming to Sandspit in the first place. But there were also quite a few who felt sorry for him and had respect for his morals. Reverend Fulk was as thin as a rake and as pale as a bleached sheet and he might have been a pimple-head with a mouth on him like a yard of elastic but everyone had a right to a fair go; this was New Zealand.

Then blow me, during the next few days there started to be more thieving and burglary going on all over town than in all Sandspit's history, according to Dad. Stores were broken into in the dead of night and goods were taken. Houses were burgled. Someone even pinched the lightbulbs from all the street-lamps along Hinemoa Street. And while this was happening the meetings in the marquee became so packed tight full of people that there were special loudspeakers put up outside so that folk who couldn't get in could sit on the Bidwell property to listen. The Bidwell sisters were rushed off their feet handing out cups of tea and keeping folk off their flower beds. People were lining up to use their lav as if it was the only toilet in town. And the more the meetings got successful and the more the

Reverend got financial from the overflowing collection plates the more there were burglaries. The Post Office was broken into and thousands of pounds worth of stamps were stolen. Radios, a hi-fi and lawn-mowers were stolen from the General Goods and then folk started stealing groceries from the Four Square while it was still open, getting caught and trying to claim that they'd no idea what they'd been doing and something had just come over them. People started to get pretty confused. Some were so upset they were flapping like dunny doors in a hurricane and the police were so overworked they had to send off for more coppers from nearby towns. Within a few days the whole place was going mental. I'd never seen anything like it. The police were running about like headless chooks trying to figure out why good honest folk were just helping themselves to anything they fancied. There were a lot who got caught but the police could only do so much so quite a few blokes and a few women got away with it, so it was said. And every night the Revival meetings were packed out and people were coming up from as far away as Whangarei and it was thought that some of them were joining in the stealing too. It was like a fever had taken over and was affecting folk's brains.

No one I knew seemed to be taking anything. Miss Maidstone said she would never steal but I wasn't sure about Charlie Gregg the Commo as I spotted him going about with a crowbar. Windows were broken in Hinemoa Street night after night until the police started to put up huge spotlights aimed at all the likely places. But by that time the thefts went on during the day as well and at night most folk were hanging about down at the marquee. The Reverend was raking it in and claiming that he'd saved more souls in Sandspit than he'd saved anywhere else in the whole Northland.

I reckon by far the worst thing that happened was that the cemetery was done over two nights running. It was said at the time that bodies went missing though that'd been just an ugly rumour put about. Whoever it was had pulled up coffins and hacked off real silver and gold handles that folk had actually paid to have put on them. One of the graves was said to have belonged to a little girl who'd died only three weeks before. Folk were buried there from all over the outlying area, not just from Sandspit. It was a huge place. It caused a real uproar. The Reverend was even seen visiting the place, preaching over the disturbed graves and crying out for forgiveness, spouting off that the Devil had come to town after him and was infecting townsfolk with evil. That had a certain effect on everyone. People started to act even more confused and panicked. Even Mum got caught up. She kept searching my room and looking under my bed as if I might be hiding stolen goods there. Dad went crook at her about that and they had a real ding-dong row one night about it out in the backyard with all the neighbours listening in. Mum had always been as tight as a duck's bum with money and so honest she wrote down everything she bought in a notebook and how much it'd cost so she could show Dad that she wasn't wasting the housekeeping. She was proud of being honest. She grew so worked up by all the thieving she kept telling Dad that she reckoned the Reverend was stirring the pot on purpose and she was sure he had something to do with it. She thought the Reverend was as mad as a maggot anyway and had poisoned minds or else his cronies had started the thieving themselves. Dad yelled at her that she was talking tommyrot but he hadn't known what was causing everything either. No one did.

Folk started buying shotguns to protect their property after the first few days. Every time Mum heard a noise out back at night she'd charge through the kitchen to the back door brandishing her broom and yelling out at the top of her voice. She became a nervous wreck. And we had nothing worth stealing. Dad wouldn't buy a gun. He hated the things and reckoned they would only lead to trouble. Sure enough they did.

Mr Ritter caught someone red-handed. The bloke was helping himself to the shop's best meat cuts. He'd broken into the shop from the front long after midnight. Mr Ritter said he'd heard a noise and taken his new shotgun to see what was up and he shot the bastard up the bum. And it was one of his regular customers. They took Mr Ritter away but there were no charges laid against him and he didn't even get properly arrested. The next morning there were so many people in the shop congratulating him that Mr Ritter closed early and hid himself away behind the shop with all the blinds closed and he stayed like that most of the time until it was all over. He wasn't proud of what he had done. He hated violence. The bloke who'd been shot left town and nothing more was said about it. Mr Ritter had only used bird slugs in the gun so the burglar hadn't suffered much damage.

The final straw for Mum was when Dad turned up one night with one of his hotel mates in an old rust-bucket of a truck. And on the back of the truck, for all the neighbours to see, was one of the actual models of the automatic washing machine that Mum had had her heart set on. It was only early evening but I'd been asleep and it was Mum's yelling that woke me up. I looked out my window and she was standing on the front lawn with her hands on her hips cursing and swearing at Dad and Dad was standing on the back of the truck leaning over the washing machine laughing fit to bust at her, as he was as full as a bull he'd been drinking so much. He stood there trying to tell her that the door had been wide open and everyone was helping themselves and why should they lose out. But his words slurred and he hadn't made a lot of sense. Well, Mum came barging back inside the house and pulled on her gumboots and set out like she had a plague of wasps up her bloomers. I threw on my shorts and a shirt and was off out after her so fast that Dad hadn't had time to catch on. Mum marched down our street not looking to her left or right until she reached Miss Maidstone's place. And Miss Maidstone must have spotted her because she came rushing out and grabbed Mum by the arm and nearly caused her to have a gutzer. They hadn't seen me as I'd nicked behind a hedge but they talked for a couple of minutes, Mum waving her arms about, and then Miss Maidstone was marching along beside Mum swinging her arms and as they passed under the street-lamps Mum's face looked as ugly as raw liver she was so mad. Miss Maidstone just looked excited. I kept on following and Mum didn't notice me, or she chose not to. They didn't stop until they'd passed down Hinemoa Street and reached the marquee. They barged inside and down along the aisle like tanks. The place was packed solid, as it was every night, but that didn't faze Mum. She only came to a stop when she'd reached the foot of the stage, with Miss Maidstone right behind her. Reverend Fulk was in the middle of shouting the odds on original sin when Mum started shouting too and the Reverend came to a dead stop and stared down at her with his mouth wide open. Mum let him have it once she had his attention. She told him straight out in front of everyone exactly what she thought of him and his

Crusade, spouting off that he was a no-hoper and a con-man and a shit-stirrer. The whole marquee went so quiet you could have heard a mouse blow off. But then a whole group of folk started getting to their feet and were clapping and cheering Mum on and then Mum and Miss Maidstone were clambering up on to the stage and the Reverend was backing off calling out, 'Now ladies, now ladies!' No one took a blind bit of notice.

Well, whatever else Mum shouted (I couldn't hear everything from the back), she'd stirred up a lot of other women and blokes. They started following her up on to the stage. There were shaking fists and shouting voices and the Reverend was backing away holding up his arms and behind him the Choir of Heavenly Hopers who'd been singing in low voices had stopped singing and started to push forward en masse. In a minute there were so many on the stage that I lost sight of Mum just as I saw her raise her fist to sock the Reverend in the jaw. Then there was a screeching, wrenching sound. Someone near me began yelling out and the whole stage just sort of collapsed inward and women were screaming their heads off and some bloke was yelling, 'Watch my flaming legs, you bastards!' There were bodies all over the show lying on top of each other and struggling. Folk who hadn't managed to get up on to the stage were leaping back in sheer panic. I tried to shove my way down to the front but didn't get far. Everyone was suddenly trying to leave. I soon got knocked over because I was only small but I managed to roll myself into a ball and I covered my head and hoped for the best. I got walloped across the back by boots and shoes and the noise was loud enough to bust your drums.

Mum suffered a broken wrist, two cracked ribs and

got a black eye. Miss Maidstone had her left leg broken and someone ripped her dress open down the back and whoever it was pinched her bra, so she claimed. Quite a few got badly hurt and they had to send out for a couple of ambulances that took two hours to arrive. Folk lay about moaning and crying and some of them were dragged across into the Bidwell sisters' house to wait for the ambulances. It was like a battle had just ended. The nearest hospital was fifteen miles away and I went with Mum and Miss Maidstone and a lot of others in the back of one ambulance. After Mum's wrist was set and her chest was taped up and they'd set and plastered Miss Maidstone's leg, Mum demanded she be taken back home. She wasn't going to stay the night in a hospital miles away from Dad. She was still in such a bad temper the hospital agreed and we got back home in the early hours of the morning and Mum got me to make up a bed on the settee for Miss Maidstone. They both slept the clock round.

By lunchtime the next day the marquee had been pulled down and the Reverend Fulk and his cronies had done a bunk without anyone really noticing. The Bidwell sisters left town that same day too and a few weeks later their house was up for sale and no one ever heard from them again. It was thought by half the town that Mum had been right and it had been the Reverend who had stirred everything up and that he'd been in on the thieving somehow, but no one could figure out why. There seemed no earthly reason for it. He was a respected Gospel Minister, it was said, and had made a lot of people happy all over the north. There'd been a heck of a lot of confusion in the days following. Some folk reckoned it might have been something in the water so the town supply was tested but that was all right. Foodstuffs from the Four Square were taken away to be looked at but there wasn't one clue as to why the town had gone haywire.

Then a week or so later a letter and a cheque arrived care of the Post Office. The cheque was for hundreds of pounds and the letter was from the Reverend Fulk. He claimed in the letter that he didn't know what had happened either and believed sincerely that it had been the Devil at work. Satan followed him all over and tried to destroy what he was trying to achieve for the country. The money was to cover for all the damage done to Sandspit and to apologise for the whole shibang. Well, that news flew all over the place like a madwoman's shit and even Mum was a bit stumped as it was the last thing she'd been expecting.

Life settled down again, eventually. My mate Roy Gonda ran off to join the Merchant Navy after getting Raewyn Scudder knocked up three years later. Miss Maidstone kept on opening the library every day and sitting in there with no customers except me. When I left school they employed me as her assistant so I might take over when she retired. We'd sit there together surrounded by books and she taught me how to play poker and gin rummy. I could have left town as Roy did but somehow I never really felt the urge. I had no ambitions. I just grew older.

Mum finally got herself on to *Try Your Luck*. She was real lucky. They asked her to appear on the very last show because she had written more letters to try to get on it than anyone else had in the whole of New Zealand. She never did win the washing machine. In fact she won nothing at all. But when she arrived home on the coach from Wellington Dad was waiting for her at the bus station with the news that he'd been saving up for a machine on the quiet and it was to be delivered the very next day. Mum was over the moon about that. I'll always remember her climbing down off the coach, dressed up like a dog's dinner, looking a bit fed up and then her eyes lighting up like globes when Dad told her what he'd done. There were still only a few families in town who had been able to afford an automatic machine so that week Mum started washing clothes for some of the neighbours and she kept that up for years until people were better off and bought their own. She never charged them a penny either, which Dad had reckoned was a bit mental, but Mum was a good sort. People never let her forget about the night she'd faced the Reverend Fulk and sorted out the town by it. Somehow the Reverend copped all the blame anyway whenever anyone brought the subject up and went on about past days. Mum had been a bit of a hero in a few folks' eyes. The Reverend went down in the town's history as a bit of a rum bastard. None of us heard anything more about him. He just disappeared off the face of the world.

And in all the years Mum used that automatic washing machine and kept some of the neighbours happy with whites whiter than white, she never once caught her own tits in the wringer.

Raise Your Right Hand

NEIL BARTLETT

◆

*'Thou shalt not bear false witness
against thy neighbour.'*

◆

*S*ince I met my David things have mostly been a lot better for me. Before, I thought being sure about things was something that other people were, married people mostly. Also, it is a lot better for me having a place to live all the time, like I have now, and I am certainly happy every day at four o'clock when it is time for me to go home and I know there is a place for me to go home to. I like there being someone there, too. David isn't actually there when I get home, which is usually at about 4.30, but at 6.30 he is there. He comes home at 6.30 most days. It is two o'clock now. I am starting writing this in a new notebook, one of the blue ones. David gets me them from work. The picture on the cover of the blue ones is always the same; it is the statue of a naked man swinging a sword.

Before, before I met him, I used to just be out mostly, just walking around and waiting to meet people. You meet a lot of people and when you have agreed on the money they mostly take you back to their place, so you get to see a lot of different flats and houses as well as the hotels. But you are really on your own all the time, even at the weekends. Now, at the weekends, we do things together, things like the shopping, which even though it is ordinary for most people, I really like, because I am doing it with him, I suppose. Also we go out in the evenings. During the week when he is at work I am on my own during the day and this is when I come to the library. I am here a lot, most days of the week at the moment in fact. Although I come here on my own it doesn't feel the same as before, because I am not waiting to meet people any more, and because there is a point to it now, I have somebody I can talk to about the books in the evening.

I like the books which are actually about things most, the reference section. I like them best because of the way you're not allowed to take them home. You have to sit upstairs and work at a table if you want to read them, and there is always a really good atmosphere of everybody concentrating. I think it is a good idea that some books are there for everybody to use. You can't take them home, you have to come and work on them here, you can't take them home because somebody might need a piece of information really urgently and then if you had taken the book home the information wouldn't be there just when that person needed it most.

When I am here, I read all sorts of books, because I think all kinds of information is useful, even things that you don't know that you need. Information makes you think more clearly, which is good for me to practise, because I don't want to go back to how I was before. When I have had a good day here, that's how I can tell; you can tell when you have been thinking properly. It doesn't matter how many things you read about in a day (sometimes I spend a very long time just with one book so that I understand it properly, I don't like to go on to the next one until I have understood it properly), and in the end it doesn't matter how many things you know, but it does matter how well you can think. Since I met my David I know that I have been thinking better.

This is because he encourages me, but also because I know that he loves me.

When we are at home I know that he loves me because of all the things that we are doing together all the time (I don't mean just the sleeping together but mostly all the other things that we do. I think that waking up and finding that he is still holding on to me, or when we cook our dinner together, that is when I am really sure). But when I am working here and I start thinking, when I am not actually with him (especially when he goes away for his job, which he does sometimes), when I am not actually with him I do sometimes feel like I used to feel, before. I can't concentrate, and then I want to take the books home with me, or just to go walking, and I do then sometimes think that maybe he does not love me at all. It is the way that everything is different now I expect, I expect it is because I'm not used yet to the way that everything in my life is different now. I think this feeling is something to do with how many books there are here for me still to read, and the idea of knowing that even if you read all the time you can never read all of them, which is like the feeling that you can never really know what is going on inside somebody else's head even if you are staring at them. Even if it is someone you are seeing every day, even if you think about them almost all of the time. Or like when you sit there and look at them but you don't know what books the other people are reading or why, or what they are thinking about them. So now I have a photograph of myself that I bring with me to work here, it is from before, a passport photo (someone I went with who really fancied me had it done in a photo-booth). I've got it out here on the table for when I am working, and I look at it when I am working, and I think about how I will get used to my life, how I want to. There is a man here who I talk to sometimes in the café where I have my lunch when I'm working;

he has photographs too. They are all pictures of women with children (he gets them out and puts them on the table in a row like playing cards, he tells you all about them, who is related to who and how old they all are), and he told me they were all pictures of his wife and her sisters and their children. He's showed them to me a lot, several times, so I've even got to recognise some of the people; I remember their names and ask him how they all are, which he likes. But now one of the women who serves there in the café told me that he shows her the pictures too, he showed them to her one day when I was not here, and he told her that they were pictures of his sisters, not of his wife and her sisters at all. The woman in the café thought she knew some of the people in the pictures too, but he told her they had different names to the ones that he told me. And so now I think that he is making the whole thing up, that he has some sort of fantasy or problem and actually they aren't even pictures of anyone that he knows. And I don't know what I will talk to him about next time he sits next to me at lunch, because he gets his pictures out without even asking and just starts telling you about them. I think that perhaps the next time he does it he'll tell me they are pictures of his cousins in America or somebody. To pretend like that I think is awful. To pretend that you are related to someone or that somebody loves you or that you are the person they love the most. The worst thing I think would be to pretend that you were ill, because that way you can make somebody love you, by telling them that you are ill. You can make sure that they are going to look after you. I read a book on makeup and special effects and I think with all the notes that I made it would be quite easy to do. I could make myself look like I had the bruise-marks on my legs. One night

when he got home at 6.30 I could show them to David
and then tell him that I was really ill and that he had to
take me to the hospital.

I had a dream where I did that. I told David that I
was ill, I took my clothes off to show him, and he
turned straight round (we were sitting in the café) and
he said to me, you know I'm not who I told you I was.
My name isn't even David. Go and look in my passport if
you want to. Nothing I've ever told you about myself
is true, not even my birthday. And then he got his
passport out of his pocket, out of the right-hand pocket
of a brown jacket (which is what the man in the café
wears), and he began tearing out the pages and laying
them in a row on the tablecloth (the same kind of
tablecloth that they have in the café), and I could see
that there was a picture of David on every page, which
I know is wrong, but it was one of those small colour
photographs you have to get for your passport and get
someone else to sign saying that it is really you, and
across every one of the pictures David had put his
signature, except that the thing was that in the dream
every signature was a different name, though I don't
remember them now. And when I woke up from the
dream, he was still holding me. Often I wake up and
he is holding me like that in the morning. And that's
what matters. The times when he's holding me, that's
what matters, that's what I'm sure about, that's what
makes things better for me since I met my David and
that's what I want to write down and to tell people
about and I wish they knew. It's four o'clock now.

I think I don't know why he loves me. If I wrote down
the list of all the reasons why I am with him, then
there would be six reasons; but if David wrote down
his list of reasons then I don't know what he would

put on it. I think it is meant to be like that though. If you knew why your lover loved you, then you could make them do it deliberately, I mean make them love you. Whatever it was that you knew they loved about you, then you could do it more, giving them money or sleeping together or keeping the flat clean for them or whatever it was.

When I look in the living-room mirror and I see us together in private then I can see that he does love me even if I can't see why, that's all I can say really.

This week I am in the POLITICS, SOCIETY AND RELIGION section and the book that I am working on (that is what I call it, I say to David in the evening, I have been working at the library today, because I think what I do during the day is work too. It is important, it has taken me a long time to get to how I am now and I do not want to go back to how it was before), the book that I am working on at the moment is the third book on the SOCIETY shelf and it is all about disguises and dressing up, it is called *Seeing is Believing*. Pierre Carlet de Chamblain de Marivaux was a French writer, he died in 1763. He wrote thirty-five plays and five novels, and all of the thirty-five plays and all of the novels are about love (this is from the sixth chapter of the book, which is called 'Lying in Public'). And almost all of them are about dressing up as someone else, which is why he's included in this book. I have been working on this book for two days now.

When he (Pierre Carlet de Chamblain de Marivaux), was a young man he fell in love very badly, or that is what he thought anyway, because I think that when you are that young you don't really know what love means yet. In all the time before I met David I don't think I really knew what it meant although somebody was always talking about it, people were talking about it all the time. Pierre Carlet de Chamblain de Marivaux lived in Paris, and the person that he thought he was in love with was a young woman who lived out in the country. It doesn't say so in the book but I think they must both have been about eighteen or nineteen at the time. He used to go and visit her every weekend, and in the book it says that he was in love with her because she was different to the Paris women that he had spent most of his time with before, he thought she was very different. 'Sweet and charming,' it says in the book. I know that before (before I met David), the men that I used to meet often made me feel that I was like that for them, that I was some sort of country boy. Somebody they could meet just now and then. Now I think that they thought I was stupid. I have red hair and I am shy sometimes but that does not mean I am stupid.

One afternoon (it was a Sunday afternoon, it says in the book), Pierre Carlet de Chamblain de Marivaux was teaching this woman to play the piano or harpsichord, and they were very happy, although they knew that at the end of the afternoon he was going to have to go back to Paris and then they wouldn't be able to see each other for another six days. When it was time for him to go she stood in the doorway of her house and waved him goodbye. And then (this scene is all described in the book, because he wrote it down in his diaries afterwards, that is how we know exactly what happened in this story), after she had waved to him she put her fingers up to her mouth as if she was going to blow him a kiss. David did that to me once, when I was seeing him off to work. Nobody saw. But then instead of kissing her fingers and blowing him a kiss she put them into her mouth. They were already sleeping together I expect, as they had been seeing each other for over a year, and this was her way of saying to him I remember, I remember what I did to you last night, I'll be thinking about it every night for six nights until I see you again. I know David and I are like that when he has to go away with his work and we aren't going to see each other for a week. He phones me every night but it is not the same. I miss him, and I think about him every night and about all the things we do together. Sometimes I stand in front of the living-room mirror to help me remember. I stand there and tell myself that this is one of the reasons why we are together, I remember how he tells me that us sleeping together is better for him than it has ever been with anybody else. I remember how we look like two white statues. So I can see why she put her fingers in her mouth like that instead of just waving goodbye. It's really important, sleeping together. It is what you think about most of the time.

It says in the book that he laughed, and that he was shocked too, because she was a girl living in the country and he did not expect her to do that. He laughed and she smiled and he thought about the next time they would be together and then he walked away and she went back into her house. And then he remembered that he had left his gloves behind.

This is the important part of the story.

He went back to get his gloves, and when he got back to the house he saw that she had left her front door open. He went in quietly. I expect he was glad that he was going to get to look at her one last time, he thought he would surprise her, and I think this was a mistake. I know it is lovely to look at someone when he doesn't know that you're there, I love it when I wake up in the night and he doesn't and I can lie there and look at him and look at him, but I think it's dangerous too. I always let David know what time I am coming home. If he has a day off or if he's going to be home before me I always tell him that I will be home at 4.30, always.

The book says that when Pierre Carlet de Chamblain de Marivaux opened the front door ('very slowly and quietly,' it says that he did it), the woman was standing in the hallway, which is where he had left his gloves, on the hall table. Over the hall table was a small mirror, and she was looking at herself in the mirror. And she couldn't see him. She was looking at herself, and he was looking at her, and he smiled because she was looking so lovely, and then she put her fingers to her mouth just like she had when he had waved goodbye, and just like when he had waved goodbye she didn't blow him a kiss but slid her fingers into her mouth. And then she did it again. And then she did it again. And each time she did it a bit more, putting the fingers a bit further in, and doing it slower. And each time she pulled her fingers out she smiled to herself in the mirror.

That is how I imagine it anyway. The point is, he saw her practising. And before that he'd thought that she'd done it especially for him, that she'd never done that for anybody before, that she'd done it just for him and on the spur of the moment and when nobody else was looking. Anyway this next bit is exactly how it happened, I am not imagining this bit, because I am copying this next bit out of the book exactly because I am going to show it to David. 'The young Parisian felt his love deserting him as the blood drained from his face; suddenly he felt chilled, even though it was a warm Sunday morning in May. He coughed politely to announce his presence, and as his surprised lover turned to face him he said, turning a phrase whose elegance and feeling quality he was never to match in any of his thirty-five plays and five novels, "Mademoiselle, you have shown me how the machinery of your profession works. The spectacle will fascinate me always, but it will in future move me less."' I like that bit about the drop in temperature. Because I think that is exactly what it feels like when suddenly you are not sure any more. And I like the bit about the machinery because I think that is exactly what you are afraid of really. Everyone is scared that that's what people are really like, especially when you love somebody. Because how are you supposed to prove it, that is what I have been thinking about while I have been reading this disguises book, and that is what I really wanted to write down.

When we are out together, I know that he loves me, but when other people see us, I wonder if they know. Because if somebody loves somebody you ought to be able to tell just by looking at them, but you can't. I think it never occurs to most people that we are living together, I think when they see us they just suppose that we are doing our shopping together for some other reason. I think even the people who live next door, the way that woman looks at me when I see her on the stairs, and the ways she asks me how is your friend, she thinks that we are just that, friends, that we are two men sharing the flat to save money or something, which is ridiculous. And once when we were in the supermarket somebody said to David, excuse me, is he with you, and it sounded as if he thought I was David's child or that he was a nurse looking after me or something. I know you might not think we are together when you see us, because the way we dress is very different to each other. David is very smart, and of course he is older than me, but when people do think we're together I wonder if they think we are boyfriends or just friends or what. And I wonder if they have any idea of how long we have been together, because I know people are often very disapproving if they think you have just met; I mean if they think you are two men who have just met to have sex together, but they are less disapproving if they think you are a proper couple. Sometimes I want to go up to them and say did you know that I have been with my David for almost three years now, three years in May, almost three years he has been with me.

And sometimes when they look at us I want to do something awful like start shouting in a restaurant, just to prove it. I want to shout at them and tell them all the things he says to me when we are in front of the mirror together. He says them very quietly in a voice which isn't like his daytime voice at all; and when people look at us funny and I can see they're talking about us I want to say all those things that he says to me, really loud, to shout them. Shout in the street like I used to, before.

When we are out we never hold hands, which is odd, I think, considering how we are at home.

I have very big shoulders which David likes a lot, very big and very white. He likes me to wear just a vest when we are at home so that he can see them. And when we are in bed he often bites me across there. I bruise very easily because of my red hair, people with red hair like mine have very white skin, and you can often see it in the mirror for days afterwards. Once he said, it looks like roses. He put his hand on my back, afterwards, and said look at that, a whole bunch of roses, a whole bunch of roses blooming on your back.

Well, one time when we are out at the weekend I would like to take off my shirt so that people can see them, the roses. Then when people looked at us they would have to say to each other oh I suppose they must be lovers. I mean how else could he have got those terrible bruises right across his back? That would prove it. That would be one way of proving it. Or if he bought me a ring and I wore it, that would prove it. A gold ring. But if I wore it when I was out on my own, if I was wearing it now for instance, if it was on my finger two along from the pen, then people would see it and they would just think I was married, they wouldn't think I was with David at all. So I think that what I need is a ring which will make people stop me and ask me what it means exactly, where did I get it and who gave it to me. So that the man in the café would ask me about my ring instead of showing me his photographs. David says that thinking is often about things, that you can make some feelings you have make sense with things better than you can with words. For instance, the picture which we have in our living-room, which is a picture of two men holding hands, and it isn't a picture of us, it's a picture of a statue of two men in Naples who killed somebody, but David says that it's still a picture of how we are really. So today I have finished the disguises book and I am looking up this idea of a ring in a book on English Jewellery. It tells you what all the different stones mean so that, for instance, if someone is wearing a diamond it means 'forever'. The best thing in the book, and the part which has been helping me to think most, is the chapter about rings. They used to have something called 'regard' rings, which I have never heard of before, and I have never seen any man wearing one. The book says that a regard ring was what you gave someone before you gave them an engagement ring. The stones are ruby, emerald, garnet, amethyst, ruby and diamond; it looks very pretty with all the different colours all in a row, and it spells out 'regard', which is how they got the name. 'Regard' is French for 'I am looking at you', but in English the ring means 'I have regard for you'. That is what I know David feels about me. When he is at work and I am here in the library that is how he feels about me. He is thinking about me even when he can't see me. Because of the way that it spells the word out I have decided that this is exactly the kind of ring that I need. I have chosen all the stones for it from the book, they are all red and white ones because those are my best colours, they go with my skin and my hair. Once, when we were falling asleep, he said he wouldn't love me if I didn't have my red hair. The ring I need will be all gold. The first stone will be what they call a Bohemian garnet, but the book says that its real name is a pyrope. The next one will be a ruby. The next two stones will be fire opals, which are a kind of solid fiery gold colour, and then the last stone will be a moonstone, which is a kind of feldspar, and it has no colour at all. The pyrope is my birthstone, August the 23rd. A ruby means devotion in marriage (because of the bit in the Bible where it says 'more precious than rubies'), and the opals mean desire, wanting something all the time, and the feldspar means honesty, because you can see right through it. And when you put them all together the stones spell it out, Pyrope, Ruby, Opal, Opal, Feldspar, you put them all together and the ring spells PROOF. I'll have to go to a real old-fashioned jewellers to get it done, one where they have all the stones laid out on trays for you to look at. And I'll ask to see the ones that I want, and they'll bring them out of the back of the shop all lying on their trays lined in black velvet, jeweller's velvet they call it, it's as black as a night when there's a power cut and no street-lamps anywhere. I'll pick the five stones out of their trays and tell them how I want it all done, and then when they phone me and tell me that it's ready I'll take David to the shop at the weekend and he'll buy it for me. I'll wear it all the time. When the weather is hot my finger will swell and I won't be able to get it off even if I want to. And when the man in the café or the woman on the stairs asks what my ring means, I'll be ready with my answer, because I will have got all the information about it from the library. It's the only ring like this that there is, I'll say. I got all the information about it from the library, and I got them to make it to order for me, I'll say, but it was my idea. And my David paid for it, I'll say, it's a gift, it's a present from my lover. It spells proof, I'll say. It's the proof of love, I'll say. And I will raise my right hand. I will raise my right hand just like you are supposed to do in a court of law, and when I am asked to give the particulars, when they ask me to give my evidence, when I am asked to bear witness, I will raise my right hand, and I will be wearing my ring with the five stones in it, and I will swear. So help me God.

◆

Other Men's Sweetness

PATRICK GALE

◆

*'Thou shalt not covet thy neighbour's
house, thou shalt not covet thy
neighbour's wife, nor his manservant,
nor his maidservant, nor his ox, nor his
ass, nor any thing that is thy
neighbour's.'*

◆

*S*arah-Jane? Sarah-Jane? Wake up. We're nearly there!'

Jane opened her small, green eyes, yawned and focused on her mother from the back of the overloaded car. From as early as she could remember, she had loathed the name Sarah and the hyphen that accompanied it. People who really loved her, like her dolls and the sweetshop lady, called her Jane. Her mother smiled and turned back to face the road. Jane shifted and winced crossly. The rear of the car was hot and stuffy and she had outgrown her safety seat.

'I'm too big for it now,' she had complained as her father strapped her in.

'Nonsense,' he said. 'It's meant for ages three to five. You can have a new one on your birthday.'

She looked down at Jones, the only doll she had been allowed to bring. ('Quickly, Sarah-Jane! Choose one quickly! We don't have all day.') Jones's eyes clicked open to reveal a baby-blue stare. Jane tugged Jones's red nylon hair and felt a little more cheerful. Then she looked out of the window. They were in the flattest place she had ever seen. On either side of the slightly raised road, fields flat as carpets stretched out as far as the eye could see. Here and there was a line of sickly trees or a sinister stream straight as a ruler. The road was straight too and seemed to stretch as far as the horizon.

'Where are we?' she asked.

'Cambridgeshire,' her father said.

'We're about to cross the border into Norfolk,' her mother added.

'Where?'

'Any... minute... *now*! Here! Now we're in Norfolk.'

They passed a sign. The road looked just the same, as did the countryside. Flat. Flat. Flat.

'Where's Norfolk?'

'East Anglia. On the east coast.'

'And why did we have to get a cottage *here*?'

'Your mum liked the idea.'

'And your dad found the perfect place.'

'And we got it at a bargain price,' her father went on. 'Can't think why no one else has discovered this bit. I mean, it was a bit grim having to drive out through the East End, but I suppose, if one kept clear of the rush hours and so forth, it wouldn't be too bad...'

Her parents lapsed into one of their usual, incredibly tedious conversations, cobwebbed with adult impenetrables like Hangar Lane Gyratory System and Miles Per Gallon and Post-War Architecture. They weren't nearly there. Her mother had lied again. Sometimes she seemed to resent Jane's falling asleep in the car and wake her for the hell of it. Jane fell to pulling Jones's hair again then tried to push out one of the doll's eyes with its own, miniature thumb.

She had twenty-nine other dolls at home and a hammock and an exercise bicycle and her own fridge for cold drinks and her own colour television and a childsize portable video camera and her own stereo system with compact disc player and remote control facility. She had her own bathroom, with a bidet and an extensive menagerie of clockwork bathroom toys and a whole wall of fitted cupboards to house the dress collection she planned to amass over the years to come. She had piano lessons and ballet classes and went to the cinema often and had only been refused a pet because her mother said she was too young to look after one. They had a lovely house in Islington, with two garages and a gym and both her parents seemed happy with their jobs. Why then had they seen fit to buy — another adult impenetrable — a Little Place in the Country.

'Sarah-Jane? Sarah-Jane? Look! We're here! There it is!' Jane looked up from her ponderings. They were pulling up on the outskirts of a village. There was a farmhouse in a cluster of outbuildings overgrown with creepers and long grass. To their left crouched a small, red brick building not unlike a rather cheap doll's house, set near the road in a patch of windswept garden.

'Oh,' said Jane.

'Well you could show a little more enthusiasm,' her mother snapped.

'Don't bully her,' her father said. 'She'll like it when she looks around. Come on. We can unpack later.'

He unstrapped Jane's harness and lifted her down to the grass verge. She followed as he walked arm in arm with her mother up the garden path. A dead rat glistened with flies under a rose bush but Jane said nothing. She would save it to come back to later.

The house was quite nice inside. It smelled of wet paint rather and there was only one bathroom, but her bedroom under the eaves was so tiny and had such a small window that it reminded her of the 'houses' she liked to build under her mother's dressing table or inside the airing cupboard. She began to understand her parents' enthusiasm. It was all a game.

'Do you like it, then?' her father asked her.

Jane bounced on her bed to make it squeak.

'When are we having lunch?' she asked.

'She likes it,' her mother said. 'Thank Christ for

that.' And Jane had to watch while her parents kissed exaggeratedly like a couple in a cartoon.

They were busy with suitcases and spice-racks after lunch and Jane found herself repeatedly in their way. Responding at last to their impatient suggestions, she slipped out to play by herself in the garden. At the back of the house was a cluster of tired fruit trees. An old tyre hung from one and she amused herself for a while by swinging on it until she felt dizzy. She tried an apple or two but they were hard and their sour juice made her tongue curl. Then she found a congregation of slugs oozing in the rhubarb patch and had fun squashing it with a stone. She needed to pee suddenly and felt pangs of hunger (lunch had been olives and salad) so she started back towards the house. Her parents were shouting at each other however, and she was frightened to go in. Instead, she relieved herself in some bushes below one of the windows. Crouching on the dry earth she gradually became aware of a delicious smell; warm, sweet, spicy. It was coming from the shabby farmhouse next door. She followed it across the garden as far as a broken part of the fence and stopped there to sniff again. The smell curled around in her head and made her stomach gurgle. The gap in the fence was not wide and she had to squeeze and shove to force her belly through.

Once she was on the other side it seemed impossible to go back the way she had come. So she went on. She was enchanted to find a small zoo at large in the yard. A cat was dozing on a bale of hay. Another was draped across a sack of fertiliser, swishing its tabby tail. An old sheepdog rose from his place by the back door to sniff and lick her face. There were ducks on a greenish pond and hens scratching in the earth. A donkey brayed and wheezed in a paddock where a huge black horse watched her from the shadow of a tree. A goat, safely tethered, paused in its munching to fix her with reptile eyes and she counted three cows grazing in the field beyond the paddock. She stopped to pat the dog and pet the cats, then she followed the delicious scent — which was making her quite ravenous now — to the open back door.

A batch of sugary Chelsea buns and two seed-dusted loaves were steaming on a wire rack below the window. Further into the room, in the shadows, a woman and a man were seated, one behind the other. She was gently combing out his black hair, which was nearly as long as hers. They were both beautiful. Not like her mother and father, who were beautiful and handsome respectively of course, but beautiful in a new, unsettling way. They didn't look altogether clean and the woman wore no make-up, but they had a kind of glow. It brought Jane to a sudden, hurtful realisation that her parents might not be the most attractive people she would ever meet. The man had been working on the farm. He had no shirt on and there were streaks of mud among the black hairs which formed whorls on his chest where her father's was pink and smooth. His eyes were shut with pleasure but the woman saw Jane and smiled without stopping her combing.

'Hello,' she said, in a faintly mocking, low voice. 'Who are you?' The man opened his eyes briefly but didn't move.

'I'm Jane,' said Jane. 'We live next door now. Can I take a bun?'

'Sure,' the woman said and, as Jane carefully picked the bun nearest her and sank her teeth into its sticky crust, she twisted the man's hair into a glossy braid and kissed the nape of his neck. The dough was still warm and one or two currants tumbled from its torn surface to the floor, where the sheepdog licked them up and sat, with a barely discernible whine, to wait for more. The man opened his eyes again then pushed back his chair and stood. He winked at Jane and walked out across the yard to the barn, where he started using a noisy machine.

'Like your bun?' asked the woman, grinning now.

Jane nodded vigorously. She would have liked another but knew this was best left for a sort of going-home present.

'I'm Jeanette,' the woman said. 'And that was Dougal. Do your parents know you're here?'

'No,' Jane told her. 'They're busy.'

'Well,' Jeanette winced. 'So am I, in a way. But you can watch if you like.'

'Yes please.'

'Come and sit on a chair then instead of standing there like a pudding.'

Jane came forward and clambered on to a kitchen chair. The woman, Jeanette, in whose honour she had already resolved to rechristen one of her better-favoured dolls, had switched on a light in a corner of the big, low-ceilinged room, and was turning her attention to a chest of drawers. It was painted dusky blue all over and someone had started to decorate it further with little clumps of painted leaves.

'Are you a farmer's wife?' Jane asked.

Jeanette chuckled.

'No. The animals are just pets and the field and paddock are all the land we've got really. This is how we make our living. Well. Our sort-of-living. We buy old bits of bashed up wooden furniture at auctions. Dougal mends them and does the base coat and I paint on the twiddly pretty bits.' She shook her yard of blonde hair away from her face and tied it impatiently in a handkerchief. Then she reached for a saucer of paint and a brush.

'What are you doing now?' Jane breathed.

'Pull that chair closer and I'll show you.'

Jane moved closer and watched Jeanette paint leaves and buds and tendrils. She had a smell that was almost as good as the buns − Jane's mother never wore scent and stopped Jane's father wearing it either because it made her sneeze. There were other good smells in the room besides Jeanette and the buns. Bunches of scented leaves were hanging from the beams to dry and there was a fragrant mound of orange peel and a pot of cooling coffee on the table. Jane watched, fascinated, as Jeanette's long, dirty fingers made deft twists this way and that with the brush. Dougal stopped using the machine and began to make gentle taps with a hammer. He sang to himself as he worked. Jane pulled her feet up on to the chair beside her. The good smells, the bun and the pleasing sense of doing nothing while adults laboured, conspired to bring a delicious drowsiness over her. For a few lucid seconds before she nodded off, she wondered why her life was not always like this, why this sense of well-fed content was so unfamiliar.

When she awoke, the cupboard was all painted and her parents were in the room making clucking, apologetic noises to Jeanette.

'She's been no trouble, honestly,' Jeanette was saying.

'We had no idea. I'm so *sorry*!' Jane's mother exclaimed.

'No bother at all,' Dougal added. He winked again as her father swung her up against his shoulder and followed her mother outside. He winked privately, so that on one else noticed.

'Come again,' Jeanette murmured, with her discreet

smile. 'Pop round.'

Her parents rarely came again however. In the week-ends that followed, they were preoccupied with adult impenetrables — Hand-Blocked Paper, a Damp Course, the demise of a Feature Fireplace and some lengthy and bad-tempered dealings with someone called Artex Removal. But Jane came. She could barely wait for each weekend to begin in order to squeeze through the gap in the fence and visit her new friends. Dougal let her stir paint and showed her how to milk the cows and goat. Jeanette taught her to plait her own hair (which seemed to make her mother cross). She gave her handfuls of bread dough to knead into shapes and bake and she used to stretch a sheet of yellowed lining paper across the kitchen table for Jane to paint on while she worked at her grown-up painting alongside her.

Jane's parents were perturbed at first, in case Jane was proving an embarrassment, then they seemed to accept the idea that Jane had adopted a second family. They chuckled, in her hearing, about the Hippies and pounced on any small infelicities that crept from their neighbours' speech into their daughter's. (Jane, un-comprehending, told Jeanette that her mother said that Jeanette had 'a terrible Norfolk burr' and Jeanette laughed and fed her some cooking chocolate.) That Jeanette could be handy as a child-minder was swiftly appreciated. Jane's mother was often unable to come to the cottage for more than two weekends in a row. On these occasions, Jane's father would bring work with him and closet himself with the portable computer in the dining-room while Jane went to play with the animals she now thought of as hers. It was not unheard of for Jeanette to invite him to come over with Jane for long, boozy meals in the farmhouse but Jane preferred it when he stayed on his side of the fence. She was not above keeping a proffered invitation secret and passing back some fabricated apology so as to keep her friends to herself.

When her nursery school began its holidays she was even left behind one weekend to spend seven glorious days as Jeanette and Dougal's guest. She fitted quite easily into their routines, rising and retiring when she felt like it, washing as little as they did and eating whatever pleasantly meatless meals Jeanette placed before her. Two things set the seal on the week's pleasure for her: lying awake listening to the loud sighs and open laughter that came from their bedroom – a far cry from the embarrassed coughs and inexplicable creakings that came from her parents' well-appointed own – and being woken by Dougal at the dead of night to watch one of the cats giving birth.

Her parents joined her for a fortnight's holiday after that and brought with them bad weather, bitterness and alteration. While Jane sheltered, bored, from the rain, they argued. Jeanette's name was raised as was that of a young Frenchman who lived with their neighbours in London. Adult impenetrables to do with Planning Permission, Fraud, Silk Purses and Sow's Ears, crackled on the air over Jane's head and when she tried to slope off to Jeanette and Dougal, as had become her habit, she was faced with an inexplicable edict.

'You are *not* to go round there any more, Sarah-Jane,' her father commanded. 'You are *not* to see them. Do you understand?'

Stunned, Jane retreated both to her room and to the temporarily abandoned solace of her dolls and their unstinting fidelity. She sat them in elegant half-circles around her on her bedroom floor, trying not to listen too closely to the angry phrases that followed her up the stairs.

'I've a good mind to go round there and have it out with him.'

'*Him*? You think *he*'s behind it? Oh no. It was her. Her name was on that form. It was her application for planning permission that had so carefully been allowed to lapse until we'd had the searches done. She's the one that took you for a ride. Simple, unworldly hippies my arse. She saw you coming a mile off and if you hadn't been blinded by lust...'

'Well if we're talking about lust, I hardly think last week's sordid revelation leaves you in *any* position to —'

Jane quietly shut the door to keep out the sounds of their anger and climbed on the bed with a pad of paper and some crayons. She drew the perfect house where she and the more attractive of her dolls would live. They had a gym and a swimming pool and a bathroom apiece and there were dogs and kittens and a cow and a donkey and a place for Jeanette and Dougal to make her buns. Her parents, perhaps, might live next door. In a slightly smaller house, because their needs were simpler and their natures undeserving.

Her mother came upstairs after a while, her hair newly tidy and lips newly red, to announce that the three of them were going to drive to the seaside for tea. For the rest of the week an unnatural parade of normality was mounted. Where they would formerly have amused themselves, they now did everything as a closely-bound trio or, rather, as a pair with Jane a necessary buffer zone. They had picnics and a boat trip. They made apple chutney and visited historic buildings where Jane was rewarded for her boredom with cake or ice cream. There were no more arguments apart from quickly stifled bickering about road directions and timetables. Jane saw nothing of Jeanette and Dougal — there was no time and the ceaseless activities left her whimpering only for sleep.

On the penultimate evening of the holiday, Jane's mother delivered a startling piece of news. Jane's father had returned in high excitement from taking a phone call and a bottle of champagne had been opened. Jane could smell it on her mother's breath as she bathed her.

'Sarah-Jane, you do realise, don't you, that we're going back to London tomorrow and we won't be coming back here?'

'No.'

'Well we won't, you see. We've just managed to sell the cottage.'

'But why?'

'We had to. It turns out the naughty woman who sold it to your dad kept lots of bad things secret.'

'What bad things?'

'Oh. Well. That there are going to be a lot of horrid new houses on all the land around here. Things like that.'

'Oh.'

'So it was very important to sell quickly and get a good price before anyone else found out. Daddy's found a buyer today and we've accepted the offer. It's a shame but there it is. Now. Let's wash your hair so it's as shiny as a little doll's. You *are* getting plump, darling! We'll have to put you back on salads for a while. Whatever can that Jeanette have been feeding you?'

Jane started to ask why her father had kept bad things secret too but her mother had turned the shower on and Jane's eyes and mouth threatened to fill with water. She cried while her hair was washed and grizzled as her mother rubbed her dry. But she quietened down when allowed a dusting of Chanel talcum powder and by the time she was tucked up in bed in her tiny room for the last time, she was utterly calm. She had forged a plan.

'Do you want me to read you a story?' asked her mother, who had unthinkingly ascribed her tears to a surfeit of tiring pleasures during the day.

'No,' Jane told her and enjoyed her mother's moue of disappointment at the small rejection. Left along with the eerie reflection of her nightlight in her dolls' eyes, Jane dwelt on her simple plan. She had tried for a while to share herself with two households. Now thoughtless decisions from adults left her no option but to choose. She had already transferred her loyalties from the household and parents she was born with, to those she coveted. Now she had merely to follow through with a bodily transfer. She would swop families. Like any nicely brought-up girl faced with a plate of cakes, she would reach for the sweetness that lay closest to her.

In such familiar territory the defection was easily performed. As Jane had suspected, the next day was taken up with frantic preparations for removal men. Many boxes of books had remained packed all summer for want of shelves but there were china and glass to wrap and linen to sort and pictures to protect. When she slipped out of the house after a perfunctory late lunch and squeezed through the gap in the fence, she was not missed therefore. She hid at the side of the barn and watched until she was certain that both Jeanette and Dougal were in the house, then she darted around the corner and through the barn door. Jules, the dog, stood and wagged his tail to see her but he was still tethered by the back door to keep him from bothering the kittens so he could not give away her whereabouts.

On one side of the barn bales of fresh straw were stacked up high over Jane's head. She had played for hours on these, drunk with their heady smell, until Dougal frightened her off with a warning that children could easily slip out of reach, deep between the bales, and die for lack of air. Against the other walls clustered a collection of wooden wardrobes, chests of drawers, looking-glasses and trunks in various stages of restoration and dismemberment. Jane walked over to a dusty looking-glass to stare at her reflection nose to nose. Then she heard Dougal talking as he left the house. She knew he would be happy to learn she was adopting him, but sensed that it was wisest not to confront him until her former parents had safely given her up for lost. She glanced around and chose a huge wardrobe to the back of the barn. She slithered over the chest of drawers in front, tugged open the door and slid inside. She scrabbled the door almost shut again with her fingernails, put an eye to the crack and waited. Suddenly her mother's voice rang out, crystal clear, from the garden.

'Sarah-Jane? Sarah-Jane?' There was a muttered curse and she called back to the cottage, 'She's nowhere in sight, Brian. Are you sure she wasn't upstairs?... Well look again, could you?'

Dougal appeared, walking towards the barn entrance with a painted bathroom cabinet under one arm.

'Oh, er, Dougal?' her mother called out. He stopped, then walked out of view, towards the fence.

'Hello?'

'You, er, you haven't seen Sarah-Jane, have you?'

'Jane? Have you lost her?'

'Well. Not exactly. I just wondered if she'd come over.'

'Sorry.'

'Send her back if you see her, would you? We're meant to be leaving soon.'

'No problem.'

'Thanks.'

Dougal came on into the barn, set down the cabinet and gathered up some electric cable which he tidied lazily into loops over his arm. As he left again, Jane suppressed an urge to jump out shouting boo as she had done several times before. She leaned against the back of the wardrobe and listened to her mother's fretful, now slightly irritated cries.

'Sarah-Jane? Sarah-Jane? Where *are* you?'

Jane smiled to herself. She would miss her dolls and her party frocks but at least, after today, she would never again be called Sarah or given a hyphen. Her mother's cries stopped and for a while there was silence except for the clucking of two hens which had appeared to scratch at the earth and woodshavings in the doorway. Jane's stomach gurgled and she rubbed it reassuringly. Then she heard her mother's voice again and her father's, followed by a knock at the back door of the farmhouse. Jeanette answered. Jane couldn't make out the words but she heard the one woman's anxiety being passed on to the other and soon her parents and Jeanette were walking towards the barn. Her mother's face looked tight and cold, despite the warm remains of the day. Her father strode on ahead.

As he walked in he seemed momentarily subdued by the barn's looming shadows.

'Sarah-Jane?' he asked quietly. 'Sarah-Jane?'

Jane bit her lip and stared out at him, her fingertips holding the door in place before her. Her mother appeared in the doorway with Jeanette.

'Sarah-Jane?' she called out. 'Don't be silly, darling. Game's over now.'

She came forward and opened a large chest then let the lid shut with a bang. Suddenly both Jane's parents were galvanised into action. They hurried here and there, in and out of Jane's narrow range of vision, tugging open drawers and wardrobes and shifting things to peer into the shadows. Jeanette stood, hands on hips, and watched them.

'The hay!' Jane's mother shouted. 'She might have slipped down inside the hay!'

The air filled with straw dust as, grunting, she and Jane's father set about tugging down bales.

'She isn't here,' Jeanette said softly. Jane's father came into view again. He started clambering over the chest of drawers to reach the wardrobe where she was hiding. Jane slid into the farthest corner and held her breath as he stretched out a hand towards the doorknob. Then Jeanette shouted, causing him to turn round. 'Look, I said she isn't here! Now would you both please get out?'

'Now listen,' Jane's mother began then seemed to run out of words. Jane heard her panting.

'Come on, Christine. She isn't here.' Jeanette said, reaching out an arm. Jane's mother gave a little whimper and ran forward in tears. Jeanette led her gently out into the fading light. Jane's father lingered a moment. He had picked up a small, carved box and turned it over in his hands, evidently admiring it. He glanced around, saw no one was looking and, to Jane's astonishment, slipped it into the deep poacher's pocket of his waxed jacket. Aimlessly he then opened a few more doors and slammed them shut again. Dougal walked across the yard.

'Come on, Brian,' he called. 'It's no use. We've called the police for you.'

In a sudden burst of anger, Jane's father turned and shoved hard on the chest of drawers in front of her hiding place. It slid back with a complaint of old wood and banged hard into the wardrobe, slamming the door firmly shut in his daughter's face.

Jane waited a moment, rubbing her forehead where the wood had struck it and wondering whether to cry, then she pushed and found the door stuck fast. She couldn't shout out to Dougal yet. Not with her father still there. She looked frantically about her in the increasingly musty space and saw light coming through a tiny crack by the hinges. She shifted her position as quietly as she could and thrust an eye to the space. Squinting, she just made out her father's silhouette as he walked into the yard. Dougal was still there, looking around at the furniture. She would wait just long enough for her parents to get clear then she would call. Or perhaps she would wait until after the police had been? Perhaps she should call out now? She wanted to pee and she was getting hungry, but if the police caught her they might punish her. She might be punished anyway.

She hesitated a moment too long. Dougal turned on his heel, strode out into the yard and swung the barn doors shut with a terrific bang then shot the bolts on the outside. Cars and voices came and went in the hour that followed but through two great thicknesses of wood they might have been two fields away. Jane shouted herself hoarse, then slumped, exhausted and tearful, to the cramped wardrobe floor. She had no coat on and the evening was turning cold. A hen emerged from its roosting place in the straw. Losing consciousness, Jane heard its clucking as it scratched for beetles.

*

As Brian drove out through Hackney and Stratford, his mood gradually lightened. He had been angry at Chrissie's refusal to join him on the house-hunting trip since it had been her idea in the first place and he had taken a day off valuable work to make it. Her refusal had been of the kind that, left unheeded, would have poisoned the entire day however, and there was nothing he disliked more than driving anywhere with her being monosyllabic and hurt in the passenger seat. It might have been fun to have brought Sarah-Jane along at least – they so rarely spent time alone together – but she was coming increasingly to mimic her mother's every gesture and mood and would only have been monosyllabic and hurt and squeaky.

A trio of Bengali women passed chattering over a zebra crossing before him, the sun catching on flecks of synthetic gold in their swirling, rainbow drapes and Brian reiterated his vow to spend one Sunday soon exploring rather more of the East End than the White-chapel Gallery and Blooms. Chrissie had bought him a glossy book on Hawksmoor churches but it had gone unread. He drove on towards the motorway, acceler-ating as the traffic thinned out, and his irritation evap-orated. He pressed a button and the car's roof folded away. It was the latest German convertible, with an engine so quiet one was said to be able to balance a fifty pence piece on it while driving at fifty miles an hour. Brian would have felt absurd testing this claim under his family's critical eye. It was a pleasure to have the car, as well as an excursion, to himself for once. He was on holiday. He would take his pleasure where he found it. He might try the fifty pence piece test on a quiet side road. He slipped on to the motorway and smiled to himself as the speedometer registered ninety with no discernible increase in noise level.

He stopped in Wisbech to pick up details from estate agents. He admired the prettiness of Georgian houses and enjoyed the bustle in the market square − such a far cry from the anger and desolation of shopping in London. Whenever he came to places like Wisbech or Salisbury he bemoaned the fact that he was not a GP or a solicitor or even a dentist − someone who could work equally profitably in a quiet, provincial backwater where there was less tension, less overt competition and more time for the good things in life. Chrissie tended to be sharp with him when he mentioned this.

'You'd be bored,' she would say. 'You know you would. You're a very competitive man. You always have been. You'd wither without the cut and thrust. And there wouldn't be any good schools for Sarah-Jane. And anyway, what about me?'

Chrissie had a good job too. She travelled so much for it that there was no reason why she shouldn't live in the country, provided she was within easy driving distance of an international airport. All she would need would be a telephone and a fax machine. But when he suggested this, she sighed, impatient but long-suffering.

'Brian,' she said, 'You *know* what I mean.'

'What? You mean parties and things?'

'And things. Yes.'

Brian looked at five cottages recommended by the agents. They were all fairly pretty, certainly, although the austere fenland landscape did not lend itself to a snug village atmosphere in the manner of rolling

Cotswold hillsides or burbling Hampshire water-
meadows. But Hampshire and Gloucestershire were
fast becoming part of the retirement belt boom whereas
prices in East Anglia could only go up. There was
something wrong with each of the cottages he saw
however. They were all close to the road, but that, the
agents had explained, was a fenland phenomenon dictated by the very gradual process by which the need
for land had triumphed over the usefulness of water.
They had gardens, they were in good condition, they
were clearly loved and they were within his price
range. The trouble was that too much money had been
lavished on them, some of it tastelessly so. 'Feature'
fireplaces had been installed, an owner's pride and
joy, as were neo-Victorian garage doors, obtrusively
modern fitted kitchens and driveways of pulsatingly
orange gravel. Even this would not have been a problem
usually. In London, where comfortable convenience
was of paramount importance in their hectic lives, he
and Chrissie had been grateful to buy a modern house
with every efficient luxury already installed, a house
needing only the addition of a couple, a child and
their groaning pantechnicon of possessions. Yet Brian
sensed that his needs — their needs — in a weekend
cottage would be different. They did not want convenience — for that, all his friends would agree, one
kept a single house in London and spent one's surplus
on country house hotels — they wanted distraction
and difficulty. Brian wanted a challenge. He wanted
somewhere he could make his own, a place where he
could mark out individual territory. (In his weekly
work, all-powerful market forces had him exploiting
originality in others, and scarcely fostered it in himself.)
  He fell to perusing a copy of the *Wisbech and District
Chronicle*. There, amid ragged columns of classified

advertisements for land auctions and lawnmower sales, he found what he was looking for.

'Fenland cottage in need of loving care,' he read, 'Brick-built, pantiled roof, c. 1850. 1 acre. Mature fruit trees. Suit young couple with small child and vision. £35,000 o.n.o.'

He called the owners on the car phone and drew up outside their ramshackle farmstead twenty minutes later. He had spoken to a man but it was a woman who emerged as he shut the car door. She had long, straight, blonde hair and was, he guessed, about his age and height. She wore a loose, scarlet dress of rough cotton that clung about her full and bra-less breasts and swished about her long thighs as she advanced. When she took his hand in hers and said, 'Hi. I'm Jeanette. I assume you're the intrepid house-hunter,' a twinge of lust stirred his loins. 'Sorry,' she went on, brushing her palms together, 'I've probably got flour on you. It's baking day.'

Brian smiled and assured her it was quite all right. There was a streak of flour on her forehead, running into her hair like grey.

'Normally I get Dougal to show people round,' she said, leading him across the grass at the roadside. 'He knows more about building and joists and so on than I do. But he's getting ready for an auction in Cambridge so you'll just have to make do with me.'

'Oh. Well. I'm sure you'll do very nicely,' Brian said automatically, then coughed to cover his embarrassment. She merely smiled to herself and passed on.

The cottage for sale was immediately next door, set a short garden's distance from the road, with a gnarled, flower-strewn orchard behind it. Jeanette explained that she had inherited it from her mother but could not afford to keep it on. She drew his attention to the interesting brickwork then led him around the inside. Her proximity in the tiny rooms was intoxicating. She gave off a heavy scent, composed of baking spices, yeast and another, sweeter odour he could not place. He was vaguely aware of peeling paintwork and the sour taint of damp but he found that he was concentrating on her lips more than on what she was showing him. Her eyes were grey and the kohl pressed thickly round their edges and the slight wateriness it had induced, summoned louche memories of earlier, freer days, before Sarah-Jane. Before Chrissie. She showed him a stained bath with clipped enamel then followed him into a minute bedroom under the eaves.

'Now this would do for... Do you have kids?'

'Yes,' he told her. 'One. Sarah-Jane.'

'Ah. Sweet.'

'Yes. She'd love it up here.' Brian crouched to peer out of the small, low window at the dyke that lay, a still, dark mirror, along the other side of the road. 'Do you have children?' he asked, turning back to her. 'You and...?'

'Dougal. No. We've tried, but no. Sometimes I catch myself peering into pushchairs at the supermarket and just, well, lusting. I catch myself planning how I could just reach in and take one.' She had to pass close by him to reach the landing again. She paused, looked deep into his eyes and pressed his erection frankly with her wrist and fingertips. 'Believe me,' she said, 'I'm tempted.'

Brian felt himself blush hotly. She released him and moved on just before he made a move so that he lunged at nothing. He followed downstairs, watching the swishing of her skirt and wondering how it would be if he seized a handful of her hair and bit into her lips. Was it other people's babies who tempted her or his all too visible lust? She had blurred the distinctions. His head was full of her scent and the cottage suddenly felt as though it had been designed for smaller, surer-footed creatures.

She stopped in the hall and swung her hair behind her shoulders as she waited for him to come down.

'Well?' she asked. 'What do you think?'

Her Norfolk accent would have been comical had it not been so intensely erotic.

'I like it,' he stammered, 'I like it very much. I think it's a good idea.'

'Are you making an offer then?'

'I'll give you twenty-eight for it.'

'Thirty-two.'

'Thirty.'

'Done.' She held out her hand. As he shook it, a sly corner of his brain, unimpeded by lust, told him he had done her out of a bargain. 'I'll put you in touch with my solicitors,' she said. Then, rather than let go, she lifted his hand and rubbed its palm across her breasts then down to where, he could tell at a touch, she was knickerless.

'Oh God,' he groaned.

'Yes?' she teased, smiling.

'Your husband...'

'Dougal's off to Cambridge,' she sighed. 'Don't mind Dougal.'

The red dress came off over her head in one liquid movement. He forgot, in his haste, to take his shoes off first, so he was caught with his jeans locked around his ankles and had difficulty keeping his balance. Surprisingly strong, she lowered him to the foot of the stairs and sat astride him but he became fearful of splinters and they tried leaning in the doorway then moved to the kitchen table.

'Yes,' she cried. 'Yes! Yes!' and she struck him hard on the buttocks with her bootheels.

At that moment, Brian looked up to see an extremely handsome, pigtailed man swing over the farmstead fence and stride through the orchard towards the cottage. Seeing what they were at, the man stopped, raised a hand and threw them a dazzling smile.

'Er,' said Brian.

'Don't stop,' Jeanette ordered.

'Your husband.'

'Yes.'

'Oh God.'

'Yes!'

Letting her head hang back off the table's end, she returned her husband's smile and, laughing, scaled a peak of pleasure on her own as Brian withered inside her.

*

'Why don't *we* get a little place in the country?'

Chrissie, who had shortened her name when she first perceived it to be a feminisation of Jesus's, had always been driven by things. As a child, she learnt to charm toys from hateful relatives. She had worked hard at school because she liked prizes. Love of things dictated her career, on the sales team of a firm of clothing chain stores. It dictated her choice of husband; Brian earned far more at his record company than her other candidates did in the City. He was also more generous. He would buy her more things. The danger of materialism, as her credit card statements reminded her with a cruel regularity, was its infinitude. Love of things was a black hole, a ravenous virus, a galloping soul-cancer. Since to acquire was a compulsive pleasure in itself, quite unrelated to the individual attraction of the thing acquired, each acquisition could only leave her hungry for more. A friend of hers, Nicci, had a similar compulsion where the telephone was concerned. Nicci used to spend hours, literally, ringing up friends, acquaintances, even total strangers on expensive services like Dial-A-Pal, Chat-A-Lot and the infamous Hunk-Junkie. Eventually, when Nicci's bank refused to extend her overdraft any further, her mother had declined to bail her out unless she visited a hypnotist. The latter successfully induced an acute jabbing sensation in her ear whenever she held a receiver to it unnecessarily. He also offered a red-hot credit card service, but Chrissie scorned to approach him. She recognised her habit for what it was and made sure she earned enough to stop it turning ugly. She gained an ironic distance on it and, thereby, a measure of control. At a conference in Houston, she bought a Barbara Kruger T-shirt which proclaimed with witty frankness: I Shop Therefore I Am.

In her youth, she had despised her parents' suburban rivalry with their neighbours; the race to the first Flymo, the first double garage, the first conservatory, the first retirement, the first brush with death. When she became pregnant, however, several years into her marriage to Brian, and the two of them decided it was time to exchange their sexy flat in Soho for something larger, cheaper and further out, she was brought to a fuller understanding. She and Brian had neighbours on either side in Islington; the Kilmers and the Pengs. The Pengs were Chinese and industrious and their house was council-owned. Not that Chrissie had anything against people in council housing − far from it − but the Pengs were somehow unapproachable. She always said hello and stopped to admire their (really very sweet) children, but she found it hard to understand why they continued to throw money away in rent when they could be investing it in an endowment mortgage. The Kilmers, on the other hand, became firm friends soon after the delivery of Brian's first Mercedes convertible.

Everything Chrissie wanted, Jade and Ian bought. Or maybe it was the other way around. They took midwinter holidays in Phuket, booked boxes at the opera, sent a son to prep school and 'had him down for a place' at Westminster. Ian played expensive, perilous sports while Jade belonged to a chic women-only health club and probably wore hand-sewn underwear beneath her kaleidoscopic array of *haute couture* clothing. These blessings of existence scarcely needed parading when the two couples got together; their abundance made them unmissable. As the younger, less wealthy pair, Chrissie and Brian could only fawn and coo. And envy. That Jade was *old* enough to have a son at prep school was small consolation to her masochistically observant neighbour, and that her figure failed to justify so much expenditure was, if anything, a goad.

Then, after five cosy, neighbourly years, three things happened to change the course of Chrissie's life. She was promoted to marketing manager for her company's expansion into Europe, Brian came to fit less and less with her image of the life she felt she should be living and the Kilmers took delivery of an *au pair* boy from a 'good' Bordelais family.

'Laurent has beautiful manners, he cooks like a dream and actually likes it *and* he's doing wonders for Sebastian's French,' Jade had exclaimed as Laurent, tall, tanned and twenty-three, set warm duck salad before them and went to open another bottle of wine. 'Besides, what would I want with some sulky girl around the house? I mean, Chrissie, can you picture it? Lisa had that Marie-Paulette all last summer. She almost had a breakdown, she and Vaughn barely speak now and Sharon still managed to fail her O-level. Ask anyone. *Au pair* girls are torture, but *au pair boys*...well!'

'What do you do all day?' Chrissie asked Laurent, once he was seated before her and had pouted becomingly in response to the compliments on his *salade tiède*.

'Oh. Not much. I take the little ones to school, I tidy the house, I do some shopping and then perhaps I go swimming or play tennis.'

'The answer to every maiden's prayer,' laughed Ian and returned to some lecture he was giving Brian on market research and demographics.

'Quite,' said Chrissie. 'Actually, if you get bored, and if Jade can spare you, of course, I'm going to need to draw up five or six French documents for some presentations in Paris and Toulouse next month and you could be a huge help. The company would pay you, naturally.'

'Of course I can spare him,' Jade laughed, 'So long as you promise not to cook for her too, Laurent.'

'*Mais bien sûr*,' Laurent said, with a smile that revealed his dimples, 'I'd be delighted,' and Chrissie, who had the figure if not the clothing account, was not surprised to feel his shoeless foot unmistakably caressing her calf.

In the fortnight that followed, it caressed her again, as adventurously as an inquisitive typist and the glass partition walls of an open-plan office would allow. Chrissie found herself stirred up to an uncharacteristic fever pitch of desire and frustration. She ached for a bed, for any discreetly situated horizontal even, but Jade could only spare Laurent on weekday afternoons, times when Chrissie's employers could rarely spare her.

As usual, her love of things or, more properly, her love of other people's, brought her a solution. Jade and Ian owned a farmhouse a little north of Banbury, where they retreated most weekends and where they had often invited Chrissie, Brian and Sarah-Jane. Whenever he was there, Brian became soft and sentimental about his 'country' childhood (spent in a red-brick suburb of Reading) and exerted pressure on Chrissie.

'It would be a good place to bring up children,' was a typical opening. 'Sarah-Jane loves animals.'

'What about schools?' she would retort. 'She'd have to board. She wouldn't love that. And if you think I'm commuting, you've another thing coming, Brian Warner.'

But later she noticed that Ian occasionally let Jade take the children to the farmhouse while he stayed behind to work, which seemed to involve his dressing in his smartest casuals and leaving the house on Saturday afternoon, reeking of aftershave (a waft of it blew through the trellis as he slammed the car door) to return in the early hours of Sunday afternoon. Brian, typically, failed to notice this dereliction. Chrissie, a childhood subscriber to *Look and Learn*, was extra kind to Jade and kept her observations to herself.

Another weekend was spent in Oxfordshire with their neighbours and Laurent's unbearably stimulating foot. Chrissie made a big effort. She cajoled them all to a nearby church fête. She taught Sarah-Jane to make daisy-chains and Laurent how to make scones. ('No, rub the butter in like this.' 'Like this?' 'Oh, Laurent. Yes. *Exactement*.') Leaning her head on Brian's shoulder as he drove them home, she asked, with just a hint of a knowing smile:

'Why don't *we* get a little place in the country?'

'So you want one now?'

'Why not? I mean, nothing large. Not like Jade and Ian's, that's too much hard work and, well, frankly I think they've made it rather common.'

'Mmm. All those paint effects.'

'And those fussy curtains. No. I was thinking of a cottage. A real cottage. A contrast to London.'

'Somewhere quite run down that we could do up?'

'Exactly. Everyone's going on exotic holidays nowadays. I think it might be rather smart to spend some holidays in England for a change. A cottage would be the perfect excuse.'

'When shall we start looking?'

'Oh God. Brian, you know how I hate house-hunting.'

'Do you?'

'You remember what I was like over Islington. I can never picture how things will look — I just see the squalor and the naff things people have done everywhere. And I get so tired. Couldn't you go on your own. I trust your judgement implicitly.'

'Well that wouldn't be much fun. Why don't you take a Friday off and we can make a weekend of it?'

'Not a weekend. Sarah-Jane's got her ballet classes on Saturdays until the twenty-fourth. Let's take off a day midweek. The roads will be clearer then. We could get a babysitter for Sarah-Jane after school and come home late. How about Wednesday? There was going to be a sales briefing but Janine had to cancel.'

'Okay.'

Their Wednesdays were taken off accordingly, a babysitter arranged and Laurent was informed by a message slipped across Chrissie's desk on the previous Friday:

'*Jettes les chaussettes — mercredi on aura un lit!*'

Then, on Tuesday night, she returned just in time for supper and announced, with a passable show of irritation, that Janine was now available again and the sales briefing was back on for the next day.

'But you've taken tomorrow off. They can't make you go in.'

'They can't *make* me, Brian,' she agreed, 'but I can hardly stay away. Now can I? You wouldn't in my position.'

They argued the question from every angle. Then, for several awful minutes, Brian threatened to spend his day off working at his accounts instead. Chrissie found herself, watched across the dining-table by Sarah-Jane's pinched and questioning gaze, protesting that of course he should go ahead, he knew so much better than she what houses would suit them and which would not.

'It was your idea after all,' she added.

'It was yours!'

'Hardly. You've been suggesting we get a place in the country ever since Ian and Jade had us to the farmhouse for the first time. You know how envious you were of them. Besides, it would be fun to have a day off. The weather's going to be great.'

'More fun with two.'

'Now don't start.'

Suddenly Sarah-Jane interrupted them with the unfamiliar sound of weeping. She hardly ever cried. She was a sensible, well-ordered little girl; her mother's child. Tears coursed down her sweet, fat cheeks at an alarming rate and she screwed her fists back and forth on her eyelids.

'Don't,' she sobbed. 'Don't, don't, don't!'

Brian lifted her into his arms and walked up and

down, rubbing her back and stilling her cries.

The subject was dropped until the next morning, when he made one last abortive effort to dissuade Chrissie from work. She had put on her smartest blue linen suit with a deep purple blouse and jet black accessories. Sarah-Jane complimented her enchantingly as they left the house together. It was a pity she was getting so fat. Even her ballet teacher had commented on it. The Fultons' little girl was so lithe and pretty.

Laurent was loading his charges into Jade's other car for the school run. As he pulled out alongside Chrissie and the children waved and called frantically to each other, he smiled at her through the racket and showed his dimples.

'*A bientôt,*' she mouthed through the glass, and smiled.

'What did you tell him?' Sarah-Jane piped up as they waited at the junction with Caledonian Road.

'I've a hard day ahead of me this morning,' Chrissie told her crisply. 'Try to be good.'

AUTHORS' NOTES

ADRIAN WESTON spent his formative years in Australia and attended university in Adelaide. His short stories have appeared in *Meanjin*, *Westerly*, *Pink Ink Anthology*, *The Australian Bicentennial Anthology* and he has been arts critic for the *Adelaide Advertiser*. He has recently moved to London and is writing his first novel.

MICHAEL CARSON was born in Merseyside just after the Second World War. Educated at Catholic schools, he became a novice in a religious order but decided the religious life was not for him. His novels include *Sucking Sherbet Lemons*, *Friends and Infidels*, *Coming up Roses* and *Stripping Penguins Bare*. He is currently working on the third of his Benson novels.

STEPHEN GRAY was born in Cape Town and educated in Cambridge. After a spell on the Writers Workshop at Iowa University, he moved to Johannesburg where he is a professor of English. His novels include *John Ross: The True Story*, *Time of Our Darkness* and *Born of Man*. He is also a poet and editor of *The Penguin Book of Southern African Stories*.

JOSEPH MILLS was born in Scotland and graduated from Glasgow University in 1989. He has had stories published in several anthologies including *The Freezer Counter* and *Oranges and Lemons*. His first novel, *Towards the End*, was published in 1990.

TOM WAKEFIELD was born of a Midlands mining family. After publishing his first three novels and an autobiography, *Forties' Child*, he was awarded the North West Arts Council Literary Fellowship 1980–82 and the 1983 Oppenheim Award for Literature. His most recent works include the novels *The Discus Throwers*, *The Variety Artistes*, *Lot's Wife* and a novella, *The Other Way* (published in the collection, *Secret Lives*).

FRANCIS KING was born in Switzerland and raised in India. On graduating from Oxford, he worked for the British Council before turning to writing. Author of over twenty novels he was, until recently, drama critic of the *Sunday Telegraph*. He has won the Somerset Maugham Prize, the Katherine Mansfield Short Story Prize and the bestselling *Act of Darkness* (1983) was the *Yorkshire Post* Novel of the Year. His most recent work includes *The Ant Colony*, also a literary guide to Florence and the novella *Secret Lives*.

DAVID FEINBERG is a New Yorker whose obsessional brand of comic writing has earned him comparisons with Woody Allen. His work has appeared in the *James White Review*, *Mandate*, *Torso*, *The Advocate*, *Outweek*, *The New York Times Book Review* and *Diseased Pariah News*. His hobbies are partial differential equations, AIDS activism, the novels of Jane Austen and staying alive. His books include *Eighty-Sixed* and *Spontaneous Combustion*.

NOEL VIRTUE was born in Wellington and caught up in his parents' religious sect until he escaped to England at twenty. There he worked as a zoo keeper – an experience he describes in the autobiographical *Among the Animals* (1988). In 1990 he returned to New Zealand with his longtime lover, Michael Yeomans. His latest novels include *In the Country of Salvation*, nominated for the 1991 *Sunday Express* Book of the Year Award, and *Always the Islands of Memory*.

NEIL BARTLETT was born in Chichester and lives in London. He is a theatre director, translator, video-maker and writer. His productions include *A Vision of Love Revealed in Sleep*, *Sarrasine*, and *Let them Call it Jazz*. His books include *Ready to Catch Him Should He Fall* and *Who Was That Man?* He is, at present, working on a new novel and producing a pantomime.

PATRICK GALE was born on the Isle of Wight and educated at Winchester and Oxford. A parson's grandson, he spent his formative years singing in a chapel choir. He lives on the edge of Bodmin Moor. His latest works include *Little Bits of Baby*, *The Cat Sanctuary* and the novella *Caesar's Wife* (published in the collection *Secret Lives*). He is writing a new novel and working on a modern screenplay loosely based on Henry James's *The Wings of the Dove*.

Forties' Child
Tom Wakefield

'Through his detailed, accurate and incisive obser-
vances and remembrances there exudes a natural
unforced sentiment which proves both genuinely
heartwarming and eminently readable ... It's one of
those books that cannot be put down, and once
finished demands to be read again.'   *Time Out*

'Beautifully evoked, touching and immensely readable.'   *Gay Times*

'He is able to touch base with the reader somewhere
at some time and you know exactly what he means
and why it is so important.'   *City Limits*

'A tender and original recollection of the way a child
puts the amazing world together.'
EDMUND BLISHEN, *The Guardian*

'I greatly enjoyed Tom Wakefield's classic autobiographical account of a wartime Midlands boyhood.'
BEL MOONEY, *The Times*

'What disarmingly polished scenes they are. Tom
Wakefield is one of our most engaging of novelists.'
VALENTINE CUNNINGHAM, *TLS*

Also published by Serpent's Tail

Lot's Wife
Tom Wakefield

'It's refreshing to come across an English novelist who knows exactly what he's doing and does it resoundingly well. Wakefield's is a welcome return to simplicity of style and construction.'

PETER ACKROYD

'A mordantly touching tale of platonic love and rebellion set in a nightmarish retirement home.'

Daily Telegraph

'Wakefield's empathy with his characters, with the plight of the outsider and the importance of personal dignity, has created a sensitive and moving book.'

Sunday Times

'This is a very funny, very moving and acutely perceptive book, which I highly recommend.'

New Statesman

The Variety Artistes
Tom Wakefield

'Wakefield possesses a keen sense of drama and draws some wonderful, almost theatrical "scenes" which can be re-read, enjoyed and savoured, and his characters are full-bodied, living creations who quickly become familiar and memorable. Warm, sensitive and witty.'   *Time Out*

'A lovely story . . . a gentle, humorous parable that says: Watch out — given the chance, there could be a lot more to that compliant old woman than meets the eye.'   *New Society*

'Full of humour, tenderness, humanity and confidence in life.'   *Gay Scotland*

'Somewhat picaresque, intensely human, richly comic, *The Variety Artistes* is an absorbing and ultimately deeply moving novel.'   *Gay Times*

Ready to Catch Him Should He Fall
Neil Bartlett

'Ceremonial, sumptuous, perverse, this novel is a compendium of a century of gay experience...*Ready to Catch Him Should He Fall* is both journalism and fairy tale – and the best gay book of the year.'

EDMUND WHITE

'Bartlett's whirling, clotted style picks up references from Wilde and Genet, Hollywood and blues songs, to throw up freshly lyrical landscapes of lust.'

Daily Telegraph

'A triumph both in its execution and its intent.'

Sunday Times

'As good a novel as you are likely to read this year... A writer who can really change the way people think.'

Literary Review

Who Was That Man?
A Present for Mr Oscar Wilde
Neil Bartlett

'. . . touching and exasperating, it makes an elegant and intelligent shelfmate to Richard Ellmann's biography. Whether or not you appreciate it may give a good indication of how you would really have felt about Wilde himself.'   *TLS*

'Always intelligent, often moving but never sentimental, this is a book which is at once critical of, and beautifully sensitive to, gay culture.'   *Gay Times*

'This is an extraordinary book. Part detective story, part literary criticism, part social history and part confessional, this "present for Mr Oscar Wilde" reveals what it is like to be gay in a city that, for the most part, pretends you don't exist.'   *i-D*

'A reflection on the links between gay lives today and those of Oscar Wilde, his friends, lovers and acquaintances.'   *Capital Gay Book of the Year*

88